The PLAN

KARLA SORENSEN

For the reader with big dreams and a big heart.
I wrote Lydia for you.

The PLAN

PLAN

Chapter
ONE

Erik

NO ONE GROWS UP HOPING THEY'LL TURN INTO A CYNICAL asshole.

My brothers and sisters had called me the latter for as long as I could remember—usually as a backhanded compliment—but the former was a fairly recent addition to my personality.

Life had a strange way of doing that, didn't it? Twists and turns we couldn't see coming added facets to our personality, usually without our permission.

I didn't like the cynicism. Didn't like how I constantly watched the people around me to make sure they weren't going to do something stupid, something suspicious. I used to do a specific variation of that when I played. I'd watch the quarterback, observing the offensive linemen to see if I could pick apart where they'd block or make space for a receiver or a running back.

It was my job to stop them. And even now, years after I'd worn a helmet and pads and cleats, I was doing the same thing. But instead of studying my opponent, I found myself looking for someone to make a wrong move just about everywhere.

Like now, for instance. Outside the small coffee shop where I was supposed to meet Luke Pierson, I found myself studying a couple as they sat intertwined in a corner booth.

They were young, couldn't be much older than seventeen or eighteen.

The girl's body language read as warm and trusting, the way her legs naturally curled over his lap, the way she touched him casually as she scrolled through her phone and drank her coffee. In her giggles and hair fidgeting, I read the full-blown obsession that often gripped newer relationships. Only the young and in love couldn't fathom sitting in a coffee shop booth without touching.

I took a sip of my own black coffee and watched the guy. He'd yet to reciprocate the easy touches even though his arm was sprawled behind the booth. Someone less cynical would think maybe he wasn't a big PDA guy.

But when a leggy brunette strolled past their booth—wearing denim short shorts and a flirty smile—his eyes lingered, his head turning without even the slightest attempt to hide it. His girlfriend had her head snuggled into his chest, completely unaware. Into my coffee, I smiled a grim, unsurprised smile.

Someone sat next to me on the bench, lowering his tall body quietly, legs sprawled out in front of him.

Without sparing him a glance because I knew him well enough that I didn't need to stand on ceremony, I jerked my chin at the couple, visible through the wall of glass that made up the entire storefront of the coffee shop.

"Twenty bucks says this prick gets up and follows the brunette."

Luke glanced at me. "This what you do for fun now, Wilder?"

"Oh, yeah. It's a riot."

In tandem, we tilted our heads when the kid reached under the table and nudged his girlfriend's legs off his lap. To his credit, he tilted her face up and gave her a monstrously obnoxious french kiss that had her a little starry-eyed when he slid out of the booth. Hands tucked into his pockets, he ambled slowly to the hallway where the brunette had disappeared.

Luke dug into his wallet and handed me a twenty. "How'd you know?"

"It's my job to peg the assholes these days." I gave him a brief glance. "Isn't that why you're here?"

"Yeah, I suppose it is." He sighed, and in that sigh, I heard absolute exhaustion. But instead of answering, he shot me a sideways look. "How you been, Erik? I haven't seen you since after your surgery. I was surprised you didn't come back after ..."

After.

That sentence could've ended right there, but the way his voice trailed off, I knew his wife—the owner of Luke's and my former team—had told him why I didn't come back after.

Outside of my family and the people in my hometown, they were probably the only ones who knew.

There were no juicy articles. No online chatter. A small miracle in the day of social media, but I wasn't one of the headliners. The one percent of players who had their every move tracked. The injury, and year of arduous rehab, was enough in people's minds that I didn't renew my contract with the Washington Wolves.

Someone younger and faster had already replaced me on the D-line, sacking quarterbacks and snagging receivers. Fans have short memories, as long as someone's out there making plays.

They didn't think about what came after. We were the ones left with that.

It was my turn to heave an exhausted sigh, and I sounded much older than my thirty years when I did. "I just ... needed a change."

"Logan said you've been on a job the whole last year, right? A tour with a folk singer?"

I nodded, taking another slow sip of my coffee. The guy in the coffee shop returned to his booth, a smug smile on his shit-eating face and a sweet, trusting girlfriend who cuddled right back up to him, even though he'd probably just saved another woman's number to his phone.

"Her head of security is a guy I roomed with in college," I explained. "He hated the bureaucracy of being a cop and found he liked private security better."

"He hire a lot of former football players?"

I exhaled a short laugh. "Not that I know of. But the job was mostly looking scary and having no problem shoving people out of the way."

"You were always very good at that," he conceded easily. "Where'd you travel?"

I closed my eyes, tried to see through the blur of the last year. Lots of stages in lots of places. Clubs and bars and festivals, and the historic cities surrounding them. "Twelve countries in Europe and Asia. All the provinces of Canada. Two cities in South America, and to top it off, a month in Australia."

He whistled. "Favorite city?"

I gave him a dry look. "This part of my interview?"

Luke grinned. "Nah, just making small talk. Should I stop?"

"Yes." I gave him a small smile because if he got his way, he was about to be my employer. A smile seemed like the least I could do to hide the asshole part of cynical asshole. "What's going on, Luke?"

Three or four years ago, I never would've called him by his first name, but I wasn't a player on the roster anymore, addressing a former QB and captain. Now, we belonged to the same fraternity.

The *former* players. The ones who had to figure out what came next.

"Ward said you might be able to help," he said, referencing my former defensive coach—one of his closest friends.

I nodded slowly. "He gave me a heads-up that you might reach out. I'm no professional, Luke."

"I know." He slid his hands up and down his thighs. The guy in the coffee shop watched another woman stroll past their booth, and Luke sighed heavily. "It's my daughter, Lydia," he said. "I don't need to give you a full rundown if you've already heard this."

"Coach didn't tell me much," I admitted. Sitting on that bench was a strange turn of fate in my life, one of many that I hadn't seen coming after that pop in my knee. When my last job wrapped up, and the year of travel that had gone with it, it was one of the first times in my entire life when I couldn't see any-thing when I stared down the future.

Going home still didn't feel like an option.

Football was gone.

And the only thing I seemed to be good at was taking care of people I wasn't related to. The people related to me didn't seem to be faring too well under my care. An irony that I hadn't made peace with. Not in the past couple of years, at least.

A call from Luke Pierson might've given me a glimpse at some sort of future, but I still wasn't sure what it meant. Or how to fix all the other things I'd messed up.

"Lydia is … I don't know what you'd call it … famous for being famous, I guess. A little bit like my wife was before she took over at Washington." He wiped a hand down his face, and the mo-tion—like the earlier sigh—showed a worried father, in the lines on his face, the tired-looking eyes. "She's got millions of follow-ers online, and she's built a really impressive business doing it too. I don't know what the hell half of it means, but I'm proud of her, you know? She's smart, and half the time, she scares the hell out of me with how fearless she is." He smiled. "When she was ten, I caught her outside a conference room in the front offices, taking notes in her fuzzy pink notebook. Told me it was so she could figure out how to be the boss."

He smiled at the memory, some of the worry melting off his face as he did.

Those were the things I knew already. In my five years at Washington, I'd seen her on and off, just like all the players had. But not once had I exchanged a word with her.

She was too young. Too pretty. And I'd been, at the time, too married for any of that bullshit. I just wanted to play.

Luke pulled out his phone and tapped on the screen a few times, handing it over so I could see his daughter's social media account.

"It just … got so big. The more she shared, the more they wanted a piece of her." He shook his head. "I hate it. I know it's normal, or for most people it is. But I don't think I'll ever make peace with this side of our life."

I didn't look at very many of the pictures, but even at a quick glance, Lydia Pierson with her blond bombshell looks and wide smile was fucking stunning. No more poetic words were needed, but I'd known that about her too.

In looking at a few of those pictures, it didn't take long to get a general idea of why the Pierson family patriarch might be reaching out to me.

The internet—for all its good and bad—was a cesspool for men with a taste for beautiful young women. My molars clenched tight at the one small sample of disgusting comments.

"Stalker?" I asked, handing back his phone.

"Which time?" Luke answered dryly. "Lydia's never been too bothered by the creeps. I think she's used to it."

I had three sisters, and nothing pissed me off faster than shit like that. "No woman should have to get used to it."

"Agreed." He sat forward, bracing his forearms on his legs.

"But, to my knowledge, nothing dangerous. Just … a little too excited to meet her when they get the chance."

"So what changed?"

His hands clenched, the skin around his knuckles going white. "Car accident two months ago. A photographer got a bit overzealous trying to get a shot of her driving her new car. She lost control, ran off the road, and hit a tree."

I shook my head. "She okay?"

"Broke her arm in two places. She's in a cast now, been living back at home with Allie and me since it happened."

There was something he wasn't saying. For my whole life, I'd had an uncanny ability to read people—for good or for bad. Only once in my entire life had someone proved me wrong on my instincts, and even though that had been a doozy, I still trusted what my gut was telling me.

And it was telling me that Luke wasn't giving me the full story.

"If you're gonna hire me to help keep her safe, I've got to know everything."

"She's scared," he said bluntly. "She doesn't like leaving the house. Won't get behind the wheel of a car. She's lost a handful of her biggest brand sponsorships in the past two months because she missed appearances, and my smart, driven daughter is … she's not herself."

"Car accident can be tough to get over," I said slowly. "Nothing wrong with that."

"No," he agreed. "But I can't do nothing either. Lydia has so much fire in her. I miss seeing it, even if it is the sole cause of my lost sleep the last decade," he said with a sad smile. "I can't force her to feel better any more than I can control asshole photographers who think she owes them a piece of her private life. But I can find ways to make her feel safe enough to take baby steps back to being herself. That's all Allie and I want. For her to get back to her life because it's killing me to watch my fearless daughter feel like she has to hide."

I nodded. "And that's where I come in."

"You're a known entity. Sort of. You understand the world she comes from, and not many people do. She and her sister Faith were raised in that practice facility. They've got NFL hall of famers as surrogate fathers and uncles and friends."

"Lydia doesn't know me, though," I pointed out. "And I'm no professional bodyguard, Pierson."

"What did you do for that singer all last year?"

I raised a hand in concession. "I've got some of the training, yeah, and my instincts are good, but I'm no warm fuzzy therapist who can tiptoe through the bullshit she's dealing with."

"She doesn't need someone warm and fuzzy. She needs someone who looks like they'd rip out the throats of anyone who hurt her," he answered dryly.

That drew a laugh from deep within my chest. I hadn't laughed in a long time. Not much cause for it in the past couple of years. But about that, he wasn't wrong.

He smiled. "When you used to line up, Wilder …" He shook his head. "You looked like you were about to take the quarterback's head off."

"Not his head. Just his arm."

"To those of us throwing the ball, there's not much difference." Luke gave me a quick glance. "You miss playing?"

No one had asked me that. Not once.

My family had been so busy dealing with the fallout of my divorce and my stepdad's health—all the reasons I'd stayed away from home for so long. The reasons I still couldn't bring myself to go back, even though I was Stateside again. They loved me, of that I had no doubt. But no one had ever asked me how I felt about saying goodbye to the game I loved.

There were too many other things to deal with.

The answer hurt coming up, the words sharp with glass edges against my throat. "Every fucking day."

Luke didn't reply because as a guy who'd played at his level, who'd hoisted a trophy over his head at the end of his career, knew exactly how I felt. Instead, he let the silence rest as it was, and I respected him even more for not offering me trite platitudes or some Hallmark bullshit cliché saying that was supposed to make me feel better.

Because no matter how much I missed it, the thought of ever going back on a field was impossible.

After a moment, Luke reached into his wallet again and pulled out a card.

On it was his address, his cell phone number, and a scrawled dollar amount with a shit ton of zeroes behind it. My breath escaped my lips in a slow hiss.

Luke Pierson and his wife Allie cared *a lot* about making their daughter feel safe and whole again.

I had a healthy savings account. Money in the stock market. I could pay my bills and then some. But what he was offering was more than I'd been given as a signing bonus when Washington drafted me.

Even the cynical asshole in me had trouble finding reasons not to do it.

"I know you said on the phone that you weren't sure this whole security gig was a long-term thing for you," he said quietly. "I love my daughter. She just … she needs a little help to feel safe again. And I think you can do that for her. Give us a few months, Erik, please."

I pinched the bridge of my nose and tried to imagine how different this would be from my last job. I wasn't one of a team. Wasn't someone who could fade in the background and scan the horizon for potential threats.

But on the flip side of the coin, what did I have waiting for me if I said no?

Nothing. Except facing a past that I wasn't quite ready to face. And that wasn't a good enough reason, not if I could step in and help.

I could do something to make someone feel better. If I shined a spotlight on all the things I was avoiding, I knew why that was so appealing. It dulled the cynicism … just a little. And that was something I could hold on to.

"I'll be by tomorrow to meet her."

This was my sisters' fault. For existing. For creating the most troublesome sort of protective instincts. Because even if Lydia Pierson was a big-ass paycheck that would manage to keep me away from home for another few months, I had a gnawing sensation in my gut that this job, this client, wouldn't be quite as easy as he was making it out to be.

Chapter
TWO

Lydia

I T WAS A MADE-UP NEWS HEADLINE AND THE SOUND OF breaking glass that had me visualizing a total one-eighty for my life.

But at the moment right before my car slammed headfirst into the sturdiest tree in the Pacific Northwest—the sickening sound of crunching glass the last thing I heard before I blacked out—I didn't see my life flash before my eyes.

Maybe things would've turned out differently if I had. I could've imagined so many great things too because my life had hardly sucked, but what I saw was the front page of a paper proclaiming my death. And all they managed to come up with for the headline was *Girl with a big Instagram following Dies. No one except her family cares.*

It was not a pleasant feeling. Neither was the broken arm and concussion that came with it, but the feeling of that headline— something dredged straight from my subconscious—was somehow even worse.

In sports psychology circles, visualization was used all the time by athletes in almost every single competition you'd ever watched in your life. In moments of stress and anxiety, elite athletes learned to harness that heightened response and picture themselves overcoming the challenge ahead of them.

The anxiety response by the brain was not an inherently bad thing, and what most people got wrong was that the goal for professional athletes wasn't to feel nothing when they lined up at the beginning of a game or a race or a skill. No response was not better. The goal was to feel that rush of anxiety and harness it into a sharper performance using clinically proven tools.

When an Olympic sprinter placed their feet in the blocks and stared down the track, you could almost guarantee that in their mind, they were picturing themselves running the race. The ability to push their body to a superhuman speed was physical, yes, but it was also mental. It was that mental piece that separated them from the rest of us mortals.

I knew this because I had a giant stack of sports psychology, sports administration, and business administration textbooks on the messy desk in my bedroom. One couldn't start a master's degree in sports industry management without them. And it all stemmed from one moment of visualization. The headline that had never existed, except in my own head.

In my twenty-two years, I'd achieved nothing of value. I wanted a career like my mom's, a legacy built and maintained that affected everyone who was part of it. I wanted a love and family like my parents. And instead, I had lots of people liking my pictures, a string of mediocre, shallow relationships, and a bank account that had been padded by wise sponsorships.

And that was unacceptable because for my whole life, I'd been able to picture exactly what I wanted to do without actually taking a single step to do it.

Which was why it was all the more ironic that one car accident and a broken arm had me visualizing one thing and one thing only: trying to achieve my dream while never leaving my parents' home ever again.

Ever.

If we were meant to gallivant all over the friggin' world, why did God give us Amazon Prime? After all the bullshit it had put us all through, what even was the point of the *internet* if I couldn't just … order anything I needed to have it delivered on the same day?

The internet owed us same-day delivery so we could stay home if you asked me.

Which was how I currently found myself, lying on my bed with the fluffy white comforter, in my childhood bedroom at my parents' house overlooking Lake Washington, visualizing the bejeesus out of placing an epic Prime order before I went back to doing my homework.

"Oooh," I said, "they have you back in stock now."

Add to cart. An instant rush of gratification. These were about the only moments when I got any sort of rush. Buying a mask online for same-day delivery. If my two million and change followers could see me now, they'd feel so epically duped.

A heavy sigh escaped my mouth before I could stop it.

I still posted pictures. Sometimes. If I felt like it.

But most of the time, I just … didn't.

Every night when I closed my eyes, there were a few seconds when it happened all over again in my head. The way the steering wheel felt underneath the tight grip of my hands, the blur of the sky and trees and grass when I yanked too hard to the side, and the terrifying pulse of silence in my ears when the tree was just … right there.

And on a loop, the sound of a windshield as it crunched into a million pieces.

I closed my eyes. Saw myself without a cast. Sitting out in the sun. Safe.

I was safe.

And there would be no depressing headlines about Lydia Pierson anymore.

I pushed off the bed with my good arm and wandered into my closet. Maybe today would be the day I'd get crazy and wear something other than athleisure.

But then I plucked at the waistband of some jeans and frowned. Fuck that. I wanted nothing binding, nothing that wasn't elastic waistbands or sinfully soft material. The tag of the jeans was sticking out after my brief study, and I grimaced at the familiar logo. An email had come through a couple of weeks earlier about some event I'd missed, and they were not happy.

Not happy enough that they dropped my endorsement deal.

Where it was tucked into the side pocket of my leggings, my phone buzzed. I slid it out with two fingers and grimaced all over again for an entirely different reason when I saw the name on the screen.

For all intents and purposes, Jill Northman was one of my friends. But she was one of those friends who didn't actually know shit about me anymore other than what I was like at an event. Her parents ran a successful sports agency, so we'd been in the same social circle for … our whole lives basically.

But even if she didn't know me all that well, beyond the superficial, she'd made more than one effort since my accident to coax me back out into public. She'd failed epically, but I had to give the girl an A for effort.

"Hey," I said, setting the phone on a shelf so I could rifle through some shirts.

"Oh, she *is* alive. What a pleasant surprise."

"I talked to you three days ago, Jill."

"Right, and you said you'd let me know if you were coming to my thing tomorrow."

My days had this weird tendency to blur together, probably

because they were all the same. It was … Wednesday. Maybe. My hand froze over a hanger. "What thing is that again?"

"Holy shit, Lydia, are you losing your mind? It's the app."

My eyebrows furrowed, my nose scrunching up in a whole confused vibe because I had no freaking idea what she was talking about.

Jill sighed. "*My* app. The dating app that's like Bumble but better."

Jill had a dating app? A previous conversation flitted up to the surface of my fuzzy brain. They asked her to promote it. Be on a couple of billboards. To say that it was hers was just a bit of a stretch. "Like Bumble but better," I repeated. "Please tell me they're using that as the tagline."

She laughed. "Close. Are you coming? You haven't been out in forever."

I ran a hand over my face because I did think I was losing my mind. Just a little. There were so many unread text messages and emails on my phone that I kinda just … got used to ignoring them.

All I'd been doing with my time was study. And sleep. And Prime.

"Ohhh yeah, the app," I said sheepishly. "I've been a little scattered since Brea quit."

"I heard. She was a garbage assistant anyway. Everyone knew that."

I stared at the phone, incredulous. "You're the one who recommended her."

Silence. "Did I?"

Pinching the bridge of my nose with my good hand, I decided to let it drop. Brea, the aforementioned garbage assistant, quit a week after my accident because I was "making her super sad with all the moping" and she "really couldn't handle that kind of negative energy in her physical and mental space."

"Whatever," Jill said. "Water under the bridge. Are you coming or not? I can pick you up from your apartment so you don't have to drive."

I winced. "I'm still at my parents' house."

"You cannot live there forever."

Watch me, I thought as I attempted a one-handed fold of one of my sweaters. A broken arm was absolutely murder on organizational attempts, but after ten weeks of the cast, I was getting pretty good at it.

In my stubborn silence, she just kept on rolling.

"We all get it. The accident was super-duper scary and everything, but you're like, twenty-two and living in your parents' basement. It's not a cute look."

I pinched my eyes shut because she had no idea how little I cared. I still couldn't get behind a wheel of a car without having an anxiety attack. The second I was out in public and a paparazzi aimed a long lens camera in my direction, my entire body went cold and prickly. But my friend—whose concern was motivated by her lack of social scene without me—didn't want to hear any of that.

Jill was far more concerned with whether my face—and my millions of followers—would show up at her party. My shiny new hermit lifestyle didn't appeal to her at all. If I'd told her about starting my master's, that wouldn't have appealed to her either. Which was why I kept my mouth shut and kept on with the one-handed sweater folding.

"Besides, the accident was *months* ago. Like … let's find a good shrink who'll give you some good pills and move the hell on, you know?" Jill pushed on, completely unaware that her blasé tone had me wanting to punt-kick my phone into Lake Washington, just beyond the stretch of my parents' backyard. "You've already lost more than one endorsement deal, Lydia. What are you going to do if they all drop you?"

Finish my degree.

Start working at Washington.

Take over when my mom was ready to retire.

Find the perfect faceless man with a great jawline and sense of humor and love of *SportsCenter* and have babies with him while we lived happily ever after.

"I'd figure something out," I said lightly. All of those things would require me to leave the house. Occasionally.

I set the sweater onto a shelf in my closet and ignored the fact that my hand was shaking a little bit. It did that a lot. Anytime someone backed me into this particular corner.

The unfortunate truth was she wasn't the first to have a mini-intervention.

My sister was concerned.

My parents were concerned. And not because they gained a blonde squatter in their basement with excellent taste in clothing. Over the past ten weeks, I knew exactly how much I'd changed and what that must look like to them. Unlike Jill, though, their worry—coming from a place of love—actually made me feel safe. Cared for. Protected. It made me never, ever want to live by myself again.

Like I'd conjured him with the thought, my dad knocked gently on the doorframe. I held up a finger and then pointed at the phone lying on the dresser next to me.

"Jill, I gotta go," I told her. "Something just came up."

"Ugh. Fine. Call me and let me know about the party, bitch."

My dad smiled when I disconnected the call with a vicious punch of my thumb.

"I hate when she calls me that," I said. "It's not a flattering nickname."

"It's really not," he agreed. "Do you have a couple of minutes?"

I eyed him. "What's with that tone?"

Dad adopted an innocent expression. "Can't a father ask his daughter to come upstairs?"

"For what?"

"Your mom and I want to talk to you about something."

I shoved my feet into my fuzzy black slippers, tugging up the hem of my favorite gray sweats so they didn't drag on the floor. Lately, they'd been slipping off my hips, as some unintended weight loss had been another unfortunate side effect. Pre-accident Lydia *loved* her curves. "Lead the way."

He studied me for a second. "Do you maybe want to"—he gestured vaguely at my hair—"brush that?"

With a self-conscious pat to the bird's nest sprouting out of the top of my head, I glanced in the mirror hanging on the wall next to my dresser. Yikes.

Maybe I did look a little … homeless. With a yank and a twist, I attempted to smooth my hair into something a bit neater, but honestly, with only one hand to manage it and the amount of dry shampoo we had going in that situation, it was kind of a lost cause.

As I tugged the last few loose strands into place, I narrowed my eyes at the look on my dad's face. He looked nervous.

He never looked nervous.

"Is there someone up there?"

Dad pinched the bridge of his nose, then let out a sharp exhale. "Okay, your mom thought we should do this a different way, and if you don't act completely surprised, she'll know I warned you."

"Oh Lord, what?" I groaned.

"Just remember, we love you, and we're worried, and that's the only reason."

"Why what? What did you do?" I set my hand on my hip.

He did some hand-hip-setting of his own, which was how I knew this was really serious. "He's … he comes highly recommended."

"Who does?"

Dad held up a hand. "And he's a former player. I got his name from Logan."

"Who is?"

"He played for five years before he left the league and ended up working in security."

"*Who?*" I stomped my foot like a toddler.

It wasn't my finest moment.

"He's a … professional driver. Sort of," my dad hedged. "And he's going to escort you wherever you need to go."

"*What?*" I yelled. There was no cold tingling in my body now and no shaking hands as I brushed past my dad and started up the stairs.

"You're supposed to act surprised," he whispered frantically.

"Too late," I tossed over my shoulder.

As I cleared the landing, I only caught the briefest of glimpses of my mom's face. Obviously, my yelling and stair-stomping had reached her ears.

She said something to my dad or me, but I couldn't hear a thing, only garbled words that didn't penetrate the buzzing in my ears as *he* unfolded his great big body from the couch in the living room.

Tall and scary. It was the only way I could describe him, with the arms and the beard and the chest and the eyes. If I crossed him in an alley, I'd run holy hell in the opposite fucking direction.

Those eyes of his, even darker than the hair on his head, never moved from my face, but I felt like he'd taken my measure in a single heartbeat.

"No way," I said. "Not happening."

His expression never changed.

If my parents thought they were saddling me with this terrifying driver/bodyguard/guard dog, they were sadly mistaken.

My mom stood from the couch and approached from the side. "Lydia, this is Erik Wilder."

He dipped his chin in a curt nod, but that was it. I recognized him from his playing days—a defensive lineman, if I remembered correctly—but even for me, the one who knew all the things about all the players, the details of his career were just out of reach.

Somehow, I snapped the tether between his hard gaze and my own. When my mom's hand settled softly on my back, I turned toward her. "You hired me a *bodyguard*? I don't need a babysitter, Mom." I swallowed past the thick wooly feeling in my throat.

I wanted *less* of this circus in my life, not more.

"We have to do something, Lydia." She cupped the side of my face. "You hardly leave the house, and that was fine for the first couple of weeks. Your dad and I completely understand, but it's time to try something new."

"I'll … make more appointments with that therapist the cop told me about."

She and I had done one session, and I never rescheduled.

"You canceled every single time we tried again," she said gently. And while her voice might have been soft and sweet and all motherly concern, her face was firm, even as she tried to settle all my highly ruffled feathers. Mr. Big, Tall, and Scary couldn't possibly know this about me, but *no one* wanted to be around me when I actually really got mad about something. Logic? Out the window. Rational thought? Forget about it.

And right now, I was the worst possible combination. I was angry and embarrassed. As my days had flown by, it never actually occurred to me that my parents would hire me a glorified babysitter.

I felt … stupid. Like a little kid whose parents have been watching them stumble around before stepping in. That saying about being up shit creek without a paddle, I suddenly wanted to throat punch whoever came up with it because my parents weren't just handing me a paddle. They were super-gluing it to my hands.

Locking eyes with my mom, I covered her hand with my own, anchoring it to my face. "Please, Mom, this is so embarrassing. I'm not … in danger or anything. I just need some time to get over this. And I will, I promise."

"How many male superfans have shown up at your apartment, Lydia?" my dad asked quietly.

I closed my eyes because, yes, I'd brushed those off more

than once. "They were harmless. They just wanted a picture and an autograph."

"One of them wanted to marry you," he said. "He had a ring. He slept on the sidewalk for two days until your neighbors called the cops."

I walked away from my mom, her hand dropping off my face. "That hasn't happened in months. And I'm hardly posting anything these days, I'm … I'm not worried about *that*."

I was *trying*. Trying to change. To craft something different that matched up better in my mind to what I really wanted. Didn't they see that?

"Because you've been living here," my mom said. "And we have security."

Right on cue, I heard the comforting beep of the front door camera when a delivery guy deposited a box. Probably my face mask because the Prime people were on the ball these days. Everything that happened on our property was recorded, monitored by someone in a cute little security gatehouse just down the road. The people in that gatehouse had a nice big scary-looking dog who walked around with them, and yes, fine, it was one of the reasons I loved staying there. But I'd still always had my freedom to come and go as I pleased.

I wasn't like, *Beyonce*. I didn't need an armed guard walking me anywhere because the world would lose its collective mind anytime I showed my face.

I was just a girl with a former quarterback dad and a mom who owned a football team, and I temporarily lost my desire to be around people or leave the house. That did not make me *needs a bodyguard* material. Especially the kind of bodyguard who looked like he would rip someone's face off if they came too close.

Under my lashes, I studied him again. He made my throat go just a little dry, the breadth of his chest and the way his arms curved with heavy muscle underneath his simple T-shirt.

Erik must've sensed my perusal because he lifted his eyes, and when they locked onto mine, my stomach went weightless.

No one, and I mean *no one,* would mess with me if he was by my side.

For just one brief second, that realization had my shoulders relaxing. And my fricken parents must see it.

"He's not a babysitter," my dad said in a quiet, firm tone. "You're an adult, and as much as we love all this time with you, kiddo, you have to start living your life again. He can help with that."

My parents traded a look, passing the proverbial baton of the conversation. "You wouldn't have to worry about photographers getting too close or weird fans approaching you when you're alone," my mom continued. "And little by little, you will be able to feel normal again."

My eyebrows furrowed. Which version of my life did they want me to return to? My parents were supportive when I started my degree, and I'd expected nothing less. But maybe they didn't realize exactly how serious I was about this change.

When I closed my eyes, I brought that picture up in my head of all the things I wanted … being trailed by photographers and a big scary dude holding everyone at bay was not what I wanted. I'd never lived the kind of life where I needed security. And starting now felt like … moving backward.

"No."

My eyes opened, and Erik Wilder's face held its first expression beyond total intimidation.

He was shocked.

My mom's mouth was open in a gentle circle. "Lydia, you don't mean that."

I looked over at her, then my dad. "I really, really do."

Dad swiped a hand over his face as he studied me. His eyes flipped to my mom and held another wordless conversation that I wasn't privy to.

This was a curveball that none of them had visualized. That was for freaking sure. I desperately wanted to cross my arms and be all nonchalant about this entire negotiation, but I was not nonchalant. I was *full* of chalant. There was a really good chance I was being needlessly stubborn about a well-meaning gesture from people who loved me.

But if this served any purpose, it was like a bucket of ice water, snapping me awake from whatever comfy little hiding hole I'd found.

The clothes.

The excuses.

The dry shampoo. Okay, no … that wasn't going anywhere.

But I could change my future and not have a glorified watchdog following me around.

And the entire time, that watchdog and his dark eyes studied me like a specimen behind a glass case. The shock was gone from his handsome face—stupidly handsome, really—and in its place was begrudging curiosity.

I held his gaze. "Thank you for coming, Erik, but I'm afraid you've wasted a trip."

His eyes narrowed slightly, lips parting like he was going to speak.

What did his voice sound like?

It was probably hot. Any guy who looked like he did—with the arms and the hair and the beard and the … everything—was destined to have a really hot, really sexy voice. And somewhere in the back of my head, I was sad that I hadn't heard it yet.

My dad cleared his throat. Erik's eyes never moved from mine.

"Walk me out?"

The sound of it had my heart skipping, which was … unexpected. My dad nodded his head, but Erik held a hand up.

"Not you," he said. "Her."

My eyebrows rose in surprise, but I found myself willing to concede this little trip out to the front porch.

Mom and Dad watched quietly while Erik Wilder matched my stride and held the door to my house open for me. Like he was walking me somewhere.

I blew out a slow breath at the size of his hand on the solid wood surface.

The weather was beautiful. Perfect.

And I inhaled the sweet smell of the fresh air, filling my lungs before turning to face him.

"It's nothing personal," I said, squinting a bit in the bright light. "I just … don't want you following me around, you know?"

He made a sound. Sort of a hum grunt hybrid. Could've been a laugh, but this man did not look like he laughed easily.

"Thank you for coming, though."

Why was he just standing there? He was staring at me like we weren't done with this conversation, but I most certainly was. The way his gaze seemed to catalog every little detail was unnerving.

My hair.

The raggedy-ass shirt.

The pants that were a little bit too big.

I didn't like it.

I huffed, folding my arms over my chest. "I'm not changing my mind, so you can stop that stare-down thing you're doing. It won't work on me."

After a moment, Erik reached into his back pocket and extended a plain black card in my direction.

Careful not to touch his big hands, I took the card and gave it a quick glance.

His name was in solid block letters, followed by an email address and phone number.

I grinned up at him. "People still use business cards? Can't I just look you up online?"

"Nope."

Just that. I rolled my eyes. "What is this for?"

He glanced past my shoulder, where my parents were undoubtedly watching. Then his gaze landed squarely back on mine. It felt a little bit like something punched a hole in my chest every time he did it.

Like that gaze alone could light something back to life inside me, and hoo boy, that was a dangerous feeling.

"If you change your mind," he said. "It's not a weakness to let someone have your back."

His deep voice ringing in my ears, I stood in place and watched him take long-legged strides back to his immaculate vehicle.

Once he was settled in the driver's seat, Erik slid sunglasses up over his nose, and even though his face didn't turn, I knew he was looking at me.

My arms tightened around my waist, and as he pulled out of the driveway, I had the strangest premonition that I hadn't seen the last of Erik Wilder.

But a guy like him … that wasn't someone I'd visualized in my life. So I took a deep breath and went back inside the house.

Chapter
THREE

Lydia

THE NIGHTMARE STARTED LIKE IT ALWAYS DID.

First, the steering wheel disappeared under my hands, a puff of black smoke that I couldn't grab onto. Everywhere I looked out of the windshield were bright flashes of light and disembodied voices yelling my name over and over and over.

Somewhere in the middle of it, I screamed my sister's name because I knew she was out there. Somehow knew her car was behind mine. But I couldn't hear her, and I couldn't see her. The tree stretched up out of the ground like a great, crawling beast, something living and breathing and monstrously huge. Before I could draw a breath and try to climb out of the car, it stretched so tall that the branches blotted out all the sun.

My hands clamored uselessly for a way to steer the car out of the way, but there was nothing I could do to control the car.

The sickening crunch of glass, splinters growing across the windshield until I couldn't see anything, and my body rocked forward with a rough jolt. Only this time, instead of the dream ending there, my body flew forward through the glass, the black of the tree rushing to meet me.

I woke with a yell, heart clamoring wild and hard against my ribs. My neck was cold with sweat, and I sat up in bed, burying my face in my one shaking hand. My arm was sore like my stupid brain sent out pain signals from the accident, zeroing in on the one spot where I couldn't hide.

Heavy footsteps tripped down the stairs and the hallway, my bedroom door swinging open to reveal my dad.

"Are you okay?" he asked, eyes worried and dark, silver-threaded hair askew.

I nodded, trying to take a deep breath but failing when my lungs wouldn't fill. My chest was heavy and tight, and I pressed my hand against it while I focused on the weight of his hand on my back. I didn't even realize I was crying until he brushed the wetness off my cheek.

"You are breaking my heart, kiddo," he whispered.

My exhale was shaky and reed thin, and I tried again to suck in the oxygen I needed. The remnants of the dream slid away as we sat there in the silence of my room.

"How did you hear me?" I asked.

Dad sank onto the edge of my bed, and it made me feel like I was a kid again, back when he used to tuck me in. "I've been up for a while. Your mom had to leave early for that remote interview with the *Today* show about women in sports."

I nodded.

He blew out a long exhale. "Same dream?"

Again, I nodded.

"You haven't had that one in a while."

"I know." I slid out from underneath the covers and sat next to him. I tugged at the messy ponytail falling over my shoulder and ran my hand through the tangled mess. "I think ... meeting with Erik yesterday triggered something. Thinking about going out and about."

He grimaced, opening his mouth to say something. Before he could, I held up my hand.

"No apologies, okay? Let's just … go watch Mom be awesome."

I didn't need him to tell me he was sorry because it wasn't his fault. My brain just … needed not to be stupid. I'd only dreamed of the accident for the first couple of weeks afterward. Settling into a new routine at their house had lulled me into some false sense of security.

Dad ruffled my hair and left my room, and as I tugged on a sweatshirt to follow him, I had to blink away the image of Erik Wilder's face as he handed me his business card.

The card sat on the edge of my desk, and as I tugged the hem of my sweatshirt down around my hips, I stared at it like it might jump up and bite me.

"Hungry?" Dad asked from the doorway. "I can make some breakfast."

Tugging my gaze from the card, I shook my head at my dad. "Just coffee for now, I think."

My desk hugged the wall next to the entrance to my bedroom, and he glanced down at the wobbly stack of brightly colored textbooks. Half of them were required, and the other half were from a list I'd been building for a couple of years. People my parents quoted often, coaches and owners and players who they'd learned from.

In my head, I could see the row of bookshelves stretching out behind my desk someday … all the spines lined up in neat rows. For years, I said I'd start working on it when I got closer to thirty.

Until crunching glass and snapped bones made thirty seem really far away. No one would accuse me of not being ready when it was my turn to step behind the desk where my mom currently sat.

His finger tapped the top book, a biography by Tony Dungy, one of the coaches Dad admired most. "I liked this one."

I smiled. "Me too. I finished it the other day."

We walked upstairs, quiet as he switched the TV on. I poured myself a cup of coffee, and we settled into our usual spots on the long gray couch.

As per the usual in the Pierson household, the screen came to life with ESPN as the channel of choice. My social media following may have grown because of my sponsorships in fashion and the photo shoots that garnered the most attention, but this was how I loved spending my mornings. And afternoons. And evenings.

It wasn't sexy, and it certainly wasn't glamorous, but sitting on the couch with my dad and breaking down what was happening in the league was my happy place.

"Ten minutes till your mom's interview is up." He glanced my way. "Keep it here until then?"

I nodded. "I want to hear what they have to say about Detroit's issues in the back field."

My dad grinned. Everyone said I looked exactly like my mom, but if they knew my family well enough, I had my dad's smile.

"What do you think their problem is?" he asked.

My forehead pinched in a frown at the question. "They keep focusing on receivers, but they don't have enough depth at the other positions, so their playcalling is easy to defend. It's not like they can force their QB to run the ball when he needs to, but if they keep relying on the pass game when there's no chemistry between their quarterback and their receivers, they'll never do what they want to while he's healthy enough to play."

Dad hummed. "Coach's fault?"

I shook my head slowly. "They'll blame him, probably even fire him after this season if they don't win enough, but they've been through three coaches, and nothing's changed. They need a new General Manager, but no one wants to admit it."

"Agreed." He took a quiet sip of his coffee. "Tough decisions to make when the GM has been around for ten years. Your mom caught a lot of flack when Washington fired the last one."

"I remember." It wasn't always fun to watch the talking heads, especially when they found a target in the woman you idolized most in the world.

Dad switched the channel when Mom's interview was about to start.

"Your mom has a security detail every game day," he said quietly. "There's security at the practice facilities. At the stadium. Most charity events we attend."

I blew out a slow breath because I knew the subject had been dropped far too easily. "I know. But she runs a billion-dollar professional sports team. It makes sense for her to have a security team."

He gave me a quick look. "And don't you want to step into that role someday?"

"When she's ready to retire, sure." I tugged a blanket over my bare legs. "But I don't need someone tailing me with a mic in their ear and a gun strapped to their hip because I'm still a little nervous about being out and about."

My dad sighed. "I know it seems like we're taking this too far, bug, but what if . . . what if you just let him drive you one place?"

"Geez, busting out the childhood nickname. That's emotional warfare." I smiled, though, because he hadn't called me that in years.

"Will it help you agree? All I'm asking is that you get to know him a little bit."

"In one drive?" I scoffed. "What will that accomplish? He had the conversational skills of a toaster, Dad."

And really dark, intense eyes.

And big hands.

I snagged the remote and tried to turn the volume up. He snatched it right back and hit the pause button, the screen freezing on Mom's smiling face so we didn't miss anything.

"I'm asking you to give this a try. You know your mom and I support you and your sister in just about anything you want. You want to burn your social media to the ground and never post another picture again? Great. I'll light the match."

I rolled my eyes. "That's not what I'm trying to do. I'm just trying to shift my focus."

"You want to start your degree and do both? I'll help you study. I'll quiz you. Help you vet business proposals so you can build your brand in a different way." He held my gaze. "Whatever you need."

"If I keep getting any proposals at all. I've lost five sponsorships in the last ten weeks, Dad."

"Yeah, well, they're probably fucking terrible people."

I smiled. "They're not. I didn't hold up my end of the bargain."

He sighed. "You still have more, though, right?"

I nodded slowly. "Yeah, I still have some. But they all require some level of showing my face in public. I've got that big one with Dior in a couple weeks."

"The perfume," he said.

"The perfume." I rubbed my forehead. "I can't mess this up. It would pay for the entirety of my master's."

My dad smiled gently. "Have I told you how much I admire that you want to pay for it yourself?"

"Only seventeen or eighteen times." I nudged him with my shoulder. "It's your fault. Faith's and my bedtime story was how you worked two jobs to offset the tuition cost when your scholarship didn't cover everything at Michigan."

"You'll never regret working hard for what you want, bug." He gestured at the TV. "Your mom is a testament to that as much as I am. She was handed ownership of a football team and had no clue what to do. But look at her now." His eyes shone with so much love and pride, I almost burst into friggin' tears. My parents loved each other so much, it was ridiculous. A lofty standard set for my sister and me, and nothing short of that would suffice.

All my life, I was surrounded by successful people, not just in love, but in life. Athletes and owners and philanthropists. Because of my dad's more blue-collar background, I saw just as much success in the people on his side of the family who worked hard at jobs they enjoyed, who went home tired and sweaty at the end of the day, and were just as happy as the people who made ten times as much. Happier, in some cases.

The clearer the idea of my future became, the more I wanted to learn about the people who'd found solid footing in theirs. Every fiber of my being believed that I could build on my mom and dad's legacy at Washington, but each step closer had me questioning whether I had it in me.

"What do you think made her so good at it right away?" I asked.

His eyebrows rose in surprise. It was the nature of what he'd done—as a player—that his strengths and weaknesses were constantly discussed, even decades after his playing days were over. But we didn't often break down what made my mom so good at what she did.

Instead of answering right away, my dad stared at Mom's face still frozen on the screen. He shook his head slowly. "How much time do you have for me to answer?"

I smiled, snuggling down into the couch.

He set his coffee down onto the table in front of us and took a deep breath. "She's never afraid to ask questions. I noticed that right away. There's a certain humility that's necessary to be willing to admit you don't understand something. When she does understand something, she knows the value of her own opinion." He gave me a look. "And no one can tell her otherwise.

"She listens to the people she's talking to—no matter what their role is at Washington. Every person, every job holds equal value to her. And she relies on the expertise of those people instead of pretending like she knows their job better than she does. Your mom figured out on day one how to set aside her ego and lead with heart." He blinked, and in the dim light of the room, I thought maybe he was getting a little misty-eyed. "That's why every guy who lines up on that field would go to battle for her. And has."

I tucked my knees up against my chest, resting my chin there while I absorbed what he was saying.

Nothing about his answer was pointed, it didn't hold any subtext about my own situation, but I found a thread of truth in what he was saying regardless. It might be years before I was in any sort of position of leadership, but would I be able to set aside my own ego when it was necessary?

I certainly wasn't now.

"I'll be right back," I told Dad, sliding off the couch.

He glanced up. "You okay?"

I nodded. "Just need to make a quick phone call."

"This early?"

"Oh." I glanced down at the time on my phone. Sunrise was a ways off. "I guess not. Most people don't get up this early, huh?"

Dad studied my face. "Depends on who you're calling."

I rolled my lips between my teeth. "Are you going to make me say it?"

His mouth twitched. "Maybe."

With a huff, I walked around the couch toward the kitchen. "I'll send him a text."

"He'll be up," my dad said to my retreating back.

I froze. "You sure?"

"Oh, yeah."

"You won't start Mom's interview without me?"

Dad laughed. "I know better than that."

Chewing on my lip, I skipped back down the steps to my bedroom and carefully plucked the business card off the surface of my desk.

The solid block letters of his name screamed out to me, and I had the wispy notion that I was making a massive mistake. That whatever future I was trying to carve out for myself couldn't be achieved by relying on some big scary hot man taking me places.

But I closed my eyes and tried to drag up a good reason not to accept the help. Tried to imagine how I was going to crawl out of this dark space if I refused to accept help.

And I came up blank.

Before I could talk myself out of it, I punched in the numbers and held my breath as it started ringing.

"Yeah."

That was how he answered. One gruffly spoken word in a sleep-rough voice.

I winced. "I'm sorry I'm calling so early."

Silence. Right.

"Umm, it's Lydia Pierson."

"Figured it was." He cleared his throat. "Where are you?"

"Oh. I'm at home. My parents' home," I amended. "I don't need you right now."

"So you're okay?"

"Yes. I was just up with my dad, and he said you'd probably be awake." My face was blazing hot because, holy shit, you'd think I'd never spoken to a man on the phone before. "Sorry, this probably made it seem like an emergency or something. It's … not. I just wanted to call before I talked myself out of it."

He made a grumbling sort of humming sound, and it tickled my ears, a pleasant shivering down my spine that I couldn't quite control.

"I'm willing to give this a shot. But you can't be this big scary silent shadow who refuses to talk to me."

Erik let out a deep sigh, and before I could think better of it, my lips curled up in a smile. He sounded so annoyed, and instead of annoying me in turn, there was a small kindling of curiosity burning under my skin.

"I'm talking to you right now, aren't I?" he grumbled.

"Yes." I was smiling widely now, so it was probably good he couldn't see me.

"Do you need me today?"

What day was it? I glanced at the screen on my phone. Friday.

"If you're free," I said. I rubbed my forehead and blurted it out before I changed my mind. "A friend of mine has a … thing … today. She asked if I'd come. I don't want to but, maybe it's a good test run."

"Where's it being held? How big of an event?"

My nose scrunched up. "I don't know, and I don't know. Can I give you that information when you pick me up? I think it's supposed to start at three. Which … is dumb for a dating app event, but whatever. No one asked my opinion."

He was quiet for a beat. "Right. How about you text me the location when you find it. I'd like to know what we're walking into."

We.

There was a nice ring to that.

"I can do that." I blew out a breath. "Thank you. I know I didn't give you much of a chance yesterday. And I'm still feeling a little weird about the whole my family thinks I need a bodyguard thing. That's why I can't handle if you're just standing there *glaring* at people and making it seem like I'm a Kardashian wannabe or something because like, hey, props to people living how they want, but I'm not trying to walk into random places with an entire entourage, you know?"

Again, Erik let out a sigh. "Uh-huh."

It wasn't as disgruntled as the first sigh. And I found it way more amusing than I should have.

I tucked a stray hair behind my ear. "Well … I guess I'll see you this afternoon then. Maybe around three?"

"I thought it started at three."

"Well yeah, so you can't show up until at least an hour later."

"Uh-huh."

I laughed. "I'll teach you proper social event etiquette."

"Please don't," he murmured.

It was strange to be sitting on my bed, where I'd woken up in a cold sweat not that much earlier and be smiling at the thought of going out.

Okay, fine, I wasn't smiling about going out. But if nothing else, I found myself calculating the hours until our little test run.

Erik Wilder and his sighs might not be the most horrible idea after all.

Chapter FOUR

Erik

GOING INTO MY FIRST MEETING WITH LYDIA, I'D BEEN QUITE sure about a few things.

Because she was younger than me, her primary concern driven toward how she looked and what image she projected, I'd be able to handle her just fine. I would've staked every penny of what Luke offered me on that.

Oh, how laughably wrong I'd been.

It wasn't the way she stomped up the stairs. It wasn't even the baggy clothes covering her body or the mess of hair on her head. It was the flash of pure stubborn anger flashing in her blue eyes that had me wanting to cover my balls and reconsider my employment options.

The singer I traveled with said four things to us on tour.

Good morning, guys.

Thank you.

I'm ready.

Have a good night.

She was polite and professional. Her schedule clad in iron and immovable. Weeks ahead of time, we knew where we were going and how big the event was and what was expected of us.

Now I was taking pre-dawn calls with zero information and a surprisingly headstrong woman who all but shoved me back into my car.

The confused look on my face had lingered until I walked back into my sister Adaline's apartment.

"What happened?" she asked.

I'd blinked. "Honestly, I'm still not sure, but she is *not* what I expected."

My sister laughed and laughed, only managing a condescending pat on my head. "Oh, big brother, if I could print and frame your face at this moment, I'd hang it on the wall under a spotlight. Welcome to the other side of the Washington Wolves—where the women reign supreme, and they will never make things easy for someone telling them what to do."

Her words rang in my ear all night as I dreamed of big blue eyes and an arm in a black cast. Tangled blond hair and her voice saying *it's nothing personal* while I tried to help her over a rushing river, and she batted my hand away.

It sure as fuck felt personal.

And now, I drove back to the Pierson family home with a renewed determination not to screw this up. It was a new day, and even though I hated not knowing what type of event I was bringing her into, I had a laser-sharp idea of what Lydia Pierson was really like.

Today she might look more of the part of what I expected if we were attending a social event, but already, I knew I was dealing with a woman far more complicated than I'd assumed.

Stupid, on my part. Because the famous saying of not judging a book by its cover was a famous saying for a reason.

Something I'd forgotten and would not be forgetting again soon.

In the hours before I picked her up, I studied her social media again, and I knew one thing for sure. The bubbly captions underneath the overtly sexy photos was not the same woman who I was picking up. And if I needed a reminder, then she proved it when I pulled up to the house, and she was waiting on the front porch.

I'd expected a tight dress with high heels, sexy hair, and full makeup.

I'd expected to have to come to the door and wait for her to finish getting ready, where I'd usher her into the back seat of my car, and we'd make the drive in polite silence.

But no. That was not what I found.

Because there was Lydia Pierson, waiting on the front porch, looking like she was about to break into someone's house.

Wearing a black ballcap and mirrored sunglasses and a boxy black sweatshirt over dark jeans, she could've passed for any normal college co-ed. The mass of her hair was tucked up underneath the hat ... somehow.

Before I got out, I took a second and tried ... yet again ... to adjust my expectations. To remind myself of all the ways I'd felt disappointment or regret in the past few years. If I had to track this girl's ass all over Seattle, I would not let this job be added to the list.

I took a deep breath and got out of the car.

She'd be nervous, I reminded myself.

This was a big deal for her, and she'd need me to stay calm and cool and in command.

I could handle this.

She stood off the front porch, hefting a rather large bag over her shoulder. I held my hand out.

Lydia stared. "Is that for a handshake, or is this your non-verbal way of offering to take my bag?"

My jaw twitched. "The latter."

"Right. I can manage, but thank you. It's just shoes and a skirt."

I eyed the massive bag. "Looks like you could fit a body in it."

She smiled. "Close."

I slid my sunglasses down and studied her face. What I could see of it. And what I noticed was that she was not looking back at me.

Down at the ground. Past my shoulder. To my car.

"You ready for this?"

Her chest rose and fell rapidly. "Why wouldn't I be?"

I cleared my throat. "You're, uh, dressed differently than I expected."

Lydia looked down at her body, which was absolutely swallowed by the sweatshirt. The hem about hit her knees.

"Right." She did some throat clearing of her own, hers full of nerves. "Well, I have a plan."

One eyebrow rose slowly on my forehead. "Do you?"

"Yes?"

"Is that a question or statement?"

"I don't know," she huffed. "You're doing this thing with your face that's throwing me off, okay? Yes, I have a plan. You weren't sure what we were walking into today, right?"

"Correct." Because she hadn't given me a single shred of information.

Lydia pulled the sunglasses off her face, those bright blue eyes like a gut punch. "So we do a lap. Like around the block. We see how many people are there, and if anything looks fishy, we'll just keep on driving."

I managed a steady look. "Miss Pierson…"

"Lydia," she interrupted. "Do not call me Miss Pierson, or I will lose my mind. I already feel like this whole driver bodyguard thing is wildly pretentious, okay?"

I slicked my tongue over my teeth and tried to figure out how the fuck she'd gotten the upper hand in … everything.

"Why would it look fishy?"

She shifted in place. "I don't know … it just might."

Her good hand gripped the arm of her bag tightly, and I let out a slow breath. She was nervous and handling that was part of my job. "Let's do a lap then."

Lydia's eyes brightened. "Really?"

"Sure. A little recon never hurt anyone."

"*Exactly* what I was thinking."

She met my much longer stride as I turned toward the car, and at the same moment that I crossed to reach for the back seat door, she crossed to reach for the passenger side door handle.

Lifting my hands up so I didn't brush against … anything … I gave her a sideways look. "Where ya going?"

Lydia pointed at the passenger side. "The car."

I gave her a look.

"You're going to make me sit in the back seat?"

"It's safer that way. You're less noticeable back there too. For recon purposes," I added.

She glanced at my SUV. The windows in the back were a slightly darker tint than the front, and I could see the exact moment she decided that what I was saying actually made sense. "Okay."

With a deferential nod, I reached past her to open the back seat and she slid in without another word.

One point for me, if I were keeping a tally.

"Plus, if I do go in to the event, I'll need to take off my pants back here and switch to the skirt, and this will be easier." She smiled in my direction. "Good call."

I sighed heavily as I shut the door, and I thought I caught the sound of her laughing under her breath.

When I got into the driver's seat, Lydia was sitting in the middle of the bench, her entire face visible in the rearview mirror.

"Address?" I asked.

She slid her phone between the seats, and I took a quick glance at the location, typing it into my phone as she took hers back.

"A garden?"

Lydia shrugged. "I guess."

She'd shed the hat, her hair pulled back in some elaborate braid that wound around the back of her head. She caught me looking, touching her hair with just the tips of her fingers. "Faith did this for me."

I watched her face carefully.

"She's my sister." Lydia hooked her seat belt. Then checked that it was tight. She took a deep breath. "Half sister, I guess. She was six when our parents met and then got married. I was born like six months after they won the Super Bowl during my dad's last year … I know you know all of this. I don't know why I feel like I need to explain it."

I'd turned the car on while she spoke, giving her a quick glance when her voice trailed off. Her cheeks were pale.

"Take a deep breath for me, okay?" I asked.

Lydia's eyes met mine in the rearview mirror. Her mouth opened, and I braced for the argument, but instead, she complied.

I thought about telling her about my own family. How many siblings and half siblings I had. The way my dad left without a second glance. I thought about telling her that if he hadn't, my mom would never've married Tim. Marrying Tim got me three stepbrothers and a half sister who tagged along about two years later.

It would've served as a nice distraction for Lydia. For me, it would've been awful. Reliving my past was the last thing I intended on doing in any job.

No matter how badly I wanted to do this one right, it wasn't worth reliving for a young woman who'd probably bounce back into her old life just as quickly as she'd snuck out of it.

No. Lydia Pierson didn't get a piece of my past.

I'd learned the lesson a little too well. Sharing any part of me only ended in heartbreak for everyone involved.

"One more." Carefully, I pulled the gear shift and eased my foot off the brake. We moved forward away from the house. And I kept my eyes locked on hers. "It's just you and me going for a drive, all right?"

She nodded. The color slowly returned to her face, and her shoulders relaxed fractionally.

"I'm, I'm better," she said after another breath. Her hand fluttered along the edge of her seat belt. "Just don't like, test your hand at breaking the land speed record, okay?"

I wanted to smile. But I didn't. Instead, I nodded and pulled the car quietly down the tree-lined streets of her parents' home.

Lydia was quiet as we drove toward the venue, and in the rearview mirror, I studied her body language.

Even with cars next to us, my speed increasing, and noise filtering in around us, she didn't look too tense. I saw her open and shut her bag, muttering something under her breath.

Someone else might have asked if she was okay, but I remembered what Luke said. She didn't need anyone coddling her.

"What's the event we're headed toward?" I asked.

She blew out a slow breath. "Some dating app launch thingie."

I must have frowned because Lydia let out an amused laugh.

"Sounds bad to you, huh?"

I grunted.

A bunch of twentysomethings, probably all as attractive as her, gathered around taking selfies so they could connect on a new app that would allow them a different excuse to screw. So yeah, it sounded like hell on earth.

"Three months ago, I wouldn't have minded going," she said, eyes trained out toward the mountains. Then she blinked down at her lap. "I *shouldn't* have a problem going. It's not going to be that big. Maybe a h-hundred, hundred and fifty people."

Her voice stuttered just a bit over that last bit. My eyes narrowed slightly in her direction.

Shouldn't didn't always have much to do with it, when your body refused to participate in what your mind wanted to do.

I knew that well.

It *shouldn't* have been so hard for me to go home, yet it had been more than eighteen months since I'd stepped foot onto our family's property. It shouldn't have been difficult to return to the league after my injury, after a recovery that happened at the same time as the signing of my divorce papers.

And it should've been easier to forgive myself for the things I'd done wrong.

For Lydia Pierson, her *should've* was going to a garden party for a dating app, even if her reason for being on shaky ground was legitimate.

"If you decide you want to go in," I said easily, "how long we stay is completely up to you. All you have to do is say the word, and we're out of there."

She smiled at me in the mirror. "Like a safe word?" she said in a teasing voice. "I hardly think an afternoon party is on par with some whips and chains."

I leveled her with an unamused look.

"I know what you mean," she continued. "And … yes, if I decide it looks not-fishy, I'll let you know."

But the moment we turned the corner and saw the line of cars, her throat moved in a heavy swallow. The pale drawn look sank back into her face. And her chest moved with the increasing speed of her breaths.

There was a wall of flowers for a backdrop, across which stood a line of photographers snapping photos of people as they strolled in.

They clamored over each other to get the best angle, jostling like they were fighting for prime spot.

"I don't …" She stopped and took a deep breath like she had earlier. "I don't know if this is a great event to start with."

I kept driving, noting the way her shoulders were tense and high. And she'd braced her feet up on the console, hugging her knees to her chest.

"No problem," I said. "Anywhere else you want to stop on the way home?"

Lydia didn't look at me, not until we'd passed the circus. Her shoulders dropped a good inch. Her breathing steadied out. And I wasn't entirely sure that Lydia Pierson was afraid of being in the car after all.

"I'm sorry for making you drive out to get me," she said, still not meeting my eyes. "It's stupid, huh?"

"No apology needed. It's my job to drive you wherever you want to go."

She blinked those blue eyes back in my direction. "Can we just … get an iced coffee or something on the way home?"

"Where do you want to go?" She'd probably want something fancy and expensive. Where snooty college kids made drawings in foam for the sole purpose of posting a picture. A cat or a fucking camel or something that would cost twenty dollars.

But Lydia shrugged. "McDonald's is fine. They've got yummy whipped cream."

"You want me to take you to McDonald's," I said.

"Whatever's closest. Don't go out of your way on my account." She leaned forward in her seat. "Can I put on some music?"

"*No one* touches the radio in my car," I said. "It plays rock and country and nothing else."

"How do you know I don't listen to those?"

I raised an eyebrow. "Do you?"

Lydia lifted her chin a notch. "No. But that's besides the point. You're making some awfully big assumptions about me, Erik."

Before I could defend myself or my music, she settled back in her seat.

"It's okay." She smiled again. "People do it all the time. It makes it all the more enjoyable when I prove them wrong."

Her words hit with the accuracy of a bullet, slicing straight through whatever armor I may have strapped on in preparation for this first strange outing.

Taking Lydia Pierson through the McDonald's drive-through for an iced coffee. What the actual fuck.

Shifting in my seat, I tried to recalibrate. Mentally tick through what this meant moving forward. Everything I'd expected was out the fucking window, and a big part of me wanted to sit Luke and Allie Pierson down and get a whole new viewpoint of my reluctant new client.

"Speaking of assumptions," she said, "do I have to wait until our second or third outing to hear your story of how you ended up driving little old me around?"

I glanced into the back seat. She might have looked innocent, and her voice was certainly trying to convey the same thing, but wheels were turning in that head of hers.

"Who says I'm going to tell you at all?"

She laughed. Until she saw the look on my face.

Her smile fell, eyes widening almost comically in her face. "Seriously?"

"Your dad didn't hire me to tell stories, Miss Pierson."

Lydia did the thing my sisters were so good at. She looked straight at me and mentally rolled her eyes without moving a single muscle. I'd recognize that facial expression in my sleep.

"If you don't tell me, I'll just figure it out the old-fashioned way."

I sighed.

"Cyberstalking," she continued. "Don't think I won't."

"You like it when people do that to you?" I asked.

Lydia frowned. "No."

The golden arches appeared down the block, and I jerked my chin at the windshield.

I pulled up to the speaker, and she shuffled forward to look at the menu, elbows braced on the back of my seat.

She smelled like candy. Her soft voice sent a silky tremor through my ears as she read through her options.

"Oooh, I changed my mind. An apple pie, umm, a vanilla dip cone. And a small french fry."

I turned my head. Her face was inches from mine, but she didn't back up. Neither did I.

"You want all three?"

She set her chin on her hand and batted her long eyelashes at me. "Judgey much? Yes, I want all three."

Once her food was in hand, I actively tuned out the happy moaning sounds she made at the first lick of ice cream.

And once I'd pulled back up to the Pierson home, without leaving my car and feeling more than a little off-balance, I wondered for the millionth time what the hell I'd gotten myself into.

Chapter
FIVE

Lydia

THE PROBLEM WITH RUTS WAS THAT YOU HARDLY EVER SAW them coming.

Ruts were comfortable. Like wrapping up in the coziest warmest blanket in your favorite chair on a snowy day. Who would want to pull themselves out of that spot?

I thought I'd taken the first step out of my stay home rut by climbing into Erik Wilder's immaculate SUV.

But by the time I polished off my fries and licked the last crumbs of the apple pie off my fingers, I refused to admit that one rut had been replaced by another. Like I rolled from one comfy spot on the bed into the other just as comfy spot.

Not that there was much about Erik that was comfortable.

On our second outing, only a few days later, I watched him underneath my lashes from behind the passenger seat. Made for better undercover viewing when I wasn't in the middle of the bench and thereby in full view of the mirror. Without complaint and hardly a word passed between us, he drove past the southern edge of Lake Washington to my favorite Dutch Bros Coffee.

"Going inside today?" he asked, big hand casually resting on the steering wheel.

Honestly, his hands were huge. Long fingers. My face felt hot as I thought just a little too hard about that.

He was wearing a short-sleeve black shirt, tight around the impressive curve of his bicep, and as the muscles shifted when he turned the steering wheel, I almost forgot what he'd asked. No … there wasn't much about him that felt comfortable at all.

But he sure made for pleasant scenery in this new rut I'd found myself in.

I blinked. "Umm, doesn't matter to me."

Erik's eyes narrowed on the parking lot. It wasn't busy, but it wasn't dead either. "Doesn't it?"

I gave him a look. "Drive-through is fine."

He let out a reserved sigh, and my lips quirked.

There were so many variations to the way he exhaled, and it probably made me a little sick in the head that I was enjoying them so much.

The rut continued, happy little punctuation marks between days spent studying and logging in for my two classes, usually topped with whipped cream and chocolate. Each time I slid into his car—which smelled like him—it got a bit easier.

On our fourth outing, we stopped at the little gourmet market down the road from my parents'. Yes, it was a chickenshit way to prove to him that I was capable of being in public since I knew just about everyone who shopped there, and the owners always left us alone. He quietly walked behind me as I filled a basket with the ingredients for the spaghetti and meatballs I would be making for dinner.

At the end of an aisle, I studied the bottles of red wine for my sauce and caught movement at the other end. Two teenage boys, dressed in designer labels with long, floppy fuckboy haircuts, whispered to each other, eyes darting in my direction.

I let out a slow breath when one of them pulled out his phone. Usually, all it took was a kind smile, and the average person would leave me alone. But that was the hard part. You could never quite tell who was average and who was a freaking psycho with a zoom lens on their camera.

"Should've worn my hat and glasses," I muttered.

Erik shifted forward, effectively blocking their view, and I gave him a small, grateful smile.

"Want me to ask them to go?" he said, voice low and rumbly.

I snatched a bottle with a black and gold label, shaking my head as I stuck it in next to the box of pasta. With Erik walking close behind me, a giant wall of muscle between me and the rest of the world, I slowed my pace as we passed the bakery. Behind the glass case, I peered in at the perfectly decorated cakes and pies and cookies.

"Want anything?" I asked.

"No thanks."

"Do you *ever* eat?"

Erik cut me a look.

"Just asking. You never order anything when we go out." The sweet old lady who owned the market came out from the kitchen, giving me a head-to-toe study as she approached.

"You look skinny, Lydia." She snapped on some plastic gloves. "Better order two of whatever sounds good."

I smiled. "I'm doing my best, Maria. Do you have any tiramisu today?"

She nodded. "Just cutting some in the back." Maria eyed Erik. "One for your … friend, too?"

"Oh no, he'd never indulge in something as glorious as your desserts." I patted Erik's shoulder. "He survives on suspicion and scary facial expressions."

Maria chuckled. "If that's your type, honey … can't say I blame you."

Erik mumbled something under his breath, and I rolled my

lips between my teeth to keep from laughing. His eyes flashed with annoyance, and I lost the battle, laughing loudly enough that the punks in Abercrombie strolled back in our direction. As I took the boxes of tiramisu from Maria, Erik's hand slid warm and heavy over my lower back.

My arms popped with goose bumps because that one touch felt an awful lot like the last time someone tried to shove their hand up my skirt.

But better. Much, much better.

"Let's go back this way," he said.

A man was touching my back, and I was struggling to breathe evenly.

The sheer shock of it had me admitting something in a rushed exhale. "I watched you on YouTube last night."

Erik dropped his hand, his jaw tensing as he kept stride with me. "Find anything good?"

My chin rose a notch. "A lot actually."

Maybe it was the class I was taking, something I didn't feel like explaining to him, about how social constructs influence the way we look at sports that had me thinking about Erik again as I climbed into bed.

Setting my iPad up onto the bed next to me, I typed in his name and found a small list of replays.

His best sacks, some interceptions that had me grinning. He was big, and he was fast. He watched the quarterback, shifting quickly as he noticed something someone else might have missed, was able to spin around linebackers easily, using those long, strong arms to disrupt even the best QBs that played during his time.

And I watched his celebrations after. His passion was contagious, such a far cry from the well-contained man who smacked my hand away when I tried to switch the channel on his radio.

"You were good," I said simply.

His wide chest expanded on a deep inhale, and I found myself holding my own breath to see if he'd sigh.

"Makes sense why they switched up their defense after you left though." I tugged the wine out of the basket and laid it flat on the conveyor, giving him a look when he was hogging space in the aisle. "Their sack average went down when they switched to the 4-3 defense, but the guy who replaced you was better containing the run."

"Thanks," he said dryly.

I laughed. "You fishing for compliments, *Mr. Wilder*?"

Oh, he didn't like that. His face bent into an impressive frown.

I knew he wasn't. Because any time I brought up football, his already limited conversation skills dropped to subzero. If he had been, though, I could've told him that watching the way he rushed the quarterback was about as hot to me as if he'd paraded shirtless down the fifty-yard line.

Well. *Maybe* as hot. I'd have to reserve that opinion if I ever caught a glimpse of what lay under all those solid color cotton shirts he wore.

"I didn't watch your injury," I continued. "That's game film I've never been able to bring myself to study."

Erik cut me a look. "You do a lot of that?"

Eyebrows raised, I nudged him out of the way with my hip to set the rest of my food on the small conveyor belt. "Girl's gotta have some hobbies."

He exhaled a short, incredulous laugh under his breath, and I found myself smiling.

I kept my tone light when I spoke again. "I did read about it, though."

Erik took the empty basket out of my hand and slotted it into a stack on the floor. All I got in response was a grunt.

"Does your knee still give you trouble?"

He sighed. "No."

The article hadn't contained much. A rundown of the play,

his stats for the season, the grade of the ACL tear, and that he'd be placed on Injured Reserve until surgery and rehab was complete. Many, many players had come back from worse.

"So that's not why you didn't go back?" I asked casually.

His eyebrows pinched in over his dark eyes. But he didn't move his gaze over to me. Didn't even pretend he was going to answer.

It was like he enjoyed knowing it was driving me crazy.

I chewed on my lip while Maria's husband scanned in my items. He winked when I handed him my card.

Erik took the bags without a word, and I slid the receipt into my pocket. The complete lack of information I had on Erik was in total contradiction to how immediately at ease I felt with him.

How often I thought about him when he wasn't around.

Hell, my *comfort level* was in direct contradiction to how he acted around me.

And I told myself that this interest was purely educational. I'd never met anyone who had so much talent, no end in sight to their career, to simply just walk away without a second thought.

As we walked to the car, I thought about telling him that. Thought about telling him about my class and that the only reason I was asking was to uncover some layer of how sports influenced culture, how culture influenced sports, and the ramifications when it came to how we viewed both.

What about it, in the game itself or his life outside it, caused so much damage that he left millions—literally—on the table in order to move on.

But I found myself holding my tongue. The last thing I could handle from him was a flippant comment about what I was doing and why. It would take any comfy cozy rut and rip me right the hell out of it. And as much as I hated to admit it, after I'd so easily dismissed him the first day, I needed Erik Wilder to get through that Dior party.

That knowledge unsettled me. Just a little.

But as the days inched just a little bit closer to the event, everything seemed to unsettle me.

My parents hovering made me twitchy. Because it was like they knew exactly what rut I was in—even if I'd edged my way out of the house—but still weren't sure how to shove me out of the nest completely.

Faith being perfectly happy and head over heels in love with her gorgeous, talented football-playing boyfriend had me riding the edge of jealousy for the first time in my entire life. Not because I wanted Dominic or begrudged her happiness. But the longer I drove around with Broody McHotpants, and the more he seemed determined not to let me in under his skin, the more I seemed to notice all the happy freaking couples around me.

And Jill …

Jill was about to drive me out of my fucking mind with her texts.

If there was a way to un-invite her to the event, I would've done it faster than Erik could manage a grumpy sigh.

I got texts about why I didn't show up to her event.

Texts asking me to meet for lunch.

Texts asking what I was wearing for the event so we didn't accidentally match.

And all of which I evaded like a mother effing professional. My excuse-making skills were so honed by the end that I could've had business cards made up.

Lydia Pierson- Professional excuse-maker and drive-through connoisseur.

It had a nice ring to it.

I kept telling myself I'd be fine by the time my Dior event came around.

I'd be fine because it was just a simple party and I'd done hundreds of them, and I should have no problem because I had Erik.

I had Erik and a great dress and the knowledge that showing

up to one party for putting my face on one perfume ad would cover all my tuition to finish my master's.

I would be *fine.*

I reminded myself of that as I emailed with my professors, firming up the topics I wanted to focus on for my primary project. I had a million tabs open on my laptop as I worked, only stopping for occasional coffee runs with the man who shared nothing.

I kept things basic, forcing Erik through the Starbucks drive-through the next day.

The line was long, and I slid to the middle of the bench, setting my elbows on the console while he studied the menu.

"Getting anything today?" I asked him.

"Nope. Just trying to see if I can guess which horrifically sweet concoction you'll poison your body with today."

"Ha, ha." His lips twitched at my dry tone. We sat for another five minutes, hardly moving at all, and I blew a raspberry. "This line is going to take an hour at this rate."

I glanced at my watch. I had a class discussion board due in two hours, and I still needed to read through one more of my classmate's projects.

"You got something to rush home for?" he asked.

Ouch. His dry tone had me let out an annoyed sigh of my own. Except it didn't make him smile. His gaze flashed to mine, and he must have seen something buried in my eyes because he narrowed his.

Did he ask, though? Of course not.

"Of course not," I said lightly. "All I do at home is paint my nails and count my split ends, Erik."

Oh, he didn't love the sarcasm dripping from my voice. His phone vibrated, and he picked it up from the console to open up his message thread.

While he was distracted, I reached my arm over and punched the button that switched to the Bluetooth setting on the radio.

He knocked my arm away, and I slapped my hand over his before he could change it.

One of my favorite K-Pop songs started on my phone, and I gleefully punched the volume button on the side of my phone when he started muttering foul, foul curse words underneath his breath.

"Sorry, can't hear you," I said.

The unholy annoyance in his eyes brought me so much joy, I probably should have worried about my mental health.

Erik set down his phone and punched the power button on his stereo so hard that the button popped off.

"I like that song," I said.

"You would." He brought the car to a stop at the speaker, the disembodied voice asking what he'd like to order. Before I could open my mouth, Erik leaned through the open window. "Yeah, I'll get a venti Iced Sugar Cookie Almond milk latte with whipped cream, chocolate and sprinkles and, uh … a grande Caffe Americano."

My mouth dropped open. It wasn't precisely what I was going to order, but okay, it sounded delicious.

Erik handed over a twenty, ignoring my hand as it held out my credit card.

I sighed, and I caught the edge of his lips twitching.

When the green apron-clad barista with big brown eyes handed over the two drinks with a fliratious smile at Erik, I fought the urge to growl at her. But of course, I was sitting in the back. Like a kid. So she didn't see me.

In the momentary jealous haze clouding my eyes, I missed Erik trying to hand me my drink.

He cleared his throat.

I took the cup blindly, stopping short when there was no whipped cream. No sprinkles. Just *coffee*.

"What?" I glanced at the front seat just in time for him to take a huge spoonful of the whipped cream and shovel it in his mouth. "That's mine!"

He licked his lips, a borderline lewd gesture that had my thighs feeling a little … restless. Then he hummed deep in his throat. "I didn't catch *you* ordering anything, but mine is delicious."

I glared, and Erik let out a low, scraping chuckle that would probably echo somewhere in the back of my brain later when I crawled between the sheets.

On principle, I didn't drink the coffee, tossing it into the kitchen garbage after he dropped me off.

My phone buzzed, and I wondered if it was Erik, who'd dropped me off with his usual 'See you tomorrow' and a steady, unbothered look in his eye.

I groaned when I saw Jill's name.

Jill: Well … since you ignored my question about the dress, I'm wearing green. Do you even remember how to show up to events anymore? Don't forget not to blink when they take a picture.

Me: Your concern is touching.

Jill: Don't be bitchy. It's pretty evil genius, actually. I wish I'd thought of it.

Me: Thought of what? Staging my own car accident?

Jill: You've managed to hide away for three months. Once you resurface, the press will have a field day with the way you've made them wait.

Jill: Everyone was talking about it at my app party. I mean, *I* didn't say it was over the top, but someone did. Don't worry, I defended you.

"For fuck's sake," I muttered. Just what I didn't want. Couldn't I just … slip in through the back door or something?

My face started feeling a little warm, my hands itchy and cold, prickles moving down to the tips of my fingers.

I almost called Erik. Told him I wasn't feeling well and we could skip the party.

Rubbing at my forehead, I wandered down to my bedroom and stared at the stack of textbooks, with the marked-up papers next to my laptop. And I pinched my eyes shut.

It was so easy to pretend this would go away on its own. That I could still manage the life I wanted without having to cross over this particular hurdle. But it wouldn't. And I couldn't make an excuse or stay in my comfy warm spot any longer.

Yup. I was feeling twitchy all right. Because I had less than twenty-four hours, and my rut was about to be blown the hell up.

Chapter
SIX

Lydia

O N MY FOURTEENTH TIME LOOKING OUT THE SIDELIGHT windows of the front door, my sister snuck up behind me, setting her chin on my shoulder.

"Whatcha doing?" she whispered.

I swatted her face away. "Nothing."

Faith hummed. "You didn't eat much at dinner, and I know I didn't make shitty chicken."

With a sigh, I turned away from my vigil at the door. Erik wasn't due for another five minutes, the man had never shown up a single minute early *or* late, so I wasn't even sure why I was watching for his arrival so obsessively.

"The chicken was definitely not shitty." I shrugged. "Just not very hungry."

My big sister eyed me carefully. In fact, throughout the entirety of our family dinner, all my family had done was eye me carefully.

Mom came home early from the Wolves office to carefully watch me get my stuff together for my event that night. My bag had been by the front door for two hours.

Dad canceled a recruiting meeting at the practice facilities to carefully watch me check and then re-check the contents of said bag. Yes, it might have been easier to get ready at their house, given that I'd lived there for a couple of months, but honestly, I could not handle all the watching—careful or not—because I was already feeling like I was going to fly apart at the seams.

"How are you feeling about tonight?" Faith asked. "You sure you don't want me to come with you?"

"Because fancy perfume events at swanky clubs are so your scene," I teased.

They didn't feel much like my scene anymore, but that seemed a bit superfluous to the conversation.

"No, but being there when my sister needs me is a thousand percent my scene." Again, with the careful watching in her eyes. I turned away, studying the empty driveway. "And you didn't answer my question," she said gently.

I knew what I wanted to say.

I didn't want to go, and yes, I very much wanted my big sister there with me. I could clutch her hand with my good one and throw on a big, carefree smile that was oh-so fake while I broke all the bones in her fingers with my super-strong grip.

I'd done so well, mild twinges of apprehension aside, and when the day of the event dawned … anything mild had disappeared the moment I opened my eyes.

Every outing had felt like practice, and as I stood waiting for my six-foot-four security blanket with the scary eyes and big arms to arrive, I had to admit that all that practice was complete and utter horseshit.

I couldn't visualize a way out of this one, no matter how hard I tried.

But if I told Faith any of that, she'd just worry.

So I shrugged. "I'm a little nervous. But it's stupid. I shouldn't be. There will be a m-million people there. All I have to do is smile for the cameras and hang out for a while, and that's it."

"It's not stupid," Faith argued. "I wasn't even the one in the accident, and I felt shaky for a couple of weeks."

Her voice wobbled dangerously at the end of the sentence, and I pinched my eyes shut. She might not have been driving my car, but she witnessed it. Powerless to do anything as my car slammed into a tree.

Skkkkkrt. Pump the brakes on *that*, I commanded my own stupid brain. Instantly, I rerouted my thoughts somewhere more immediate, somewhere anchored in the present.

"Did you know that Erik still had three years on his contract when he walked away?" I asked Faith. "Only played for five years."

At the abrupt change in topic—my pretty blatant non-answer—she drew in a quick, surprised breath.

"I guess I never really paid that close of attention," she admitted slowly. "You always watched the roster more carefully than I did."

I stared out the side window, waiting for him to appear. "He ruptured his ACL in the second half of his last season. Never came back to play."

Faith hummed. "Some people don't want to risk another injury, I guess."

The night before, I'd spent hours watching footage of him. Again. It gave me a safe thing to obsess over when I pretty much did not want to think about the fact that I had to take his giant scary ass with me to that giant scary event. Jill's words about my grand triumphant return triggered some pretty shittastic mental images in my head. Walking the red carpet, press clamoring for photos while I did my best not to puke on that red carpet.

So naturally, I let Erik and his blank slate of a past cram into every busy, restless part of my brain.

"But like, what's up with that?" I turned and gave her a look. "Can you imagine Dominic quitting after an injury that a lot of guys completely recover from?" I asked, referencing her boyfriend, a tight end in his first season with the Wolves.

"No," she answered immediately. "He loves it too much."

I gestured to the empty driveway like Erik was there on display. "See? It's weird. How does a professional football player just quit like that and then end up doing something super random like … sort of a bodyguard? He never tells me anything. I've asked a dozen times."

Faith studied me quietly, running her fingers through the ends of the messy curls tumbling down my back, the ones she'd helped me with earlier because one-handed curling was not something I'd mastered yet. "Are we doing like transference right now? Is that what it's called?"

I sighed. "No."

"Mmkay." My sister squeezed my shoulder. "You will do great tonight. No one will make a big deal out of you being there, and then you'll realize there's nothing to worry about. You know what you're doing."

The words, comforting and sweet, were still hanging in the air as the rumble of an engine crawled up the driveway. And something eased in my chest, just a little. My fingers were still cold, and my shoulders were rock hard with the tension I was carrying around, but the iron band around my rib cage loosened enough that I could take a full breath.

Mom approached behind Faith and me, setting her hand on my back. "You need us to talk to Erik about anything? I know you guys have gone … *out* quite a bit, but this is a different kind of scene."

We both knew she didn't need to talk to Erik about a single thing. He needed no guidance on how to do his job. In my mind, I got a flash of his hand on my back, the way he shifted his big body to block me from view. Plus, my mom's question didn't come from mistrust, just her own worry. I gave her a small smile when I glanced over my shoulder. "Being a parent must be weird, huh?"

Mom's eyes, big and blue like mine, glossed over instantly. "The absolute weirdest," she said. Then she gave Faith a kiss on the cheek, her hand squeezing on my good arm. "Like your heart is living outside your body."

The three of us stood together quietly in front of the window by the front door while Erik opened the driver's side door of his black SUV.

When I finally got a full view of him, I hissed out a slow breath. He looked *good*.

Something about his perfectly tailored black pants had his long legs looking even longer, his slim waist encased in a black leather belt emphasizing the broad span of his chest in the crisp light-blue shirt. I gulped audibly when he paused to adjust the button at the top, tugging it away from his neck like he couldn't breathe very well.

Erik Wilder cleaned up *nicely*.

Mom laughed softly, then tapped a finger underneath my mouth, which was gaping open ever so slightly. "At least if I have to let you out into the world tonight, knowing you're a little unsure, you'll be going with him."

I snapped my mouth shut.

Erik's muscular chest expanded on a deep inhale, and through the sunglass, I felt his gaze like a touch. I thought about what Jill said. How over-the-top people thought me, like my absence had been some scheme to create interest. If they thought that was bad, what the hell would it look like to show up with a freaking bodyguard? It would come off pretentious at best, hysterical and paranoid at worst. I could already imagine the whispers among them.

Nope. My brain didn't like that thought process either, so I kept my eyes lasered on the man in the driveway, on his long legs and big hands, the golden skin and dark beard that made him look like he spent all his free time chopping wood or knocking over trees with his bare hands or harvesting grain or some shit like that.

He didn't move from beside the car.

I knew him well enough now. He was going to make my ass walk out to the car unaided. Because he *knew* I didn't want to go.

Which was why I didn't budge from between my mom and sister. I liked the little Pierson-women sandwich we had going. Once I moved out of it, there was no going back. It meant the careful watching of my family was going to be replaced by the careful watching of Erik the Mute.

"Are we waiting for him to come to the door like a date?" Faith whispered.

Mom snorted.

I tilted my head to the side as I studied him. Gawd, he looked stupidly gorgeous in those clothes. I wasn't sure if that made things better or worse.

"Mom? Why didn't Washington renew his contract? After his injury, I mean."

She hummed quietly. "It, it wasn't our choice. He still had time left on his contract, but he decided to leave not long after his surgery."

I gave her a look, but she didn't say anything else.

"And?"

Mom raised her eyebrows. "Not my story to share, bug. You know how it goes."

"Drives me insane," I whispered. "All so he can play Kevin Costner to our collective *Bodyguard* fantasies."

It was Faith's turn to snort.

"Lydia," Mom chided gently.

"Lydia won't touch him," Faith interjected before I could say anything. "She just likes to look. You know that."

Erik's eyes never strayed from where I still stood framed in the window. I knew it, no matter whether I could see his dark eyes or not. I broke the connection long enough to grab my bag and give Mom and Faith a quick kiss on the cheek.

"Erik will survive me, I promise," I told them.

Dad appeared from the kitchen. "Will he, though?"

I gave him a kiss on the cheek too. "You hired him. If he doesn't, whose fault is that?"

They stood together, all careful, careful watching, and I gave them as big of a smile as I could manage.

"You're going to wait up for me, aren't you?" I asked.

"Of course not," Mom said in a weak voice.

Faith nodded.

Dad winked.

It was enough to have me genuinely laughing when I walked out the door.

But as I neared the car, the laughter faded. Erik watched me carefully, reaching for the door into the back seat. I stopped walking.

"What is it?"

"I can't sit back there," I said.

The tinted windows might have helped before, might have made me feel some false sense of security, but I didn't want to be so separate tonight. The rut no longer felt like a real thing, and being by myself on that big long bench sounded like the worst thing in the world as we rolled up to the event. Nothing about tonight was cozy and warm, in fact, it was all I could do not to shiver where I stood.

I pointed at the passenger door. "I'm sitting there."

He regarded me warily but stepped back to open that door instead. "Care to explain why?"

I tilted my head. "If you tell me why you stopped playing football."

Erik's jaw clenched, eyes darkening with annoyance, but he didn't say a damn word. Just as I expected.

He held the passenger door open, and I slid in. Once the door was firmly shut behind me, I watched him walk around the front of his car. He was moving differently tonight, the clothes showcasing his body in a way that the T-shirts and jeans just … didn't.

He was hot in both, no avoiding the truth of that, but tonight, he looked the part of the big, mean, and scary man. It was in the arrogant tilt of his jaw and the cold set of his mouth.

A role he was playing. And it was something I could understand.

There was this idea of me, one that I'd cultivated for as long as I could remember. That idea was always held firmly in my control, no matter which side of me I showed. Lately, it was Lydia, the homebody, with her fluffy drinks and favorite face masks. It used to be the sexpot, the model. Occasionally, it was the hot mess or the girl who wanted to be a mogul like her mom. But no matter what I posted, how much I engaged or allowed to be shown, I was the one steering those images and that version of me that they saw.

And as Erik got into the vehicle with me, filling the space with his big body, delicious scent, and overwhelming presence, it hit me that tonight—with him—was the very first time when I felt like I wasn't in control of how others viewed me. I wasn't in control of anything, really.

What a horribly shitty realization.

The rut—for all its good and bad—had still sheltered me from view.

The vise on my chest wound tighter and tighter, and I took a big deep breath, then let it out slowly as he turned the key over.

I turned to Erik, laying a hand on his arm. "Wait."

He paused in the motion of shifting the vehicle into reverse. "What?"

"What are we doing tonight?" I asked. His eyebrows rose slowly. "I mean," I hastily added, "how is tonight going to play out? Like … you and me. We've never done anything like this."

"I will never be far away, Lydia," he said. His voice was set to calm. It was soothing and low and quiet. It was the same voice he used when he told me to take deep breaths. "I promise."

I laid a hand on my chest. My fingers shook a little. "It's not that, I just …"

"What is it? I can't help if I don't understand."

"I can't do this if you're just … hiding away in a dark corner. Watching every move of everyone around me. I'll feel like I'm on display."

With the forehead furrow again. Honestly, Erik studied me like I was an escaped animal from the zoo.

"Aren't you … like … on a giant billboard outside the event?"

I rolled my eyes. "You know what I mean."

Erik let out a slow breath, his eyes steady on mine. "How would you like to do this then?"

In my mind, I pictured the red carpet or whatever garish color they were going with. Imagined the flashing lights and the journalists calling my name. I didn't want any of it. But there was no backing out now. Not if I ever wanted to move forward. And I *did*.

Two weeks ago, Erik Wilder would have been the last person I'd have chosen to spend the evening with.

I would've conjured up the same faceless man with a great smile and big heart and good taste in clothes and who could read my mind, just like my dad read my mom's. Instead, I found myself staring at the guy who never smiled, who hated my music, and didn't know there were variations of T-shirts beyond black, white, and gray. I wasn't entirely certain he even knew how to laugh or whether he possessed any sense of humor, and somehow he was exactly what I needed to feel brave enough to get through this big scary thing.

I couldn't imagine anyone else there with me. There was no one else who could make me feel as safe, no one who could distract me from my own fears and understand exactly why I had a role to play. One that would get me—and him—through this unscathed.

A smile curled my lips before I could stop it. He narrowed his eyes.

"What?" he asked. His voice was full of suspicion, and before I even spoke, I knew he'd *hate* what I was about to say.

It was perfect.

"Erik, I have a plan."

Chapter
SEVEN

Erik

HAVE A PLAN.

Such innocent words. It didn't take me long to realize that coming out of Lydia Pierson's mouth, they were the most terrifying words in existence.

This woman, and her plans, should've sent me in a tuck and roll out of my own moving vehicle. It would've been the safer option. Because I found myself at her lushly decorated apartment in downtown Seattle, waiting for her to appear from the bathroom while she hammered me with shouted questions.

"High school mascot?"

I didn't answer. Just like I hadn't answered the last few—my favorite home cooked meal (my mom's cinnamon rolls), my favorite movie franchise (Avengers, which is why my sisters used to call me Cap), and my astrological sign (like I had a fucking clue).

Instead of bending to the sheer force of her will, which I already knew was impressive, I studied the space where I waited to try to gain clues about her now that I was finally seeing her living space.

On the white walls were tasteful art framed in a solid dark

wood, none of them screaming any of her personality. The furniture was well-built, in brown leathers and gray flannel, but it was in the bedroom that I finally saw Lydia as I knew her.

Instead of framed photo shoots, pouting lips, or sexpot shots, Lydia's massive black dresser was covered in framed photos of her family. The largest was a shot clipped from a *Sports Illustrated* shoot after the Wolves won the championship early in her mom's reign of ownership. Luke held the trophy over his head in one hand, his hair and face coated in sweat and dirt. And tucked under his arm with a massive smile on her face was Allie—Lydia's complete doppelganger. There was such a strong resemblance between the two, in the big blue eyes, the hair and the wide, big smile, it was almost eerie.

Her king-sized bed was made in varying shades of white, but when I saw a fuzzy black edge, I lifted the pile above it to find a small plush wolf. His ear was worn, the Washington tag around its neck showing stray threads like both areas had seen the tips of her fingers over the years. And she'd hidden it underneath all the polished décor. An understanding hum escaped my mouth before I could stop it. My sister Greer used to do the same thing to one of her childhood blankets, and it was a grounding reminder in the middle of Lydia's constant barrage of inquiries. Because of her fucking *plan*.

"You don't have to tell me that one," she continued, undeterred. "You went to Sisters High School, and your mascot is the Outlaws."

My head whipped toward the bathroom. "Lydia, you told me you wouldn't dig personal shit up."

"I just googled it five seconds ago. Calm down."

"Great," I muttered. Her words were the perfect reminder of why I didn't want to go along with her idea.

Lydia heard me, and her answering laugh was a light, tinkling sound that echoed in her big tile-covered bathroom. Absolutely nothing about this was going as I'd expected.

Yet again, she'd taken all my preparation for the night and blown it to fucking smithereens.

"What about your family? I know you have one sister because I met her not long after Molly hired her." She dropped a bottle of something and swore. "Two working arms would really come in handy right now, you know."

I rubbed the back of my neck.

"Fine. No family questions. Moving on."

"Excellent."

"Why didn't you go back to playing?"

I'd faced three-hundred-pound linebackers who weren't as relentless as Lydia Pierson, something I'd never, ever admit to her out loud. Knowing her, she'd take it as a compliment, and I did not mean it as one.

Whatever my gut told me would happen over the course of that evening, it had betrayed me greatly. As I dressed earlier that evening, pulling my nicest dress shirt and slacks out of the dusty, ill-used portion of my closet, I imagined how all of this would play out. Lydia would be nervous on the drive over to her apartment, we'd talk through all the security protocols for the night, I'd tell her everything I learned from the manager at Vue to ease her mind, and the rest of my time would be spent watching. Watching her. Watching the people around her. Watching exits and entrances while she drank or danced or took pictures.

Once she was ready to go, we'd make the drive back to Luke and Allie's house, where I'd safely deposit her into her parents' care and wait for our next outing. Easy money, I thought.

"You're still not answering my question," she yelled from the bathroom.

"No shit," I mumbled under my breath. I pinched the bridge of my nose while I heard more clattering of bottles and brushes and who the hell knew what in that bathroom. I took a steadying inhale. The innocent drive-through visits had not prepared me for this. In fact, nothing I'd ever done in my life had prepared me for the situation I found myself in—the victim of Lydia Pierson's mad plans for a fancy party. "Maybe I didn't hear you."

She popped her head out of the bathroom with a long swing of curly blond hair that fell over her shoulder. Her eyes were done up now, somehow looking bigger and bluer and … lashier. "You heard me just fine."

I met her stare with one of my own.

Lydia disappeared back into the bathroom with a huff.

Her huff didn't hide anything from me. I knew exactly what Lydia was doing; focus on me so she didn't have to think about her evening out.

Lydia's body language on the drive over was strung as tight as a guitar string. She might have played unaffected, an Oscar-worthy performance rooted in her easy chatter and endless questions.

But in her fisted hands, the bone of her fingers fairly splitting the skin over her knuckles, I saw her nerves like she'd painted them on her face.

Her voice came through the open bathroom door. "My plan won't work if I don't know more about you."

"That's not why it won't work." I stood from where I'd been sitting and studied the apartment, the lock on the metal door, tested the massive glass slider that opened to a patio overlooking downtown Seattle. I thought about my own place back home in Oregon and shook my head. She was only twenty-two, and quite literally, had the world laid out before her. Picking her up every day at Luke and Allie's house made it easy to forget just how different she and I were.

"Why?"

"I never agreed to your plan."

Whatever she'd been doing in the bathroom halted immediately, the bottles and sprays and whatnot, and then she appeared in the doorway again. But instead of just a peek of her head, she stood fully in the opening. The dress she was wearing was clearly undone because she held it against her chest with her good hand.

It was black and tight to her body, and once the zipper was done—hopefully sometime really, really soon—it would be held up over her shoulders with thin gold straps.

"My idea is *great*."

I kept my face even because that was what the situation demanded. But it took every ounce of discipline not to stare, not to study the parts of her she was showing that I'd never seen before. "Your idea is flawed, and I'm not going along with it."

When her mouth dropped open, I knew I could've said that a bit … more nicely. Then her eyes flashed in a calculated shift I didn't particularly love. "Don't you technically work for me?"

"I work for your parents, not you." I gestured to the front door. "Do you want to know what's wrong with your front door?"

Her eyebrows rose slowly. "No?"

"One good kick and that lock is basically useless. You should always lock the dead bolt behind you."

Lydia's gaze darted to the door and back to mine. "I didn't think I needed the dead bolt since I had you with me."

Crossing my arms over my chest, I held her gaze. "People act on instinct in almost every situation. When you walk into this apartment, you're likely to act the way you always do, regardless of whether I'm with you. You didn't lock the dead bolt because you probably never lock the dead bolt when you're in here. That front desk and the guy in the uniform make you feel safe, right?"

She shifted uncomfortably. "Well, they *did*. Thanks for ruining that." Lydia's cast-free hand tugged on the neckline of her dress when it also shifted uncomfortably. It was uncomfortable for me, at least because the tops of her breasts were showing just a bit too much for my own personal comfort.

"Not here to ruin anything," I told her. And it was true. "I'm here to pay attention and make sure you're careful and safe. I know you want to hide away, but if I can help you figure out how to be aware, that means that *careful* and *safe* come next. I know you don't want to have someone like me following you into that place, and you're trying to make it sit better that I am. But going into that party and pretending I'm your boyfriend when I'm not is just a Band-Aid."

The words came out as gently as I could manage them. Which wasn't saying much, but still.

Her chest rose and fell a couple of times before she spoke.

"I thought you were supposed to make me feel better tonight, not worse."

No matter how good she'd been at hiding everything bubbling under the surface, there was the slightest quaver to her voice that had me feeling like a giant jackass. I let out a deep breath, a weariness settling deep into my bones. She wasn't wrong.

My teeth clenched tight because as soon as I heard that quaver, I decided that I might like the scheming version of her better. If she cried, I'd fold. I'd picture her ordering ice cream and fries, picking horrible expensive red wine and nudging me out of her way with her hip when I crowded a bit too close. Much to my dismay, I'd come to like the Lydia of the past couple of weeks.

She was funny and bright. She was determined and sweet. And none of those things mattered tonight. Tonight, I had to set aside what I'd learned about her and focus on keeping her safe.

Because her plan was nothing more than a security blanket. Only … it was more complicated. And after everything I'd been through the last few years, I'd avoid complicated if it was the last thing I did.

"I'll promise you one thing, Lydia, and one thing only." I held her eyes as I spoke. "When you're with me, you are safe."

She inhaled big and exhaled even bigger. Then she nodded.

"I'll remember that when you're rude and don't answer my perfectly innocent questions."

I snorted. Perfectly innocent, my ass.

Lydia turned, swiping the mass of her hair off her back with a quick toss of her head. "Can you do me up? I'm ready to go other than that."

With a thick swallow, I wanted to say no. Everything was happening off-kilter like she'd shaken a snow globe with far too much force, and I was just waiting for the mess to settle so I could see clearly again.

Her back was bare, the opened zipper stopping down at the base of her spine. If I'd wanted to, I could've counted each and every notch of bone that made up her spine, not a single shred of material interrupted the view of her flawless golden skin. And as carefully as I could manage, I grasped the metal edge of the zipper and started to pull. The dress was about halfway closed when she shifted restlessly, and my fingers brushed against the skin of her back.

Just that one brush, one glimpse of how soft she was, and my skin felt too tight over my bones.

Lydia went perfectly still, as did I.

Her breath left her mouth in a shaky exhale, and the sound of it had me closing my eyes.

It had been over two years since I'd touched a woman in an intimate way, and the fact that it was her sent a slow roll of thunder through my veins.

The last time I did was the night after my wife told me she was leaving me, that she'd been sleeping with someone else for the last year of our marriage. Sleeping with a stranger, under the haze of too much alcohol, it wasn't me. And since then, no one had tempted me enough to make it worth the risk.

I pulled the zipper up slowly, and in an uncharacteristic display of self-torture, I allowed my finger to brush the full length of her back as I did.

Lydia didn't move, even though I let my hands drop. Her rib cage expanded on a deep inhale, even as I struggled to pull myself back in check.

After today, we were back to drive-throughs and iced coffees, and that was fucking it.

She was the last woman in the *world* I should be touching.

Lydia smiled over her shoulder, eyes bright and blue, adjusting the impossibly thin golden straps until they were in place.

Even with the simple cast, she was stunning. But I wouldn't be the one to tell her that.

When neither of us spoke, she nodded resolutely.

She gathered her purse, giving her cover-worthy reflection one last look, and there was no mistaking the resolve she was forcing into her entire frame.

I carried her bag as we descended the elevator in comfortable silence.

I opened the door for her as she stepped carefully back into my car.

Lydia didn't attempt to fill the silence this time, and now, I felt her nerves wrap around the space like a tightening vine. There was no attempt to distract herself, and in some dusty corner of my jaded heart, I knew I was probably responsible for that with how I'd reacted to her. But lying to her served no helpful purpose.

Lies, even those told out of misguided altruism, still chipped away at the foundation of any relationship. People fooled themselves into thinking that an omission of the truth shouldn't be categorized similarly as a lie. Omitting anything of my perspective tonight wouldn't aid Lydia in regaining her footing, and that was what she needed.

"I hate the media," I admitted steadily like we'd been on the subject, instead of sitting in silence. "The cameras and the attention. I never got much notice from them when I played, and I was thankful for that. You don't need it to be a good football player. Turning any of that toward me now won't help me do my job tonight either."

She gave me a curious look but didn't respond.

The car crawled through traffic, and I watched, from the corner of my eye, as her entire frame wound tighter and tighter with each moment we got closer to the club. As I'd expected, valet was set up just down from the official entrance. Lights flashed as some of Lydia's peers posed in front of journalists. And above the entire event, there was a massive billboard on the side of an old brick building, Lydia's face watching down on the chaos with a sweet, soft smile on her face as she held a bottle made from pink glass.

"My plan would've worked," she said. Her eyes weren't on the billboard when I glanced in her direction. They were locked onto the crowds of people and the jostling group of media. Her cheeks shimmered with some sort of makeup she'd brushed on them, but underneath that, Lydia looked pale. "I know this crowd. They'd pay less attention to you as my arm candy than my security."

A huffed laugh escaped my mouth.

Lydia turned her head in my direction, one graceful eyebrow arched. "You don't believe me? There are entire social media accounts dedicated to hot bodyguards."

When I frowned, she was the one doing the quiet laughing. It wasn't the same tinkling sound from her apartment. This felt more real and more her, somehow. Then my frown deepened because dissecting Lydia Pierson's laugh wasn't something I should be worried about.

"If you need to leave for any reason, no questions asked, say you're craving cinnamon rolls." My hand turned the steering wheel smoothly, pulling us closer to the curb. "There's a back door that the manager said we can use if we want to avoid leaving through crowds."

Because the windows of my car were cracked open to allow in some of the cool summer night air, I heard the shouts of the people holding cameras, the constant click of photographs being taken, and when I did, I saw her hands start to shake.

But she lifted her chin and let out a slow breath.

"I thought you were supposed to make me feel better tonight, not worse."

Lydia smoothed those shaking fingers along the hem of her dress, her fingertips running back and forth in a small pattern until her breathing slowed. It made me think of that stuffed wolf hiding on her bed.

Her chest heaved, her breathing not so slow and steady any longer. Cameras turned in our direction, and the first journalists recognized her in the passenger seat.

In my head, all I could see were cameras pressing around her while I stood to the side, her face pale, her lips tight with tension.

My eyes closed briefly just as I pulled the car up to the valet. I'd probably regret this.

"Fuck," I whispered.

Lydia's head turned. "What? Is something wrong?"

I held her gaze. "Let me get your door for you."

The valet paused before opening the passenger door, and I motioned him to my side. When I stood, the cameras pointed swung in my direction, probably wondering who I was, and then they all pivoted immediately back to Lydia, her name loud on everyone's lips.

"Lydia! Lydia! Where've you been?"

"Who are you wearing?"

"Is the cast from the car accident?"

"Who's your date, Lydia?"

She wasn't even out of the vehicle, and the vultures descended immediately. I rounded the front of the vehicle and caught sight of her through the windshield. Her eyes were trained on me, probably because of what they were doing.

With a glare at a photographer who came too close, I opened her door and held my hand out. She paused with a foot extended out to the ground.

When her fingers curled around mine, I leaned down. "My mom's cinnamon rolls," I said into her ear as she stood.

Her eyes widened.

"It's my favorite food," I continued. Cameras flashed around us. People shouted her name. And I was probably about to fuck up this entire job by going along with this craziness. Before she could pull her hand out of mine, I slid my fingers between hers, linking them together, and helped her out. Even though she wore dangerously spiked heels, the same gold as the straps on her dress, the top of her head hardly cleared my shoulders. I felt like a giant as I towered over her, her cool fingers wrapped in mine. We stood like that for a moment, and her lips curled in a hesitant smile. "In case anyone asks what your date's favorite food is," I clarified.

"Really?" she whispered.

I ducked my head down again and spoke against the silk of her hair. "Nothing besides holding hands, got it? Your dad will string me up and flay me alive."

Lydia laughed, and as she did, I watched her shoulders relax. Inside my chest, something warmed, something I decided to ignore.

I should've known then just how completely she'd be able to wreck me.

Chapter
EIGHT

Lydia

"Y OU DID IT," HE WHISPERED INTO MY EAR.

The perilous red carpet behind me, I kept my chin up, smile pasted firmly on my face. "Did I? I felt like I blacked out there for a second."

Under his breath, he exhaled an amused sound. Almost a laugh. It was a sound from him that was even better than his sighs, which was hard to imagine.

"If you blacked out, then someone else was crushing the bones in my hand."

I gave him a rueful look. "Sorry about that."

He grunted. "I'll manage." His eyes tracked over the crowded space, landing on the VIP area where the hostess in a tiny blue dress was leading us. But even as he joked about it, I had managed to stand on the carpet all by my lonesome, turning and smiling for the longest minute in the entire history of the world.

Seriously. A thousand camera shutters went off in that single minute, and by my way of thinking, if they couldn't manage one good picture out of the whole lot, then it was *not* my problem.

The entire time, my stomach was queasy, my skin cold and prickly. My ears swam with a *womp, womp, womp* sound that probably came from my thundering heartbeat. But I'd done it.

Erik settled his hand on the lower part of my back as we followed her. I almost tripped. What *was* it about my back and this man? A whole new favorite erogenous zone had popped up out of nowhere, courtesy of one Erik Wilder.

For a split second, I let myself imagine the whole of his weight, pressing up against my back, his hips wedged onto my backside. He'd be so wonderful and *big* and heavy.

Before I thought better of it, I shivered. Erik pinned me with a concerned look. "You're cold?"

I rolled my lips between my teeth. "Mmmhmm."

Sure. Yup. So very, very cold.

When the velvet rope of the VIP area was pulled back, Jill was already rushing toward me, fake-ass smile firmly stretched across her face.

"Oh my gawd, you are alive," she said, dropping an air kiss next to my cheek. "I *literally* told Imogen that I didn't think you'd actually show."

I gave her a sunny smile. "You didn't tell her figuratively?"

Jill's eyebrows bent in confusion, then she waved it off. "Haha. Very funny." Her gaze snagged on Erik, widening as she took in the whole-ass picture. "Umm, who is this?"

I laid my hand on his stomach, which jumped underneath my palm. Oh yes, all muscle. Just … hard, hard, hot muscle under there. "*This* is Erik."

A song pulsed through the speakers, loudly enough that Jill would've had to yell over it to answer. She made no effort to hide how deeply she was checking him out, and I smothered a laugh at the flush in his cheeks.

As we took a seat on the plush black velvet couch, a blue dress-clad server appeared and offered us both something to drink.

"Water for me," Erik said. "Thank you."

Jill sipped her vodka soda, the same drink she always ordered, and watched him with interest. She was not something I'd factored into this plan. And that also had me feeling a little twitchy.

"Chardonnay, please," I told her.

Erik stretched his arm out on the couch behind me, his thigh pressing tight against mine. When I gave him a quick glance over my shoulder, he was watching the dance floor, the exits, and the entrance to the bar.

Jill cleared her throat, sliding closer to the other side of me.

"Okay, but like … two days ago, you said you were coming alone," she whisper-hissed in my ear. "Who *is* he?"

No lies, Lydia. The plan would only run smoothly if it were based firmly on the truth.

I gave her a little smile. "I told you his name. He used to play for Washington. Retired early after an injury."

The word retired had her nose crinkling up. She knew what that meant—less of a paycheck, less of the spotlight. "He's so not your usual type."

I cocked my head. "Do I have a usual type?"

I didn't, and Jill knew it. It bothered her to no end because she did. She liked her men equally as pretty and slightly dumber than her. It was something she'd never understood. Dating the guys I'd met up until that point just … didn't interest me. I could think of far more pleasant ways to spend my evenings than listen to a perfectly groomed pretty boy list off all the reasons I should be flattered. And ugh, there were so many of those in the world. I seemed to attract them like fruit flies. Annoying and invasive and every-fricken-where I looked.

What I wanted was the relationship that my parents had.

What Faith had.

Anything less than that was a gigantic waste of my time.

"He's not very friendly," she observed. The observation was

loud enough for Erik to hear and from that big bear chest of his, I caught a very long-suffering sigh.

I grinned.

"Oh, he's friendly enough where it counts," I purred.

His sigh repeated itself, and I struggled not to laugh.

Jill's eyebrows popped up. "I guess he does have a certain … rugged, scary hot thing going."

"Indeed he does." I sipped my chardonnay.

"Like how friendly?" she whispered.

I glanced at him over my shoulder with a devilish smile. He did nothing more than hold my eyes in a level, very annoyed gaze. Being in this place with him, the high of getting through the gauntlet of the cameras had me feeling just a touch reckless.

"You see his arms," I told Jill. "He can toss me just about … *any* way he wants."

Erik leaned in, the heat of him a shock after not sitting close enough to feel anything other than the side of his leg. His mouth sought out my ear again, and a shiver rolled sweet down my spine. "Enough, Lydia," he said gruffly.

I closed my eyes. I wanted to hear him like that when he was pinning me somewhere, holding my arms behind my back in a way that I was helpless to move.

"Gawd," Jill scoffed.

I turned my chin over my shoulder and met his gaze. "Sorry …" At my easy acquiescence, his frame relaxed. "Babe," I added.

His dark eyes turned stormy, and I struggled not to laugh.

I turned back to Jill. "He hates it when I call him 'babe.'"

For as much as she'd drank already, her surprisingly astute gaze flickered between Erik and me, and whatever she saw, it shifted her mood from friendly curiosity to petulant attention-seeking.

Jill was pounding her vodka sodas at an unattractive rate and kept leaning over me to engage Erik in conversation. Much to his obvious regret. His frown had hardly moved all night, and somehow, it just got more and more entertaining to her that I'd brought this giant, unfriendly asshole.

"You have to tell me *something* about the two of you," she said. Then she directed her attention to Erik, who looked like I'd strapped him to an electric chair. "Lydia never brings guys around. I was starting to think she was wearing one of those iron chastity belts."

I rolled my eyes because I knew Jill wasn't looking at me. After Faith, she was the first one I called when I lost my V-card at the age of seventeen to a guy named Bradley whose parents ran in the same circles as mine and wasn't a total douchebag. We dated for about six months, and because his IQ was slightly bigger than his ego and he never judged my upbringing, it felt like a solid choice at the time.

Jill wasn't wrong in her drunkenly-delivered, jealousy-laden observation.

"You know I'm picky," I told her. "I don't want to bring just anyone to these things."

She gave me a tight smile. "Yeah, imagine if your date got more coverage than you? Your head might explode."

I narrowed my eyes, hurt making the skin along the back of my neck prickle. Drunk or not, it was the first time she'd ever been downright mean.

Erik gave me a sidelong look because he saw my reaction, and then he sighed heavily.

"Seriously, *where* did you guys *meet*?" She reached past me to playfully slap Erik's hands, and when he drew backward so she couldn't reach, I had to roll my lips between my teeth not to burst out laughing.

Her emphasis on meet, like it would change his desire to answer any of her questions, had me snorting quietly into my single glass of wine.

"We met at my parents'," I answered smoothly. "Football thing."

At my side, Erik shifted, and the material of his dress shirt brushed against the bare skin of my arm.

"Can't he answer for himself?" she asked.

"Maybe I don't want to," Erik said, his tone so dry and annoyed that I burst out laughing.

Oh, the drunk girl to the other side of me did not like that. "He's a dick, Lydia. And not the good kind."

I pulled in a slow breath through my nose because talking shit about the people in my life was a surefire way to unsnap the super-human leash I kept on my tongue at events like this. It was a lesson Mom drilled in us early.

When you lived in the spotlight—by choice or by circumstance—people would use anything we gave them as ammunition. It could be innocently said, well-delivered, intelligent, and thoughtful. But if there was one piece of you that they could misconstrue, dissect, and offer up to make us look stupid or trashy or trivial, then that was what they'd focus on.

Normally, Jill wasn't worth the effort of channeling my inner bitch, but whether he liked it or not, Erik was someone I'd risk it for. Between the market and the iced coffees and the radio he protected with his life, I had to acknowledge that I didn't just like being around him. I didn't just feel better when he was near.

I was staring down someone I'd known my whole life, and I was ready to throw the fuck down for saying something about him.

I sent her a silky smile. "Well, that's not too flattering, is it? But then green has never been your color, Jill."

He must have sensed the edge in my tone because he settled that big hand on my back again. I fought the urge to press closer, let his calm and steady seep into my veins.

The alcohol might have lowered her inhibitions, but it certainly hadn't dulled her ability to understand me. Her eyes flashed, and her cheeks reddened.

"Think carefully about what you plan to say next," I said in a low voice, a fake smile pasted on my face lest any cameras be pointed in our direction. "I like him a lot more than I like you. You make one more comment about the man next to me, and you'll find out just how much."

My voice wasn't low enough that Erik didn't hear me because he whistled under his breath. There were people, I'd learned, who knew how to react to situations like this with grace and thoughtfulness. Jill was not one of those people.

Jill clucked her tongue. "You and Faith used to avoid the players. Give that whole 'you can look but never, ever touch' vibe, considering you've always thought they were beneath you." Then she snorted. "Shouldn't surprise me that you followed in big sister's footsteps there because she's definitely letting someone touch. Can't believe Mommy and Daddy let one of their perfect girls get dirtied up by one of the guys in a jersey. At least Faith is getting screwed by someone worth a bit more than she is. She must be better in bed than you."

My smile dropped, and when I slid forward so my face was inches from Jill's, I hardly registered the way Erik's hand curled up over my shoulder. If he was going to try to hold me back from this bitch, there wasn't enough bodyguard training in the *universe* for that.

"Jill, I genuinely didn't think you had it in you to surprise me because you're so painfully predictable," I said. "You get your rocks off by making snide comments about me, and I'm about two years past saying something, but apparently you're stupid enough to bring my sister into it." I leaned in closer. "You do that again, and I will rip every fucking piece of fake-ass hair out of your head, you got it? I hear her name from your mouth one more time, and I will bury you, you insecure piece of shit."

Her face went pale underneath all her makeup, and the blood pumping in my veins was hot and powerful. Not once in my entire life had I ever threatened someone, and I wasn't even entirely sure I'd know how to chick fight if it came down to it, but I would've staked my entire future on my ability at that moment to break her scrawny ass in half.

Jill sucked in a breath, and I sat back.

Erik's fingers tightened on my shoulder. Not stopping me. Just … there.

"You can leave," I told her.

Her mouth fell open. People around her started whispering, and her cheeks flushed red.

She stood, wobbling slightly on her feet, and in her haste, her drink spilled over the edge of her glass. Onto my lap.

I sucked in a breath. "Jill?" I said calmly. My eyes held hers. "Do me a favor and lose my number."

Her mouth gaped like a fish, but she left without another word.

Small miracles, folks. I'd take it as a win for the night.

Someone handed me a napkin, but I saw a few smirks. They came from the same people who oohed and ahhed over my dress and shoes and snapped flattering selfies they could post, heralding my return to any sort of social scene.

With those smirks, my face went blazing hot, the rush of my anger toward Jill seeping away with ugly clarity.

I'd never disliked my life before. Not ever.

But something about the past couple of months, the car accident, the broken arm, even the man sitting stoically at my side, who flagged down a server for more napkins, had me seeing things differently.

Even if I hadn't been actively working to change the way my future played out, I couldn't go back to the way things were before. Not for any paycheck in the world.

My dad used to have this big telescope sitting out on our deck, and when I was little, he tried to show me the stars. But no matter what he did, I couldn't tweak the knobs and dials to the point where the constellations came into view clearly. I'd squint into that dark hole without seeing a single thing as he described it.

And with Jill's ice-cold drink seeping through the front of my dress, it was like someone pushed those knobs into exactly the right position at exactly the right time.

Everything was right there, all the things I hadn't been able to see, or didn't want to. In perfect, black and white clarity, I could see what had been fuzzy and indistinct before.

I'd had hints of it. A reckoning of sorts, when I sat in the hospital bed and watched my dad lose the battle against his tears at the sight of me. My big, strong, tattooed dad, who was the absolute bedrock of our family, was reduced to tears. He loved me, so the reaction was easy to understand. But everything else—all the things I'd treated with such ease and flippancy before—suddenly looked very different. What did I want to do with my life?

I didn't want to waste my evenings for photo ops. I didn't want to be known simply for my face and my family, two things that were entirely out of my control. And all those hints, the reason I'd started my schooling in the first place was because I didn't want *anything* the way it had been before. Not even a little.

Erik stood quietly, and I couldn't bring myself to look at his face. I didn't want to see any judgment or pity or consternation.

He held out his hand, and finally, I glanced up.

"Let's get you cleaned up," he said gruffly.

I took his hand, proud that my own was steady as I stood. With his massive frame in front of me, the glittering night crowd at the club parted in front of him with ease, like a drunken Red Sea. The way he'd wrapped his fingers around mine made it easy to grip his hand as tightly as I wanted without any fear of hurting him.

Staring at his broad back, I was suddenly so, so tired. I wanted to be home, in bed, in my pajamas, and my new face mask bubbling away on my face. I tugged on his hand, and he stopped instantly, his head turning in my direction.

"What is it?" he asked over the music.

Before I could answer, a really short, really drunk guy

approached with a loud hoot, his camera held up in our direction, blocking his entire face except for his spikey black hair.

"Holy shiiiiiit," he yelled, "it's Lydia fucking Pierson. You are *hot.*"

I closed my eyes. Not in anger or fear, but gawd, it was just mind-boggling the things that men thought would be successful when approaching a woman.

But when I heard a sound, a low rumble coming from my big, terrifying escort, my eyes popped open. Erik pivoted to the guy, the harsh features on his face carved into an implacable expression.

"Point your phone elsewhere, or I'll fucking break it," he growled.

The phone was gone in the very next breath. "Sorry, bro."

I stared up at Erik, a smile breaking slowly over my face when he turned his gaze back down to me.

"What?" he said in that same growl, a slight blush covering his cheekbones.

I wanted to kiss him. I wanted to slide my hands up his chest and know what it felt like to have his fingers press into my ass while I did. I wanted to know how we'd fit together and if he made that same growling noise when I kissed the spot underneath his jaw that looked particularly delicious.

"Nothing," I said quietly. "Only … you're very, very handy to have around, Erik Wilder."

But he studied me, and it was there in his eyes that he could see more than what I'd said. That look in his eye had me a little breathless because suddenly, the faceless man who would be exactly what I wanted wasn't so faceless anymore.

Erik opened his mouth to say something but then severed the connection by looking away.

He sighed, eyes tracking over the rest of the crowd that separated us from the exit. "Now what?"

"I think I'm ready for cinnamon rolls now."

His eyes locked back onto mine. "Yeah?"

I nodded. "Yeah. Let's go."

As we left the club, his hand firmly holding mine until he helped me safely back into his car, I couldn't help but wonder about him even more. Having a raging crush on one's reluctant bodyguard was inconvenient but not impossible.

And if I'd learned nothing else from the last few months of my life, if I saw something clearly enough for my future, then I'd make it happen.

Erik Wilder might not be ready to admit it yet, but he was a face I could see in my future. Which meant I had a new plan—and he was it.

Chapter
NINE

Erik

Lydia: Would you be able to take me to my dr appointment today?

Me: What time?

Lydia: 2. Office is downtown on Broadway, just down the road from Swedish First Hill.

Me: You still out at your parents' or are you back downtown at your place?

Lydia: I feel like you know the answer to this since you dropped me off here.

Me: Makes a big difference in commute, just making sure.

Lydia: You know, Erik, I am a girl who appreciates candor. If you're asking to prove a point that I'm making my own life more inconvenient by staying out here, just say it.

Me: It's not my job to say that to you, just here to get you safely from one place to the next.

Lydia: … Now you're not going to ADMIT that you were thinking it because I pointed it out.

Me: I'll pick you up before 1.

Lydia: ERIK. Are you trying to be frustrating?

Me: I'd never.

B Y NATURE, I WASN'T A VENGEFUL PERSON. I WASN'T THE guy who teased my sisters or beat up on my brothers because I felt like it was my job to keep them in line. But after what Lydia put me through at that club, I found my hidden evil streak.

"What's that look for?" my sister asked, drinking her green tea.

Sure enough, the second Lydia sent that text with my name in all caps, I'd started grinning.

I set my phone down and finished the last couple of bites of the omelet on my plate. Living with one's younger sister might sound embarrassing at the age of thirty, but Adaline had a second bedroom and hated being alone. It was a perfect situation.

Once I finished chewing, I stood and set the dirty plate into the dishwasher. "Lydia Pierson made me sit at a nightclub last night that was playing music that made my ears bleed, and in the middle of a bunch of socialite assholes who have nothing better to do than stare in a mirror all day to admire themselves."

Adaline laughed. She was no athlete, but she was just as immersed into the Wolves world as I had been, as Lydia was now. Two years earlier, with a freshly printed associate's degree, she was hired by Molly Ward—who was married to a former Wolves player and now some bigwig at Amazon—as her personal assistant/right-hand woman/schedule keeper/nanny and unofficial member of their family.

"Lydia isn't like that," Adaline chided gently. "Not that *I* wouldn't stare in the mirror all day if I looked like her ..." she said with an un-self-conscious shrug.

I gave my little sister a look. "You're beautiful."

Adaline had the same features I did that we got from our dad—the asshole didn't give us much else to be proud of—dark hair and brown eyes, a dimple to the left of her wide smile. Her dimple and smile got more of a frequent workout than mine, to no one's surprise.

She held up a finger. "I find no complaints with my looks, don't get your big brother panties in a twist, I just mean ... she's like, make you see heaven *hot*."

I hated the way she enunciated that last word.

I hated it because I dreamed of Lydia again. This time of thin gold chains and delicate zippers that melted away under my hands. Black lace covered her body and a bathroom counter that was just the right height.

Clearing my throat, I gave Adaline a level look.

"She's just a person," I muttered. "Everyone acts like she walks on water because she was born with good genes."

"Oooh, touchy." Adaline's brown eyes widened, and I hated that too. "A girl can't help but wonder why."

"Wonder all you like, little sister." I dropped a kiss on the top of her head. "I need to take her to a doctor's appointment downtown."

"Her cast coming off?"

I nodded. "You working today?"

She glanced at her watch, wincing when she caught the time. "Yeah, I have to get Molly and the kids packed for one of Emmett's games this weekend, and we have eighty thousand errands to run before we leave."

My eyebrows popped up. Traveling with her boss to her boss's brother's college football games was not normally part of Adaline's responsibilities. "You're going with her?"

"I'm going with her because Noah had some commentator thing he agreed to do way before Emmett's schedule came out." Adaline stood and stretched. "They had an extra family ticket."

Adaline was going with her because she'd been starry-eyed over Emmett Ward since the day she was hired, but I wasn't going to be the one to say it out loud. She'd rather swallow hot coals than admit it.

"Why so many tickets? Is it a big game or something?"

She gave me a look. "Rivalry weekend, bro. You should remember such things."

I snorted. There was a lot about my football playing days that I'd forgotten. The ease of college was one of them. It was a phase of life that could've been an eternity ago. Lines were so clearly delineated then, the game was played out of sheer love for it. It wasn't about money or stature or recognition. There was a simplicity to playing college ball that cemented my love for it until the realities of the next level blurred all the lines, smudged them into something unrecognizable.

My knee ached as I had the thought, and I shook my head. What a strange world I'd found myself in. Still surrounded by a brown and white ball, a green and white field. But I couldn't quite touch either.

"Have fun," I told her. "I'll keep the parties to a minimum while you're gone."

"Ha. If you threw a party, I'd die of shock and awe, brother." She patted my cheek. Hard. "Have fun with the bombshell. Don't let her singe your eyes because you stare for too long."

"I don't stare at all," I barked.

Adaline's laughter echoed through the room. "Mmkay."

I flipped her off, grabbed my keys, and with the sound of my little sister's laughter trailing along in my head, I made my way through traffic to Luke and Allie's house. As I did, I wondered which side of Lydia Pierson would appear for discovery.

The night before practically gave me whiplash.

The schemer, the model, and the woman who just about threw the fuck down in the middle of a club because someone insulted her sister.

I shouldn't have touched her when I saw those hackles rise, but I couldn't not touch her either. That single brush of my finger against her back lowered some invisible draw bridge between her and me, a wall that I didn't know existed beforehand.

Lydia, the protector, was the role that kept me tossing and turning in my bed the night before. Why I woke hard as a rock and cursing her name in my head.

They were only dreams, I told myself. That was something out of my control, and now that the event she'd been dreading was under our belt, I could more firmly plant myself in a role that Luke had intended. No more pretend. No more blurring the lines, no matter what walls disappeared while we sat on that ugly velvet couch.

Once cleared through the security gatehouse, I pulled down the curve of their street, towering trees leaving dappled shadows across the road. When I turned my vehicle into their driveway, Lydia was already waiting out on the large front steps. A worker was standing in the driveway, leaning against a shovel and laughing at something she said. With her good arm, she was gesturing widely, the blond of her hair catching the light much in the same way it had filtered through those trees.

The man was easily two decades older than her, and as I parked, it was impossible not to notice how easily she interacted with him. How easily Lydia seemed to interact with everyone.

Something tugged at the back of my head. A niggling thought that I couldn't quite grasp. Other than brief glimpses, shifts in her body language, she didn't come off as a woman filled with fear, as someone locked down with anxiety.

It was the car, and I'd known that for a while. Once she cleared the line of cameras, she'd relaxed.

And here at her home, she was completely herself.

It was almost like the idea of what scared her kept her from living normally, rather than the thing itself.

The worker turned and assessed me but nodded when Lydia said something to him. I lifted my hand in a wave. Just as I went to exit the vehicle to open her door for her, she'd bounded off the steps and pulled open the passenger door.

"I was wondering something earlier," she said, hopping into the seat and yanking her seat belt over her simple pink shirt.

I grunted.

"Aren't you going to ask me what?"

My eyes stayed focused on the road. "Sorta sounded like you were going to tell me anyway."

"You're the oldest in your family. You have to be."

As much as I didn't want to—and I didn't want to, with Adaline's *singe your eyeballs* warning—I turned and stared at Lydia. My sister, that little prick whom I loved, was not wrong.

The woman sitting in my car, with hardly a stitch of makeup on, was so beautiful that after a moment, I had to look away.

"Is that a question?" I asked.

She smiled at my surly tone. "An observation. You *act* like an older sibling."

I let out a slow breath. Somehow, it still felt like Lydia was the one holding the reins of every interaction, and it made me shift uncomfortably.

"So I'm not wrong?" she asked.

I cut her a glance. "Didn't say you were right either."

Lydia pointed a finger in my direction. "Such a big brother thing to say. I mean, I know Adaline is younger than you. But that doesn't mean anything. Maybe it's just the two of you. Maybe you have eight brothers who look just like you." She sighed happily. "Imagine that."

"Lydia," I warned. My face was hot at that happy sigh, the way she settled comfortably into her seat as she said it.

"Okay *fine*, I'll drop it."

Before I could change the subject, her phone started jingling in her purse.

"Oh *shit*," she muttered. After a beat of hesitation, she declined the call.

My brow furrowed. "What?"

I pulled the car to a stop at a red light, and Lydia's eyes were wide in her face, hesitation stamped all over those finely carved features. She'd never, ever be able to lie. Or at least, not well.

"Just … a phone meeting with someone." The phone in question started ringing again. Her lips pursed to the side as she frowned.

My curiosity was officially piqued.

"You can answer it," I said casually. "We've got about twenty minutes before we get there."

"No, no, it's fine. I, umm, I need some privacy for this meeting." She answered so quickly. Too quickly.

Her phone still sat face up in her lap, and I glanced down at the screen while we were still stopped. *Prof Pena.* Lydia's fingers tapped against her bare thigh in a rapid drumming motion. Now she was chewing on her bottom lip furiously, and I tucked away each little piece for later.

"How long do you think your appointment will last?" I asked.

Lydia blinked, scratching idly along the top of her cast, something she'd probably done every single day for the last few months.

"Not very long, I don't think." She glanced down at the cast. "My arm is gonna look all weird and toothpicky."

"Toothpicky?" I repeated.

"Mm-hmm." Lydia sat back, propping her sneaker-clad feet on the dashboard. "This okay?"

I gave her a sidelong look. "Would you listen if I said no?"

"Yes?"

She must have taken that as an answer because she dropped her feet back onto the floor. Which was good because I didn't need Lydia Pierson's naked legs stretched out in my peripheral vision.

This was Adaline's fault. I refused to give a whole lot of thought to Lydia's attractiveness because it just *was*. One became used to certain things when one had lived and worked in the field of gifted individuals—be it sports or entertainment. After a while, you took for granted watching a great quarterback heft a ball fifty yards down the field and land perfectly into a receiver's hands. Only a handful of people in the world could do things like that, and when you witnessed it every single day at practice, it became … normal.

It wasn't like I was numb to a beautiful woman, even after my self-imposed celibacy. It was just … par for the course because it existed on the edges of every professional sport in existence.

That was the irony of how my own marriage had played out. One of us was surrounded daily by women who graced covers of magazines, who mingled effortlessly with the athletes, who'd have no compunction opening their legs to any number of players on the team.

And I'd been the faithful one.

So no, Lydia simply existing with her shiny hair and big blue eyes and flawless skin didn't register at first. Not the way people expected it to. Because I knew well enough that a pretty face and a glittering smile could hide all sorts of nasty shit.

But now, it wasn't quite as easy to write her off as I had in the beginning.

I knew what was underneath her pretty face and centerfold's body, and as much as it pained me to admit it—her looks were a small part of what made her so intriguing.

Lydia again itched the top of her cast. "I'm so ready to get this thing off," she said.

I hummed.

"You didn't wear a cast, did you?"

I sighed. "You know I didn't."

She tucked her legs up against her chest, setting her chin on her knee as she aimed a sweet smile in my direction. "You gonna tell me why you quit playing?"

"Oh, look," I said, "we're almost here."

Lydia rolled her eyes. The tall square building, with blocky windows and not a curve in sight, got bigger as we drove closer.

"You can drop me off at the front door," she said.

Given we still had a few minutes, I didn't argue.

Somehow, in the midst of the party and zipping her dress and her horrible friend and that fucking train wreck of a party, Lydia ended up with the wrong impression of what my role was. Maybe she felt more confident now, and that was a good thing. But she still needed a reminder of what I was doing there. And maybe I needed the reminder too.

Instead of aiming the car toward the primary entrance, I turned into the parking garage.

"I said you could—"

"I know what you said," I interrupted easily. My wrist was resting casually on the top of the steering wheel, and for some reason, she chose that as the thing to glare at as I maneuvered the car up a few levels until I found some open spaces.

Lydia's phone buzzed again, and she swore under her breath, punching the button to ignore the call.

"Professor Pena really wants to talk to you," I said.

Her jaw fell open. "How did you—?" Lydia's voice trailed off when I pulled my car into a spot and jammed the gear shift into park.

I turned in my seat, stretching my arm out to grip the back of her headrest. Then I leaned closer. "I'm not dropping you off at the door. And you are not in charge, despite what you think after last night."

Her blue eyes flashed bright. "Excuse me?"

"My job is to get you safely from one place to the next, and how that happens in that time is my decision. Last night, I let you take the reins because that was *your* world, not mine. But when we are out and about, you will stick close, you will follow my lead, and if I tell you I'm delivering you straight into the hands of the doctor, then that's what I'm going to do. You got it?"

Lydia's pretty face, with the wide smiles and the easy laughter, was fucking gone. She looked like a rumbling thundercloud with blond hair, a dainty lit match held over a pool of gasoline, a pissed-off kitten who wanted to claw my face off.

"There's a lot about you I don't understand, Lydia," I continued, voice low and quiet. "Like why you hang out with assholes or why you're scared to be alone, or why you think you have to pretend *anything* in order to feel more comfortable. The fact that you weren't comfortable is why I kept my mouth shut when that woman kept harassing me and why I let you pretend we were sleeping together." Her bottom lip fell open another inch. "But if you let me do my job and quit trying to use my personal life as a distraction from those things, you and I will get along just fine."

For a split second, I thought she'd cry. Her eyes shone, catching the overhead light of the parking garage, and I had a moment when I wondered if I could handle the sight of her tears.

"I like you, Lydia," I admitted, voice harsher than it should have been considering what I was saying. "I didn't want to, but I do. So let me do my job, okay?"

A big brother I was, as she'd guessed, and if I had kryptonite, it was a crying woman. All my sisters had to do was shed a single tear, and I was fucking putty, willing to do or say anything to make them stop, make them feel better.

But that sheen of tears was gone with the next blink of her big, long lashes. In their place was grudging admiration.

"I didn't always hang out with assholes," she said quietly. "Jill was the only one."

It took everything in me not to smile. But I managed.

Lydia and I, we weren't friends. We didn't need to be. But damn if she wasn't too easy to like in those moments.

"And I'm not afraid to be alone," she said quietly. "I just … I like being around people better."

After a moment, I nodded slowly. "We good?"

"Will you stop giving your Erik the terrifying face if I say yes?"

Now I was the one who probably looked like a rumbling thundercloud. Lydia's lips curled up on one side.

"We're good," she said, sliding her bag over her good shoulder. "And you can walk me in, but you have to stay in the waiting room."

In tandem, we got out of the car.

Over the hood of the car, I held her eyes. "Deal."

She sucked in a breath, her next question coming out on the exhale. "Is it okay if we swing by the Wolves practice facility after this?" She licked her lips. "I, uh, I haven't been there in a while, and a visit sounds nice. My mom wanted me to check in after my appointment anyway."

The request knocked me back on my heels before I recovered. I'd gotten so used to our small outings, each one a baby step to just … surviving her party last night. I never anticipated having to walk back through the doors of the place I'd left behind.

But her face—and the anticipation it held—I'd never be able to say no.

I nodded, walking to the side of her as we passed a whispering group of girls. Lydia didn't pay them any mind, but once we passed, they all turned and watched us.

If befriending Lydia was something I wanted, or to dig into her head a bit, I might've asked her if she ever really got used to it. I'd ask if it bothered her to constantly have people watching what she did, what she wore, how she acted.

But I didn't ask because I *wasn't* curious.

After pressing the elevator button to take us to the office building, I stepped into the car after Lydia. As the doors slid shut and she knew no eyes were watching, I saw her shoulders relax and her face smooth out from the polite smile.

I wasn't curious about her, I reminded myself.

But even then, I knew I was lying.

Chapter
TEN

Lydia

To my utter delight, Erik was incredibly hot when he got all preachy.

I mean, he was incredibly hot when he did nothing except sit there and exist, but for the first time in my short life on this earth, I understood the appeal of the domineering alpha-hole.

So few people in my life—basically just my family—actually knew me, so to have Erik nail what was going on in my head with such precision, I couldn't dredge up a single ounce of pissiness at his tone.

And he had a *tone*.

It was an *I am no longer listening to your plans, and if you try to push me on this, you will fail miserably* tone which I should have hated. It should have rankled, raised the hair on the back of my neck, make me want to hiss like a cat because he used it on me. And instead, I shuffled from the parking garage, to the medical building, to the waiting room, to the appointment with a hazy Erik cloud around my head.

If that man had followed up his tone by moving one single inch closer to my mouth, I would've eaten him alive. I would've mounted him like a friggin' bike.

But he didn't.

So, unfortunately, I didn't either.

The thing that made it inconvenient was that after he got some tone with me, he slipped right back into quiet rock-face mode. He walked next to me into my appointment. Sat in the corner of the waiting room where he could survey all exits or whatever, and when I emerged cast-free, he did not give my skinny little arm a single shred of notice.

As we drove to the Wolves practice facility, the building I'd practically been raised in, he tapped his thumb against the steering wheel to the song on the radio, some quiet country tune that I didn't recognize.

What an odd day it was turning out to be. The excitement of having my cast off was only made slightly less exciting by the reminder that I'd been staying at my parents' house for three months. I didn't want to move back downtown, even if going out and about was getting just a little bit easier.

When I found myself scratching the top of my arm, pausing when there was no cast there, I caught Erik giving me a sidelong glance.

But of course, he didn't say shit. Because he'd turned off his conversational skills again.

"Feels weird," I said, rubbing the skin on my arm. It was no longer sore where the bone had snapped, but sometimes, I swore I could feel the spot throbbing along with the thump of my heart, like the blood ran differently in that space on my body. "You get used to doing something for so long that you forget not to do it anymore."

He made a grunting sound that had me rolling my eyes.

"Was it like that for you after you stopped playing?"

Erik went almost comically still, giving me a look that hardly required an inch of movement from his great big body. How did he do that? Tones in his voice and *looks* without any movement. The man was skilled in so many ways that shouldn't be attractive, yet there I was, imagining what else he could accomplish with tiny shifts of his body.

Finally, he answered.

"No."

I sighed.

"What?" he asked.

"That's it? Just … *no*."

Quite maddeningly, Erik didn't elaborate, just leaned forward to flip the volume higher on the song.

I reached forward and hit the button to switch the music to my phone.

"This music is shit, Lydia," he ground out.

"It's energetic and sexy," I said primly. Then turned the volume up. "You should give it a try."

He punched the button to turn it back to the radio. "I'd rather swallow nails."

I laughed.

We came to a red light, and I turned, setting my elbow on the console and resting my chin in my hand. Instead of ignoring me like I thought he would, Erik turned and faced me.

"No more touching the music. You know that's a rule in the car."

"You have a *lot* of rules all of a sudden. It's quite confusing."

He leaned in, holding my gaze. "What's confusing about it? I'll happily clear things up. Do as I say, and there will be no problems whatsoever."

The blood hummed in my veins, warm and syrupy, and I wondered what he'd do if I leaned forward and slipped my tongue into his mouth.

"Is that all?" Suddenly, I wanted nothing more than to knock him off this little *I'm in control* kick he was currently on. Just to see what he'd do. Our eyes locked steady as I dropped my voice to a sultry whisper. "Did you know that if you hold eye contact with someone for two minutes, something crazy happens?"

His mouth opened, his pupils dilating just ever so slightly. "What?"

I licked my bottom lip, and he exhaled a soft puff of air. "It releases a chemical in your blood," I said. "I don't remember the name, something long and horrible to pronounce."

"What does it do?" he murmured.

Just a fraction of an inch, I leaned forward. "It stirs … feelings of love and passion."

Erik blinked, sitting back in his seat.

Someone behind us honked. "Light's green," I told him.

He looked like I'd hit him in the face with a two-by-four. Then his eyes narrowed, and I sent him a wide, sunny smile.

"Don't you like learning new facts?" I asked.

Erik grumbled under his breath.

But he wasn't done.

He started singing.

Like … singing really well.

It was all I could do not to gape like a fish.

He was tall and muscular. He had an excellent beard and thick hair that made me want to dig my hands into it. His nose was perfectly symmetrical, his eyes deep and fathomless. He was wildly unimpressed with my public persona or what my parents did. He noticed small details and saw through me like I was made of cellophane.

And he had the voice of a fucking angel.

I was *doomed.*

"This is not fair," I mumbled, sinking down into the passenger seat and wedging my feet up against the dash. His deep baritone layered over the song on the radio, and it took everything in me not to plug my fricken ears because before I knew it, tiny little goose bumps popped all over the length of my toothpicky arm.

Erik, the hot singing jerk, still held control of this little trip, and I was not sure how I felt about it. But as we neared the Wolves facility, I started watching the shift in his body language.

"How long has it been since you've been to the facilities?" I asked.

Briefly, his brow furrowed.

My cheeks went a little warm when he didn't answer right away. "I'm not ..." I swallowed. "I'm not trying to distract myself by prying."

Erik's eyes held onto mine for a moment, then moved back to the road. "The day I got injured."

"Shut *up*," I said.

He sighed heavily, and a small laugh escaped my mouth. Gawd, I could get off to the sound of his sighs, which was deeply disturbing.

"Not literally," I told him. "Just ... most guys do their rehab at the team facilities when they're on injured reserve."

Erik shifted in his seat, a small tell I'd noticed when he didn't like the direction I was steering the conversation.

But I continued as if I hadn't noticed it.

"But I guess your injury was past the halfway mark of the season, wasn't it? Maybe it was easier to rehab back at home."

He grunted again. I'd give that sound a seven point five on a scale of one to ten.

"Was that the day your bodyguard dreams were born?" I asked lightly.

Erik cut me another look, and this time, I didn't hide my delighted laughter.

"Not exactly," he muttered. "Who's Professor Pena?"

"A professor." I cut him a look of my own, which—based on the epically restrained eye roll—he did not appreciate.

But his question found its mark as he intended. I could pry and pry and pry, and Erik would not open easily. How absolutely infuriating. I really liked to think that it infuriated him in equal measure that he didn't have full clarity on me either, but when I gave him a sidelong glance, his handsome face betrayed nothing of the sort.

Instead, he watched as we approached the security gatehouse at the Wolves practice facilities on the outskirts of Bellingham. Even more than the stadium in Seattle, this single sprawling piece of property was the playground where my sister and I grew up. Faith—who I only shared a dad with—had fuzzy memories of a time when Mom wasn't in charge at the Wolves. But for me, born shortly after my dad and mom got married, all I knew was the dynasty of Allie Sutton-Pierson overseeing the Washington Wolves franchise.

It was my history, and if I got my way—my future.

As we slowed by the guardhouse, I leaned into Erik's space, his bicep warm against my arm, and I earned myself another aggrieved sigh. When the tall, broad-shouldered security guard looked past a frowning Erik and caught sight of my face, he grinned widely.

"Miss Lydia, we've sure missed seeing your face around here. How's that arm doing?"

I flashed him my skinny limb. "Newly freed from its prison, Martin. We're here to see my mom."

He nodded at Erik, only the smallest flash of recognition lighting his features. "Go on through. Have a good day, young lady."

I waved. "Tell Angela I made that spaghetti sauce recipe she passed along, and my dad loved it."

At the mention of his wife, his smile widened. "I will."

Erik pulled his SUV past the raised gate arm as I settled back in my seat. He didn't say anything while I pulled out my phone, propped my feet up on the dash, and snapped a quick picture of them there with the massive Wolves logo perfectly framed in the background. With a few quick taps on my editing software, I uploaded it to my story, tagging the athletic shoe brand I was wearing and the caption, *Home Sweet Home.*

As I did, I felt his eyes on me.

Something about his quiet, steady attention had my cheeks

going warm, and not because I was sitting directly in the sun. Self-consciously, I smoothed a hand over the ponytail holding back all my hair. Still, he watched me, even as he turned the car into an empty spot.

There might have been some women who could've tossed out a graceful, witty comment over his notice, but I was not one of them.

I turned in my seat and faced him, eyebrows raised. "Do you have a question you'd like to share with the class?"

But instead of angling himself away, Erik mirrored my movements, turning his big body in the seat until his chest was toward me. Still warm in the face, I refused to drop his searing gaze.

This was new. And I liked it.

Neither of us moved to get out of the car.

When Erik made no sound, no attempt at the distinctly human trait of polite conversation, I huffed, finally breaking the little stare down we had going. The edge of his mouth curled up, and I narrowed my eyes.

"I'm not even sure I need to say what's about to come out of my mouth," he said steadily.

I regarded him with unabashed awe. "That's so amazingly cryptic, even for you. I'm impressed."

Erik's eyes sparked at the dig, but if he felt the urge to respond, he had a tight fricken lid on that impulse.

He lifted his chin at my phone. "You do that often?"

Ahh.

I knew exactly what he was getting at. I could've made it easier on him, but Lord knows he wasn't making anything easier on me. Holding up my phone, I tilted my head. "Use my phone? Daily."

He held my gaze.

I held it right back, even though my tummy went all weightless and swirly at the prolonged eye contact. "You know what I mean."

I sighed. "No, I don't post my location in the moment very often."

"Why did you now?"

I leaned forward and gently patted his face. "Because I'm with you. If someone tries to kidnap my ass, you can just channel your inner Kevin Costner and throw yourself in front of the proverbial bullet, right?"

Before he could say anything, I booped his nose and hopped out of the car.

It took Erik a moment to join me, and when his head appeared over the roof of the car, his expression was stern.

"No."

My eyebrows popped up. "What?"

"Whatever you just did with my nose, that's a no," he said more firmly.

I gave him a sunny grin. "Copy that. Shall we go in?"

He glanced past me, and for just a moment, a shadow crossed his handsome face. I narrowed my eyes, but the expression was there and gone before I could study him any further.

Then Erik took a deep breath, his broad chest expanding. "Your mom is expecting you?"

"Ermm, yes?"

His dark eyes sharpened.

"I mean, yes, she a thousand percent is," I amended. "I think."

He didn't want to go into that building, that much was clear, but when I turned and strode toward the practice facility, Erik sighed, jogging to catch up.

When his big hand wrapped gently around my toothpick arm to turn me toward him, I had to fight the urge to ask him to like … touch all the parts of my arm because it just felt so good. The heat of his hand, the strength in those fingers on a stretch of my body that hadn't felt anything except a cage for months, actually took my breath away.

"Before you storm the gates," he said evenly, "let's make one thing clear."

I stopped, a chunk of hair blowing into my face. "What's that?"

"This is not a place where we pretend anything." His eyes held mine, so intense and unblinking that it almost felt like he was still touching parts of my body, even though his hand had dropped to his side. "No hand holding, no flirting, no show. Got it?"

With a quick glance at the building behind us, I realized that something about this place probably made Erik feel very, very out of control. It represented something to him. I just wasn't sure what.

I held out my cast-free hand. "Deal."

Erik raised an eyebrow but slid his hand against mine. His fingers curled around my palm, and that heat of him seared straight up my arm.

Before I let go, I tugged him just a little closer. "And don't worry, if anyone's mean to you, I got your back."

He didn't smile. He didn't let go of my hand. But his eyes … they took on just a hint of the warmth in his skin. "Deal," he said gruffly.

Our hands broke apart, the moment well and truly severed, and with a deep breath, I led us into the building.

Chapter
ELEVEN

Erik

WALKING THROUGH THE DOORS—SLEEK AND SILVER AND full of glass—and seeing the massive wall of red and black, the displays of photos and history of decades of the Washington Wolves, was like getting hit by a truck.

Or two trucks, maybe because such conflicting feelings coursed through my body at the sight of it, the smells, the sounds. Nothing about the building had changed in the years since I last walked out, but I was someone completely different.

I missed it. I missed it desperately.

And at the same time, I hated being there.

It reminded me of years of my life dedicated to a sport I loved and how that sport tore away at the foundation of my life outside of it. At a time when I thought I was doing everything right—creating the kind of life I'd wanted since I was a child—I still didn't see all the wrong until it was too late.

It reminded me of everything absent from life in the years that had passed. Someone I once loved. My family. And a future that I could no longer see.

Until Lydia paused next to me, a curious expression stamped all over her face, I hadn't even realized that I'd stopped walking and was staring at the framed photos on the wall.

Players who I knew and respected. Coaches I'd idolized and worked under. An owner who was second to none, and managers and VPs who helped shape a culture that had no rival. The shot directly in front of me was Lydia's father, hoisting the trophy over his head, face streaked with sweat and dirt and a triumphant smile. We'd won trophies since then, but that one kickstarted a dominant decade and a half, the tail end of which I'd played on.

"I wish I could've seen that game," Lydia said. Her voice was hushed like we were in a church, and she didn't want to disturb the peace. And for some, that was exactly how they'd see this hallway. Something sacred, something revered. "I've watched the replays, of course. But the fact that Faith remembers being there is probably the only thing I've ever been truly jealous of with my sister."

The fact that she hadn't been born yet hit me like a third truck, straight into my gut. A timely reminder that I was too old to be thinking the things I'd been thinking about Lydia Pierson.

Thinking about the new crackling energy that pulsed through the car every time we locked eyes.

I found myself thinking about chemicals and eye contact and hoping she was full of shit. And I found myself thinking about what she might have done if I'd gripped her hair in my fist and kissed her thoroughly enough that she stopped fucking pestering me.

Then she turned to me. "Do you remember it?"

Her eyes were big and round, like a little kid who wanted you to tell them a story they'd heard a million times.

Begrudgingly, I nodded. Lydia had done nothing but be inquisitive and kind, wanting to get to know the grumpy old asshole who was charged with driving her around. But in the wake of the last day and a half, it felt like I was conceding something important by handing her any piece of me.

Maybe it was being back at the facilities that had me opening my mouth, matching her hushed, worshipful tone.

"I'd just turned nine. My stepdad didn't have the money to replace our TV, which had broken a few days before, so we watched at my grandpa's house, which is just down the road. We ate cheese pizza, and my mom let us have two big glasses of Kool-Aid, which she never ever let us do."

Lydia smiled. "What flavor?"

"Watermelon." I gave her a sideways look. "It was horrible. When your dad scored the last touchdown, I was so excited that I dropped my glass, and my mom never bought the stuff again because it was so hard to get the stain out of his carpet."

She hummed, looking back at the photo of her dad with a proud glint in her eye. "Do you—?"

Whatever she was going to ask got cut off by the fast click of very high heels.

"Lydia! I didn't know you were stopping by."

I gave her a look, and she winced before turning to greet Allie. "Hi, Mom." She waved her arm. "Wanted to show you this."

Allie smiled, grasping her daughter's hands before leaning in to kiss her cheek. "Oh honey, that's great. How does it feel?"

"Skinny."

Allie laughed, then turned her warm smile in my direction. "Erik, good to see you. Lydia's not making your life too difficult, is she?"

"She's certainly trying, ma'am," I answered evenly.

Allie laughed. Lydia frowned.

Glancing at her watch, Allie gave her daughter an apologetic smile. "I wish I'd known you were coming. I have a meeting in about fifteen minutes that I can't reschedule."

But instead of disappointment, Lydia simply waved her mom off. "No worries. Dad's down at practice, yeah?"

Allie nodded. "I'll walk over there with you."

My eyes sharpened as Lydia took off at a fast clip down the hallway that led to the outdoor fields. The campus was massive, as were most facilities for professional teams. There were indoor and outdoor practice fields, weight rooms, PT rooms, offices, and meeting spaces. The stadium held a lot of the magic, of course, but the official facilities were where the day-to-day sweat and dedication built a team.

If I'd chosen to, it's where I would've rehabbed, but instead, I asked to go home and do my work in Oregon. The last time I walked out of the Washington facilities, I didn't realize it was the last time.

Maybe I would've studied the hallways differently, captured the smells and sounds to memory. As I walked behind Allie and Lydia, I thought about all the choices I'd made that kept me from returning to the job I loved.

A decision to go home, to try to craft a life after what came out of my failed marriage. A bad decision, as it turned out because the woman I'd known and loved my entire life preferred someone else in her bed. Because she'd never joined me full time in Seattle—a desire to keep the job she loved so much back in our hometown and thanks to my desire to keep her happy—the irreparable rift in our marriage had happened before I could even realize anything was wrong.

Allie slowed down when she noticed my slow pace, and I gave her an apologetic smile. "Sorry, I'm not doing a very good job keeping up with you two."

She gestured at Lydia, who was all but sprinting down the hallway now that we were nearing the door that would take us outside. "Trust me, keeping up with her is a task that very few are equipped for." She eyed me carefully. "Just so you know, you'll be here a while."

"I had a feeling," I said dryly. "I'm glad she's excited, though. I think ... I think the idea of going different places has been scarier than actually going."

Allie hummed. "You're very astute, Erik. I'm glad she's got you."

My face felt warm. Lydia didn't have me, but it felt wrong to correct the woman who used to be my boss.

Allie glanced back at her daughter. "Lydia and her sister treated this building like their playground growing up. Faith always loved the relationships, you know? Getting to know the guys and their families. But Lydia …" She hummed, a proud look lighting her beautiful face. "She loves the game. Every chance she gets, she wants to watch the inner workings. She used to beg me to let her sit quietly in the corner during management meetings and draft discussions. Sometimes I said yes, sometimes I didn't. But when she was able to come, she'd soak up every piece of it like a sponge."

Ahead of us, Lydia slowed her steps and took a moment to peek through the glass on the doors. I knew, from memory, what she saw. The endless spread of green, striped with white. The red and black uprights on either end of the field, the organized chaos taking place in the yards between them. Even from where we stood inside, I caught yelling, whistles blowing, guys heckling each other, loud bursts of laughter.

And at the window, Lydia smiled like someone was about to hand her a million dollars on a silver platter.

It looked like that hadn't changed, and I tried to search my memory of my years at Washington, but I couldn't remember her hovering on the edges. "I don't remember seeing her all that much. Here and there, but not often."

"You wouldn't." We stopped, Allie shaking her head with a rueful smile when Lydia turned her phone on herself, flashing a peace sign while two members of the receiving team stood behind her, arms spread wide and tongues hanging out like idiots. Allie sighed. "Luke and I were careful with how much access she and Faith got to the players when they were in that younger than eighteen age bracket," she said carefully. "Even after she turned eighteen, he watched her like a hawk whenever players were around."

"Smart," I murmured.

She was twenty-two, and I felt myself wanting to edge her away from them, the same rolling wave of irrational anger when the drunk guy at the club approached. If he'd laid a hand on her, I might have ripped his arm out of the socket.

"I'm assuming you guys can find Luke from here," she said.

I nodded.

She touched my arm. "It's good to see you again, Erik. Thank you for keeping an eye on her."

It didn't feel like I was doing much of anything, if I was honest. This was not a place where Lydia had to worry about her safety. Leaving a trail of wagging tongues and broken hearts behind her, maybe, but not her safety.

The players chatted amiably with Lydia, and she turned the camera toward them, filming more footage she'd no doubt use on her social media. I didn't know either player. They were new within the past couple of years, and they looked impossibly young.

And as Lydia laughed at something one of them said, I had to remind myself that they were exactly her age. In her tight denim shorts and blush pink shirt with a deep V, cropped just high enough that anytime she moved, I caught glimpses of a toned, flat stomach, Lydia must've represented every forbidden fruit to those players.

She was untouchable because of her mom and her dad but so delicious to look at, it was impossible—even for me—not to imagine ... things.

Allie and Luke had been wise to keep her at an arm's length from a bunch of partying players who knew exactly how easy it was to get what they wanted from women.

I'd never been one of those guys, but at the right time after the implosion of my marriage, if someone like Lydia had approached me, I would've expelled all manner of pent-up sexual frustration onto her. Someone with her smile and legs, the golden hair that swept down her back and looked nothing like the dark curls I'd been used to for so many years. Someone with big eyes and sleek skin, a body that I could worship.

I blinked, shocked at the winding trail of my own thoughts.

It wasn't me. To fantasize about someone too young for me, someone I had no right to imagine.

Just before she disappeared through the doors, she cast a quick look over her shoulder in my direction. And it was then that I saw it, the slight relaxing in her shoulders, the way her frame relaxed at the sight of me.

Even here, she kept something coiled tight inside her and feeling alone only wound it up further.

My phone vibrated in my pocket, and I held up a hand for her. She paused.

My sister Greer. Again. I sighed because I'd been avoiding everyone's calls.

Lydia appeared at my side. "You can take it if you want. I see my dad with Coach."

I tucked the phone away with a shake of my head. "No, it's fine."

Lydia, like her mom had, set a hand on my arm. Her fingers were cool and light against my skin, and simply because I registered how they felt, I took a step back. Her brow furrowed, but she didn't comment.

"Seriously, I'm okay. I'm going to go talk to my dad, but you should come in too when you're done on the phone. I know everyone would love to see you."

I exhaled a dry laugh. "The few guys who'd actually remember me."

Lydia rolled her eyes. "Oh, please. You've been gone for a couple of years, not a couple of decades."

A whistle blew on the field, and I struggled not to snap to attention and line up with the rest of the defense. She was right. They'd remember me. I just wasn't sure I could handle being out there with the reminder of what I'd given up.

My phone buzzed again, this time with a text.

Greer: ANSWER YOUR FUCKING PHONE, BIG BROTHER. I'll keep calling if you don't.

I grimaced when Lydia poked her head next to mine.

"Ha!" she shouted triumphantly. "I *knew* it."

Holding her gaze, I found it almost impossible to keep my face even. Being around her was like being surrounded with the most irrepressible form of energy. And given the vein of my own undisciplined thoughts, the very last thing I could do was think about how that energy might play out … elsewhere.

"Go," I told her quietly. "I'll be in after I call her back."

"Don't hide out here too long, Erik," she warned.

"Like you'd let me," I called after she turned.

Chapter
TWELVE

Erik

BEFORE I CALLED MY ANNOYING LITTLE SISTER BACK, I WALKED to the doors after Lydia disappeared through them with a flash of blond curls. From my vantage point, it was interesting to watch the reactions. Almost every player greeted her with either obvious enthusiasm or clear deference. The coaching staff was a little different.

Not in obvious ways, but I saw a few of the newer guys, who maybe hadn't been with Washington quite as long, stiffen at the presence of the beautiful owner's daughter barging into their time. The offensive coordinator, a new addition since I'd left, clenched his jaw and tried not to stare at her ass.

He failed.

His O-line coach shoved him sideways with a stern look, someone who'd probably known Lydia for a decade, if not longer.

Coach Ward, who'd been my defensive coach, held out his fist for a bump from Lydia, hardly removing his eyes from his clipboard.

Luke Pierson, not an official member of the coaching staff but a steady presence within the team for a lot of the day-to-day operations, met his daughter with a huge hug. As he did, I made sure to lift my hand in a wave so he knew I was there. He nodded, keeping his arm curled around Lydia as she chattered happily, pointing at the way the offense was lining up to run a play.

She belonged here, and it was obvious. Her entire demeanor, the way she carried herself, was a different person than I'd seen so far.

Another side of her. I couldn't help but wonder how many more I'd discover in whatever time I had left.

A part of me wanted to observe it further, but just as the thought appeared and before I could tear it apart, my phone buzzed again.

I hit the button with a sigh.

"Holy *shit*, Greer, I'm working," I said by way of greeting.

"Ahh, yes, the elusive new job that no one but Adaline knows about." She clucked her tongue. "Just admit it, you're selling drugs."

"How'd you know?" I answered dryly.

"The fact that Adaline won't tell me shit is how I know it's good." Greer and Adaline were Irish twins, born less than twelve months apart, and they told each other everything growing up. It was only different career paths that separated them in adulthood. Greer was still back home in Sisters and managed the design side of Wilder Homes. "You know, if you need a new career path, you could come back here and let me boss you around."

"So tempting." The offense ran a play, a beautiful bootleg that completely fooled the defense lined up against them. The quarterback's fake handoff was so smooth that even I was fooled for a second before he tailed off into the opposite direction of where the defense pushed, dropping back to heft a thirty-yard pass down the field to the waiting tight end. I hummed in appreciation. "Is everyone okay?"

"Yeah, why wouldn't they be?"

"Because you called me five times in five minutes."

"Ahh, well, Mom wants to know if you're coming home for their big anniversary party. She said you didn't respond to her text last night."

I winced. She'd sent it when I was at the Dior party with Lydia, but I couldn't really even blame it on that.

Sighing, I tucked myself against the wall so I wouldn't use the practice as a distraction from the real reason I hadn't answered my own mother.

"Twenty years, Erik," Greer said. "You have to come."

I pinched the bridge of my nose. "When is it again?"

"Family dinner Friday night, football game Saturday, big party is Sunday. You can't be the only one who's not here."

That had my eyebrows going up. "I'm the only one who hasn't answered?"

"Yes," she said, exasperation clear in her voice. "As long as you can manage to carve out time in your top secret schedule, the whole family will be home for the first time in years. Come on."

If I'd allowed myself, I could've closed my eyes to imagine my mom and Tim's house, the one they raised our entire family in. I was young enough when they got married that all my best memories included Tim and the siblings he brought into my life. Some of those memories were good. Some a little bit less good.

The last time I was home was one of the worst days of my life, a call from my ex-wife erasing any future plans I'd been making with an efficient and emotionless phone call. Now all I could remember of that house was my mom crying in the kitchen. The look on my stepdad's face when he said, "She'll be okay, Erik. She just needs some time to grieve. We lost them both too, you know."

I hadn't been able to bring myself to go back home and face their heartbreak.

But I could only avoid it for so long. Tim was sick, and we all knew he wasn't getting better. My mom wanted me there, and even though that should've been enough to commit, the thought of seeing their faces after years away, the aging they must have done in that time, just made me relive my failure all over again. Failure as a husband, as a brother, as a son. The sounds of football being played in the background only served to underscore just one more level of my failure. Because I'd walked away from that too.

Greer didn't press in the silence. Just as they hadn't pressed my absence from home.

"Shit," I muttered quietly with a pinch to the bridge of my nose. "*Everyone* will be home?"

She hummed feelingly. "Everyone." Greer delicately cleared her throat. "Ian is getting in Friday. His flight lands after lunch, I think."

The piercing sound of a whistle had me blinking because I didn't really want to think about facing my stepbrother either. For different reasons. That particular reunion had been over five years in the making, and to have us both home would probably make my mom so happy that she'd forgive us for absolutely anything.

Even years of not showing up for the two people who raised us.

"I'll be there," I said gruffly.

Greer sighed audibly. "Oh, thank God. It's only a few days. You'll hardly even see Ian."

"I'm not worried about Ian," I told her. "I mean, he's annoying and stubborn, and he never gets over anything."

"Who does that sound like?" Greer mumbled.

I ignored her. "My point is that if Ian can behave, then so can I. He's probably coming for the same reason I am. It's for our parents."

"Poppy is gonna cry when I tell her."

At the mention of our youngest sister, the only biological child that our mom and Tim had together—the perfectly spoiled and universally adored cherry on top of our crazy Brady Bunch family—I smiled a genuine smile for the first time all day. "How's she doing?"

"She's a *senior*, Erik. I feel like she was born two years ago, and she's about to graduate high school. It doesn't even seem possible."

Her statement had me resting my head against the cinder block wall behind me and closing my eyes against the tidal wave of utter exhaustion. So much was wrapped up in that passage of time. The ways I'd failed the people who mattered to me, and the complete disappointment in myself that I'd let it keep me away from them.

"I can't wait to see her." I cleared my throat because something was wedged there. A brick or a boulder or a giant ball of thorns. "You either, G."

She laughed softly at her nickname. "You'll ride down with Adaline?"

"Most likely."

"If you back out, I'll hunt you down, Erik Christian Wilder. You've been gone way too long."

"I love you too," I told her. "Tell Mom I'll stay at my place, okay? She doesn't need to get a room at the house ready."

"Or worry about you and Ian under one roof."

I sighed. "That too."

Greer disconnected the call, and I let out a slow, heavy breath.

With the call over, my surroundings slowly sharpened back into place. The sounds and smells of my past, which I'd chosen not to revisit. And with it, the weight of someone's study.

I glanced to the side and shook my head.

Two someones.

Lydia was watching me with unconcealed interest, and next to her was the grumpiest-looking football player I'd seen in a while. Besides me.

He was tall and broad, covered in tattoos, and looked at me like he wanted to punch me in the balls. I straightened, pulling in a deep, steadying breath in case I was about to meet one of Lydia's lovestruck horde.

"Stop trying to look scary, Dominic," Lydia said, nudging him with her elbow.

He didn't.

She rolled her eyes. "This is Dominic Walker, my sister's boyfriend. He, uh, wanted to meet you."

The fact that he was Faith's boyfriend shouldn't have made me relax, shouldn't have made me feel any sweeping sense of relief, yet … it did. I ignored that. Ruthlessly.

"Walker," I said. The name was familiar from another team, but I must have missed his trade to Washington while working overseas. "First year at Washington, right?"

He narrowed his eyes. "Uh-huh."

A rookie walked past us, his eyes glued to Lydia's ass. A low growl started somewhere down in my throat. But Walker beat me to it.

"Hey," he barked. "You wanna find yourself traded to Detroit? Look elsewhere, asshole."

The kid, young enough to be scared and new enough to know not to argue, snapped to attention, eyes locked down the hallway. Lydia rubbed her temples.

Walker crossed his arms over his chest. "What are your intentions toward Lydia?"

"Oh, my gawd." She sighed. "Seriously, Dominic."

I'd met guys like him, and as he sent me a dark, challenging stare, his reputation as a shit starter at Vegas came back to me. My eyebrows rose slowly. "Is that any of your business?"

She blew out a hard breath. "This is fun. So, so fun." Slapping a hand on the tight end's chest, she shoved him back when he tried to take a step closer. "I told you we're … friends."

Her pause was conspicuous. And my eyes narrowed because I would have assumed that the sister's boyfriend would know why I was hanging around. She narrowed her eyes right back.

Walker nodded. "You're, what? Thirty? She's a pretty young friend to tag along with."

I laughed incredulously under my breath. "You trying to pick a fight, kid?"

Lydia's eyes were wide, and she glanced back and forth between us.

"Not trying to pick anything. Just making sure you're not taking advantage of someone I care for."

He *looked* like he was trying to pick a fight. He looked like he was ready to rip my face off, and I didn't think Luke Pierson would appreciate me getting into a fight with one of the players. Didn't really fit into any code of professionalism I could conjure up.

But I hated what his assumption was. It sat thick and uncomfortable over my shoulders.

"Lydia, how does he not know this?" I asked. She glared at me.

Then she turned her attention to Dominic, talking through gritted teeth and a fake smile. "The better question is why is he acting like this?"

Dominic's face eased into a tiny smile as he glanced down at her. "Because I like playing the overprotective sibling when Faith isn't here to do it."

"I don't need you to! It's … a professional situation," she said.

Understanding dawned in his eyes. "Ohhhh."

"Yes."

"He's helping you with your paper," Dominic said. "Faith told me about class this semester. It sounds fucking *hard*."

Lydia's face froze. "Eh …"

I leaned forward. "With her …?"

Lydia widened her eyes meaningfully at Dominic, but he was studying me instead.

"It's not weird for you to have her pick apart your career like that? I know how it is when she's got her teeth in something." His tone wasn't mean. There was genuine interest in his face, but still … it hit me like a sledgehammer. The idea that she'd been digging for something other than her own curiosity.

Lydia snapped her hands on her hips. "I'm not *picking it apart*. And my paper isn't even about him."

I gave her a look even though my head was spinning. The

missed calls in the car earlier today suddenly took on a different meaning.

It still didn't answer why she hadn't explained anything to me, though.

"You better not fuck anything up for her. She's smarter than half the people working in most NFL front offices, and she'll have the degree to back it up now."

I crossed my arms over my chest. "*Why* would I want to do that? You don't even know me."

Lydia raised her hand. "I vote that this conversation stops. Right now."

He ignored Lydia. "You're correct. I don't know you. In general, I do a shitty job of befriending strangers, and I'm especially wary when I can't figure them out." He held his arms out. "You have a double whammy. I've heard stories about how you walked away from the team and never looked back—which I don't understand— and now you're tagging along with my girl's sister, which makes me feel extra unfriendly."

"You treat all the guys on the team like this? No wonder Vegas wanted to get rid of you."

He grinned. "Why don't we go step outside, and I'll show you, old man."

"Enough!" Lydia yelled.

Dominic looked down at the ground, and with a clenched jaw, I locked my gaze onto Lydia. She'd straightened to as tall as she could manage, standing between two men who dwarfed her. I waited for her to put me in my place because the snap in my temper was uncharacteristic.

But she smacked Dominic in the stomach. "You are not appointed my keeper, so keep your cavemen tendencies locked down when it comes to me, okay? I'm an adult, and I don't need you snapping and snarling at the people in my life."

He flipped his gaze to me and nodded. "Got it."

"And," she continued, "you don't *ever* make a former member of this team feel unwelcome here. No matter what the circumstances are behind Erik's departure—which is no one's business but his own unless he chooses to share it—it is not your job to be a gatekeeper. Maybe that's how they did things in Vegas, but it is not how we do things here, and I know you know that, Dominic." Her voice rang down the hallway. "Once a player wears this jersey, they are always part of the family."

With a small tilt of my head, I watched her transform in front of my eyes. It was remarkable, actually. Her posture changed, the timbre of her voice, the gleam in her eyes.

It was different than when she unleashed her impressive temper on Jill the night before.

This was a *woman*—completely in control and unafraid to show it. I wondered briefly what chemicals would course through my veins if we locked eyes now.

He took a deep breath, letting it out slowly. "My apologies," he said to me. "I've always had a bit of a … temper problem. But I'm working on it. Some days are better than others, I guess."

I nodded. "Apology accepted. I'm sorry, too."

He held out his hand for me to shake, which I did. When he stepped back, Lydia smiled at both of us. "There. Was that so hard?"

Dominic grinned. "Not as hard as it's going to be for the defensive line coaches to explain to Ward why you picked apart their 4-3 scheme in there."

Lydia laughed. "Quite true."

Dominic gave me one last look. "Sorry again. I think I'm still getting used to the protective instinct that these Pierson women bring out in me."

I choked on a laugh, clearing my throat when he gave me a strange look. "Water under the bridge."

He gave us a wave and jogged back to practice.

A huge part of me still wished I was going with him. And no

matter why he thought I was here, or what Lydia had been hiding from me, I wasn't ready to explain why I couldn't. Why it was so hard to remember the time in my life when I'd left.

And with that thought, I glanced quickly at Lydia as she watched the guys line up for another play.

"He's a good guy," she said quietly. "My sister loves him … like, stupid loves him. And he's really good for her. I had no idea he'd question you like that."

"You don't have to protect me from him." I stood next to her and watched. "But I would love an explanation of what he was talking about."

Lydia, with cheeks puffed out, exhaled slowly. "We can't just … forget he said anything?"

I thought about how many times she'd gently tugged on the threads of my past, and I'd resisted. I thought about how she'd overcome so much of her fear in just a few weeks simply by facing the things that crowded her mind.

Like most people did when they struggled to move past something hard, Lydia would only be helped by the things that made her feel in control.

"For now, yeah." I glanced at her profile. But I wanted to know. Wanted to understand what he was talking about. Maybe this is how she felt every single time she asked me about my past.

No wonder she was so relentless.

And today, no matter how my evasions affected her, she'd been relentless in her defense of me. To someone who had a much greater claim to be part of her life. It was dangerous, how that made me feel.

So instead of pushing her on it, I gently touched her elbow. She blinked away from the team and turned all of her focus toward me.

Every time she did, it felt an awful lot like someone socked me in the gut with a crow bar. There was so much impact to Lydia Pierson, and I wasn't sure she was aware of just how much.

"You ready to go?" I asked. "Or do you need to make the

coaches aware of any other deficiencies in how they're doing their job?"

Lydia tipped her head back and laughed—loud and long. And impossibly, I found myself smiling at the sound of it.

"I think I've harassed them enough for one day," she said, smiling happily. "But there's always next week."

"They must love your visits," I said dryly.

The sound of her laughter echoed as we walked down the halls slowly, and just before the glass doors slid open, Lydia carefully tucked her hand into my arm. The weight of her hand, curled around my bicep, was as dangerous as anything she could've done. Because the first thing I noticed was how warm her hand was, and wondered how it would feel against bare skin.

I blinked the thought away as we walked to the car.

"Need anything else this afternoon?" I asked her, opening the passenger door so she could slide in.

"You're off the hook," she teased. "I'll give you a break from me for the next couple of days. I've, uh, I've got a lot to work on."

I cut her a quick look. "We're going to revisit that, Lydia."

She set her elbow on the console and started fiddling with the radio. "Are we? You show me yours and I'll show you mine, Erik."

I sighed, and caught a flash of her grin as I did.

We drove away, and I refused to name what was growing under my rib cage, something new and inconvenient. Her feet propped immediately on my dashboard, and she switched the music to something hideous and pop-laden and her bright pink toes tapped along to the beat.

This time, I didn't make her change. Because it made her happy, and somehow, that mattered just a little bit more than it had before.

And I knew why I refused to name that feeling. Because if I did, I'd have to do the right thing and walk away.

Chapter
THIRTEEN

Lydia

"YOU'RE GOING TOO FAST," FAITH HUFFED NEXT TO ME.

"Come on, Pierson, keep pace to the beat," I yelled over the thumping speakers. My feet slapped against the treadmill, and next to me, Faith muttered a curse word and hit a button on her own machine to match my pace.

Working out sans cast felt so fricken good, and I was already struggling not to push myself too hard. My arms swung as I ran full tilt, sweat sliding down my spine, my blood pumping hot under my skin.

The song—an irrepressibly catchy pop song with a racing beat and thumping bass—came to the end, and Faith and I slowed our machines in tandem.

"Holy shit," she gasped. "You were more fun to work out with when you were taking it easy."

I laughed, popping open my water bottle to take a cold swig. "I'm going to hurt tomorrow if it helps."

She gave me a look. "How does the arm feel?"

With a stretch, I glanced at my reflection in the floor-to-ceiling mirrors in our downstairs home gym. Still a bit skinnier than my other arm, but I felt strong, if not sore.

"Good," I told her.

Faith swiped a towel along the back of her neck. "I finally got a chance to catch up with Dominic last night."

"The perils of dating a professional football player, eh? Not much alone time during the regular season."

She smiled. "Not with as busy as I've been."

I arched my arms over my head, falling forward to brush my fingers against the ground while I stretched my legs out. "And what did the love of your life have to say?"

"He told me what happened at practice the other day."

I grimaced. "I'll bet."

"He also told me he was a giant ass to Erik." She laughed. "My little hothead. He really did feel bad."

"He should." I pulled one ankle up behind me and gave her a look. "Erik was just there, and Dominic acted like he was shoving his hands down my pants or something."

Which sounded *lovely* under any other circumstance, but that was besides the point.

"And," I added, "he totally outed me about my master's program."

Her eyebrows popped in surprise. "Erik doesn't know you're doing that?"

I shrugged. "No."

"Lydia," she sighed. "I do not understand why you feel like you need to hide this."

"I'm not hiding it."

Faith laughed. "Okay."

I sat on the black rubberized floor and tucked one foot up against my inner thigh. "He doesn't tell me anything either. So we are very even in that regard."

"No need to get defensive," she said lightly.

"I'm not."

I was.

For the past three days—the longest stretch I'd gone without seeing him since we met—I thought over and over about why I hadn't told him about my schooling. I thought about why all these changes in my life were so much scarier when they were offered up for public consumption.

Faith didn't respond because she knew me well enough not to.

Finally, I sighed, flopping back onto the floor. "I couldn't stand it if he laughed or something. If he questioned my ability to see it through to the end."

She hummed in understanding. "I can understand that."

"I actually thought about, I don't know, switching up my semester research project."

"The one you've been working on for two months?"

I nodded carefully.

Her eyes found mine in the mirror. "What's your topic now?"

"The effect of media on cultural mindset toward sports, and how that can be harnessed to create a strong infrastructure of a sports team."

"I like that. What would you want to change it to?"

I cleared my throat. "The traumatic effect of injuries and anxiety in high profile athletes, and how team turnover affects long term performance."

Faith's eyes held mine knowingly.

"What?"

"You interviewing someone particular for that?" she asked pointedly.

"Like he'd tell me anything," I said, and if I'd ever sounded pouty before, it was nothing on how I felt saying that out loud. "And he already drives me crazy on a good day. I've never met anyone who pushes my buttons like he does, and letting him see this really big thing that I want for my life seems so …" my voice trailed off.

"Vulnerable?" Faith added quietly.

I nodded.

She watched me with those big sister eyes. "You care about his opinion a lot."

My face was flaming hot. Maybe because I'd just finished a thirty minute run at a dead sprint, but also maybe because my harmless crush on Erik was blossoming into something else much, much bigger.

"I mean, I like hanging out with him, and he's not bad to look at," I feigned a careless tone.

Faith saw right through it, rolling her eyes. "You are such a bad liar."

"What do you want me to say? I like him? Fine. I like him." I sat up with a huff. "I *more* than like him. He's ... nothing like what I thought I'd like. He's so grumpy and stubborn and for *hours*, he'll just go mute and I don't understand where his head is at." Bracing my folded arms on top of my knees, I buried my head with a groan. "But sometimes, he looks at me in a certain way ... and I've never felt anything like I do in those moments."

Faith was quiet, and when I lifted my head, her forehead was pinched with worry.

"Look, I'm not going to tell you it's a bad idea to change your research project. The topic idea is a good one, and I think you could find a lot of content to study."

"But ..."

"But make sure you're doing it for the right reasons. Don't change your topic because Erik is a closed book and that drives you crazy because you're having feelings for him. I worry about you."

I gave her a frustrated look. "Faith, I'm not a kid. I mean, I'm not *middle aged* either, but I know myself well enough to know what I want. And whether someone's worth any sort of emotional investment. Between you and Dominic, I'm starting to feel like my own family doesn't trust me to know my heart and my mind." I stood off the floor, holding up a hand when she opened her mouth. "I get it, I do. You love me, you worry, but he's done nothing to warrant all this. He hasn't objectified me. He hasn't talked down to me. He doesn't dismiss how I'm feeling. He listens. He pays attention to the things I don't say. So what if he doesn't spew his whole past to me," I said hotly. "Maybe he worries that I'll judge him, just like I'm sitting here worrying the same."

Faith approached with a contrite smile. "You're right."

"*And*," I continued, drawing short when her words registered. "I am?"

My sister nodded. "You are. I have to remember that you, my badass little sister"—she cupped the sides of my face—"are not afraid to go after what you want. That's a gift. And I needed that gift of yours when I couldn't admit how much I wanted Dominic."

I laughed. "You really did."

"Without your *loving* interference and excellent scheming skills, who knows how long I would've had to wait for my first date with him."

"Very true."

She gave me a tight squeeze. "I'll leave it alone. I promise."

And like his ears were buzzing, my phone dinged with a text from the man in question.

Erik: Free this afternoon?

Erik: I have an idea.

Me: Free as a bird. What's the dress code?

Erik: Tight and comfortable.

Erik: I mean … leggings and a tank top or whatever. Not a tight dress.

Erik: You know what I mean, right?

Me: No mini-skirt, got it.

I laughed, imagining the blush on his face. The desire to toy with him, push some buttons of my own was so great. Faith got one look at my face as I typed out my response and let out a groan of her own. "Oh my gosh, look at you right now," she teased. "He either just offered you sex or a million dollars."

"Ha, ha," I drawled. "I'll take option one please."

She peered over my shoulder at the exchange. "Leggings and a tank top. Doesn't he realize that this is your *only* outfit choice the last three months?"

I nudged her back. "Don't you have somewhere else to be? I didn't hassle you about Dominic."

"Ohh, it must have been someone *else* who dragged me bodily into a locked bathroom so you could interrogate me after our first date."

Middle finger up in the air, I jogged toward the hallway to the sound of her laughter. "I have to go shower. He's picking me up in thirty minutes."

Faith cackled. "You? Showered and ready in thirty minutes? Oh, I'm staying to watch this unfold."

"I hate you," I yelled.

I cranked the shower up, shucking off my workout clothes, ripping my hair from the ponytail holder and almost falling over when I couldn't tug my sweaty sports bra over my head.

"Oof," I groaned when I gave it one final pull. "This is so much easier with two arms."

The spray was colder than normal, but with Faith's disbelief in my ears, I tried to calm my still racing heart at the unexpected time with Erik.

"Not a date," I whispered harshly. My hands lathered my body soap, I had to force brisk and efficient movements.

No thinking about long eye contact. My fingers trailed around my stomach.

No thinking about his hands on my back. My palm coasted over my hip.

Curving around my shoulder.

It wouldn't take long.

His long, strong fingers locked around mine. I imagined them on my body.

My breath started coming in pants when I closed my eyes, conjuring the image of him in there with me. I had a decent size shower, but he'd dwarf the space. I'd have no choice but to brace my back against the wall. Unless he sat on the tiled bench, spread his long legs out and brought me to him. His mouth would reach my stomach, my ribs, and as my hands slid slow over my skin, my breasts.

He wouldn't rush us. If I knew Erik Wilder—and I did—he'd torture me. He'd skate his hands over every inch of my body, he'd have superhuman patience, he'd set a rhythm that wasn't punishing because of its speed. No, the insanity would come because he'd tease, he'd go slow, he'd have me mindless.

My back arched, a helpless moan escaping from my parted lips while I played it out in my mind.

He'd have me begging, arching underneath him, trying to urge him faster and harder with my hands and nails, tugging his big body as he ...

That was when Faith banged on my bathroom door.

I slipped sideways. "What?" I yelled, only a little out of breath.

"It's been fifteen minutes, Lydia," she yelled. "You're about to prove me right."

I clenched my jaw and knocked the water just a little colder, yelping when the icy spray hit my skin.

After a quick shampoo and condition, I hopped out and toweled myself down. My walk-in closet was connected to my bathroom, and I dropped the towel into the laundry basket, tugging open the drawer to snag some black lace underwear.

A girl could not wear anything else when going out with a man who just inspired *those* types of shower thoughts.

It was warm outside, and honestly, with wet skin, the thought of wearing leggings sounded like way too much work. I dug out a comfortable knit bra for underneath a Washington tank top and slipped on some black athletic shorts. There was no time for makeup, and nothing more than a quick braid to keep my heavy, wet hair out of my face.

When I tugged my tennis shoes onto my feet, I whipped the door open with a shouted, "Eat shit, Faith! I told you I could do it."

She was in my desk chair, flipping through my books. "It's a miracle."

I kissed her on the top of the head. "I'm going to go wait upstairs."

"Have fun," she called. "And don't forget to use protection when you get him to crack."

I was still laughing when I approached the front door. Through the side windows, I watched his dark vehicle pull into the driveway.

Oof, the butterflies. They were wild and swirling and dipping, through all parts of my body, not just my stomach.

Erik leaned over to push open the passenger door, greeting me with a cautious smile as I hopped into the car.

"What's that face for?"

He exhaled a short breath of laughter. "What face?"

I pointed. "That one. You look worried."

Erik waited until I'd hooked my seat belt and then eased the car back into drive. "Aren't you curious about where we're going?"

"Umm, yes."

He glanced sideways. "Just curious?"

"Cut the cryptic, Erik. What are you trying to ask me?"

"Not scared?"

I sat back. "Oh." He drove past the security guards and I waved absently. Not once since he texted me did I feel fear.

There was no worry about where we were going. What we might be doing.

"No," I answered slowly. "Not scared."

He grunted.

All of it, the days not seeing him, the conversation with Faith, and my little shower fantasy had me staring openly. He shifted in his seat, and I smothered my grin.

"Because it's you," I added.

His gaze locked onto mine.

"I'm not scared because I trust you."

Erik's jaw clenched, and after a loaded moment, he tore his eyes away from mine. "Good," he said, rough voice coming from deep in his throat.

I wanted to hear that voice in my ear while his hips snapped tight against me.

As I stared out of the window, I blew out a slow breath.

"Now will you tell me where we're going?" I asked, once my raging Erik sex hormones were under control.

Sort of.

Because his hands were … big. And holding the steering wheel the way they were, I imagined them on my hips, tugging me back toward him.

"A race track."

I blinked. "What?"

He shifted in his seat again, and it took me a moment to realize that Erik Wilder was nervous.

"We're going to a race track." He locked eyes with me again. "You're going to drive."

My mouth fell open. "The fuck I am. I don't *want* to drive."

He laughed. The asshole. "I thought you trusted me."

I crossed my arms over my chest. "I take it back."

"You can't," he said easily. "Come on. It'll be fun. And completely safe because it's just you and me."

My heart raced. Not from fear of a car, or even from fantasy Erik. But because it was the last hurdle.

Don't get me wrong, I would've gotten over it eventually. And I would've survived just fine in the meantime. Millions of people all over the world didn't drive, and no one was dropping their asses off at a race track.

If I closed my eyes, I could see myself avoiding it for a very, very long time. And I didn't want that.

I'd taken so many steps, created so much change, to be the version of myself that I wanted most. And this was one more thing that I could accomplish on the way.

Not because it was his idea or even because I thought he'd force me if I said no. Maybe that was the point. Erik saw so much of who I was. And he'd have known if I wasn't ready.

And he wanted to help me hop over this hurdle.

Knowing him, he'd rather break it in half so I could walk through it, but that wasn't really much of an option.

"Okay."

His lips twitched. "Okay."

"But I get to pick the music *both* ways," I said.

He sighed.

A perfect ten kind of sigh.

Chapter FOURTEEN

Erik

EVERYTHING STARTED JUST FINE. BORING, ACTUALLY. IF ONLY it had ended that way.

We had to fill out some forms.

Watch a video.

Let a very serious driving instructor do a simulation with both Lydia and I so we understood every piece of equipment in and out of the car.

Then we had to pull on our driving suits.

I did *not* watch while Lydia pulled hers up over her bare legs, doing an excited hop that she couldn't quite hide while the sleeves hung fetchingly off her hips. I pinched the bridge of my nose because her tank top was white, as was her bra. The driving instructor kept his eyes trained above her neck at all times, which was good for my sanity.

She zipped her suit up over the white tank top and white bra, and I breathed a bit easier when the ripe curves of her chest were hidden from view. But even then, with her helmet tucked under her arm, she strolled from the building out onto the race track, and my gaze landed unerringly onto the perfect sway of her perfect ass.

I was losing my mind. There was no other explanation.

Two years of celibacy was too much for me. At the first opportunity, I would find someone to scratch the itch, cool the heat pumping dangerously through my veins at the sight of her.

That was all it was, I told myself.

When she cleared the doors, she stopped and took in the sight of the empty stands, the immaculate blacktop and the two gleaming cars parked specifically for us.

"Whoa," she breathed. Lydia stepped forward and ran her hands along the top of the first car.

It was lipstick red and low to the ground, gleaming black tires and shining chrome accents. The hood was sleek, waxed until she could probably see her own reflection.

"You want that one?" I asked, my voice coming out huskier than I'd intended.

She glanced at me over her shoulder, pink lips pursed into a considering smile. "Yes."

"It's a beauty," I said.

"A Ferrari Four-eighty-eight GTB," she said quietly. "Six hundred and sixty horsepower, top speed of two hundred and five, zero to sixty in three seconds."

I whistled. "She knows cars too."

Lydia laughed, holding up a paper I hadn't seen clutched in her hand. "It's on here."

"Ahh." I cleared my throat. "I think we just need to wait for the kid who's going to strap us in there."

She smiled as she turned back toward me. "You're riding with me, right?"

Her eyes as she asked it, so big and trusting. I wanted to warn her not to put so much faith in me, I wanted to look away because of how good that trust felt. But I didn't. I risked holding her gaze just a bit longer. "Yeah. For the first couple of laps, at least."

I took the helmet from her hand and checked the straps. Not that I really knew what I was looking for, but it gave me something to do with my hands that didn't involve touching her.

"What happens after the first couple of laps?" she asked.

"Then you do one on your own, if you want."

She opened her mouth to answer, and that was when I had the first inkling that the day was going to shit in a hurry.

The kid approached us from the opposite side of the track, long legs and bright red hair, eyes covered with wrap-around sunglasses.

My shoulder brushed Lydia's as we stood there, and when he glanced up from his clipboard, I saw his steps slow.

Then stop.

He glanced up.

Back down at the clipboard, his mouth hanging open.

His head snapped back up as he gaped in our direction.

"Here we go," Lydia whispered.

"I figured we'd be safe from your fan club here," I said back. "Sorry."

"Erik fucking Wilder," the kid yelled. "No *shit*."

I frowned.

Lydia burst out laughing.

He jogged up, sliding the clipboard underneath his scrawny arm. Before I could blink, he snatched my hand and pumped it between his. Vigorously. "I am such a huge fan, holy shit. I can't believe you're here. This is the greatest day *of my life*."

Carefully, I extracted my hand from his. "Thanks, man. What's your name?"

He stammered nervously over the answer, cheeks bright red with excitement.

I glanced at Lydia, who had her smile covered with one hand, her blue eyes dancing big and happy in her face.

"I've been following your career since college," he said on a rush. "You're the reason I wanted to play defense."

With a careful glance at his wiry frame, I knew he couldn't have weighed more than one twenty soaking wet. "It's always nice to meet a fan. I'm glad you said hi."

"I'm more than a fan," he answered seriously. "I recorded every game at Washington, and when you tore your ACL"—his voice dropped—"I cried for three days straight."

Lydia's lips were rolled between her teeth when her hand dropped, and when the kid leaned in as he spoke, I fought the urge to hide behind her, use her body as a human shield.

"Yeah, me too," I answered dryly.

He whipped his phone out of his back pocket. "Can I? Can we?"

Lydia held her hand out. "I'd love to take a picture for you, if that's what you want."

His profuse thanks came out on a rushed exhale, and I glared at her as they traded places. Above the phone, she winked at me. "Smile, Erik."

The kid wrapped his arm around my shoulders. Tight. And with a grin, Lydia snapped a few pictures.

"Perfect," she said.

He scrolled through the pictures. "This is the best day *ever*," he whispered. "I'm going to show everyone I know."

I rubbed the back of my neck, and Lydia wound her arm through mine. "What was your favorite Erik Wilder play?" she asked. "Or is it too hard to choose?"

I extracted her grip from mine, holding her eyes when she wouldn't let go of my fingers. "I'm sure he doesn't know off the top of his head," I ground out.

"Oh, I know," he said. "The AFC championship in your second year."

Lydia hummed. "Oh yes. Against Indianapolis. The strip sack in the fourth quarter?"

The kid brightened. "Yeah. You know what I'm talking about?"

"I'm a huge fan of his too," she said seriously. "In fact, I *just* watched that replay last week."

I tightened my fingers around hers, so hard I was surprised her bones didn't snap, and she breathed out a laugh.

I cleared my throat. "So uh, you're going to hook us in here today? We're looking forward to driving."

He snapped to attention. "Right, yeah, for sure. Umm, are you driving or is she?"

She raised her hand. "Even though I *love* when Erik is in charge, I think I'm behind the wheel first."

The kid blushed furiously, looking at me like I'd just grown another foot in his mind.

I was going to kill her.

He stayed professional, showing us the seat belts and safety features, hooking our helmets on and making sure they were tight. And when Lydia turned the key, I saw only the slightest shake in her fingers.

"You're doing good," I told her smoothly.

The kid stood back and waved at me. I lifted my hand as Lydia laughed.

"I like him," she said simply.

"You owe me so big for that little show, Pierson."

She hummed, running her hands over the wheel in a way that was almost obscene. To me, at least.

Then she glanced over at me. "Ready?"

"If you are."

She let out a slow breath, fiddled with the mirrors, and then eased her foot off the brake.

And that was it.

We coasted for about fifteen feet, and I gave her a look. Her knuckles were tight. "Lydia?"

"What?"

"You can … push on the gas a little, you know."

"It's a fucking Ferrari, Erik," she hissed. "I'm not trying to break any records, *you know*."

I took my helmet off, and she gave me a panicked look.

"What are you doing? Put that back on."

"You're going eight miles an hour, Lydia. I want you to hear me clearly."

She tightened her grip on the steering wheel, taking us up to twenty.

I nodded. "Pay attention to the sounds that the car makes. The leather under your hands."

Lydia let out a slow breath. "It smells nice too," she said absently.

Thirty.

"It does." The skin on her knuckles wasn't so white anymore. "There's no one out here but us."

She nodded.

Forty.

"It's … smooth." She glanced in the mirror. "Maybe I should give myself one for my birthday."

I grinned. "Maybe you should. Go crazy and take it higher than fifty."

She laughed.

Watching her face, I couldn't help but be fascinated at the play of her emotions over her face. The way her eyes flickered behind the visor.

Fifty.

"Tell me about your school," I said softly.

Her eyes flicked to mine.

Forty again.

Then back to fifty.

Lydia swallowed, the graceful line of her throat moving underneath the edge of the helmet. "I'm … I'm getting my master's in sports administration from Gonzaga."

Fifty-five. She hugged the curve, steering the car with one hand resting along the bottom, one holding the top.

"Are you?" I asked.

She nodded, lifting her chin. "I knew I would. Eventually." She checked her mirror and pressed down on the gas pedal a little bit more.

Seventy.

I grinned.

"My car accident kinda put things in perspective," she said next. "When I take over Washington someday, I'll know everything. Every inch of that organization. And no one will question that I'm capable."

Eighty.

Her chest was heaving, her hands maneuvering around the corners with ease.

And I wished that helmet was gone because I desperately wanted to see her face while she told me this amazing thing. Lydia Pierson had a future—a bright one. For the first time since we met, I knew I didn't deserve whatever this relationship was with her.

I was a man, unable to face my past because of all the ways I'd failed, fighting feelings for a woman who knew exactly what to do with her future.

"Lydia," I said slowly.

She glanced at me, the speed declining slightly as she did. Her eyes were wary, and her fingers tightened incrementally on the wheel.

"That is fucking *amazing*," I told her. "I'm really proud to know you."

Her grin was wide and happy.

"Come on, boss lady," I said over the purr of the engine. "Show me what you can do with her."

She laughed.

And then we flew. Like a freaking pro, she slowed as she

approached the corners, then hit the gas on the straightaway, and I was pressed back against my seat with a shocked burst of air.

Ninety.

Ninety-five.

"Okay, that's good enough," I told her. "Slow down, please."

With a mischievous grin, Lydia slowed the car back down and pulled it to a stop. She yanked the helmet off, breathing hard, like she'd just run a marathon. Her hair was a disaster, wisps and curls of hair coming out of her hair all around her flushed face.

Head resting on the seat, she turned to me with a hand resting on her heaving chest. She looked like she'd just been screwed.

Hard.

I was out of the car in the next breath because if I sat there for too much longer, I'd do something stupid. I'd reach for her. I'd yank her across the console and tug her tight onto my lap. I'd grip her hair and suck on her tongue.

I wiped a hand down my face, willing my body to get under control as I strode away from the car.

Then I heard the slam of her car door.

Lydia was smiling, so wide and happy and beautiful. I simply stood there while she ran toward me.

And I didn't stop her when she leaped.

I caught her.

Her arms were tight around my neck and her legs tight around my waist, her body warm and soft as I wrapped my arms underneath her backside to hold her safely.

She leaned back, laughing breathlessly, her fingers sliding into my hair, tightening into greedy little fists that had my skin ablaze. "Holy shit, Erik, that was *incredible*."

I couldn't find words. All I could do was stare up and wonder how it had gotten this far. How I'd lost sight of what I was supposed to be doing.

How suddenly, the most important thing I could do was take one hand and slide it against her soft face.

My thumb traced the line of her lower lip, and she exhaled shakily.

"Thank you," she whispered. Her mouth brushed the pad of my finger when she spoke.

She dropped her chin, tightening her hips onto my stomach, and I inhaled sharply when our lips were a fraction apart.

That was when I saw the kid in my peripheral vision. A flash of red hair and a movement of his arm. I yanked my head back, and she blinked.

"He's … watching," I whispered.

Lydia nodded slowly. The color was high in her face as I gripped her waist and helped her down.

I blew out a harsh breath and darted my gaze back to the kid.

Just as he tucked his phone away.

Chapter FIFTEEN

Lydia

I'D LEARNED A LOT ABOUT ERIK WILDER'S SILENCES SINCE THE day we met.

This particular silence had sharp teeth. It had my skin tense, as tight as his thick fingers wrapped around the steering wheel as he drove us home.

It wasn't cold or mean, but so much was weighing it down that I had to struggle not to fidget restlessly as a result. Even I didn't dare try to knock it down with any attempts at conversation. I knew I would fail miserably if I tried, and I knew it the moment he realized someone had been watching us.

A moment that had been so carefree and light and wonderful, seconds away from knowing what his mouth would've felt like on mine, and now we drove home in utter, terrible silence.

Something shut down in his face when the kid tucked his phone back into his pocket, something locked tight in his stern jaw and shuttered eyes.

But it wasn't anger aimed at me. It wasn't even really about the camera—or I didn't think so at least.

Knowing him, I suspected it was the lowering of his guard. The allowance of that moment. A pulsing, throbbing moment when he held me weightless off the ground and touched me like I was precious.

Like I was wanted.

Erik turned down my parents' street, and still, not a single word had passed between us since he guided me with strong hands back down to earth. My feet touched the ground, the hard, hot track, and nothing was the same afterward.

Words crowded my throat, messy and unrehearsed and desperate to escape.

Why did you touch me like that?

What did I see in your eyes?

What did you see in mine?

I want more. Do you?

That was the scariest one of all, in truth.

Because this big, quiet man had me wanting him in a big, scary way.

It was easy to pass it off as a crush before.

Nothing about it was easy now, and I had no idea how to navigate it. Because every man in my past—and it wasn't like there'd been a lot—were so easy to predict, so easy to see through. We'd all been on a fairly level playing field in terms of experience and background and what we wanted. The playing field with Erik was more like a minefield, it seemed. One step forward and three back.

And still … I wanted nothing more than to clutch his hand and help us make more steps forward.

I wasn't alone in this. And I knew it now.

We passed through the security gate with a friendly wave from whoever was working inside. As the end of my parents' driveway appeared, something in that silence shifted imperceptibly.

With a quick glance over at Erik, I saw something new in his eyes when his gaze met mine for a brief second.

The moment he allowed it, I saw an apology.

My brow furrowed as he pulled his vehicle up to the front. Carefully, he slid the car into park and then relaxed his other hand off the steering wheel. Erik reached over, and the breath caught in my throat, thinking he was reaching for me.

But his arm extended into the back seat, and I fought a cold wave of mortification as he pulled my purse into view.

Right.

I took it from him quietly, risking another glance at his face from beneath my lashes.

He made no move to get out of the car to open the door, so I allowed myself just one question.

"What's wrong?" I whispered.

Erik didn't look at me right away. He was staring blankly through the windshield. Then he closed his eyes, clearly wrestling with something.

When he opened them, I didn't see an apology any longer. I saw resignation.

"I'm not the right guy for this job, Lydia." His voice was rough when he spoke. A little harsh. A lot regretful.

My heart stopped. Dropped straight out of my suddenly empty chest.

"What?"

"I'll call your dad when I leave," he continued. "But I don't—I don't think I'm the right person to fill this role."

Earlier, it'd felt ridiculous and overly flowery to say that his silence had teeth, but now, I felt them rip straight through all the softest parts of me. I liked Erik, even before I wanted him.

And the idea that what happened had him shoving me away with such precision, such immediacy, I could hardly let the rejection sink into my skin.

"Erik, please," I said, turning in my seat to face him, "you are the right person. I feel safe with you. I trust you. Look at how much you've helped me."

He eyed me carefully, mouth tight with tension.

"I …" I swallowed, not wanting to trip over the words. "I won't beg you to stay, but I don't want you to quit. I don't want you to leave."

I'd never thought of myself as someone with any superhuman amount of restraint. Usually, I was known for the opposite. But as I sat in that car with Erik, the thought of not seeing him again because of some barrier he'd erected around what had happened, oh, made me feel so awful inside.

It was different than fear, different than the nerves or the jumpiness or the wish to avoid all the things that suddenly frightened me. This was a sadness I'd never experienced.

Even as he sat inches away from me, I knew unequivocally that I couldn't reach him no matter what I did.

It was in his eyes—dark brown and ringed with green—that it wouldn't matter if I begged. If I gave him a list of a hundred reasons I felt like I needed him to stay. Maybe not even need, maybe want was a strong enough word to cover how I was feeling.

"It doesn't matter what I say, does it?" I said quietly.

He averted his eyes. And in that, I had my answer. His jaw clenched, a muscle popping underneath the surface where he must have been gritting his teeth.

Slowly, I nodded. It was on the tip of my tongue to make a joke about that kid and how he'd ruined this for me, but somehow, I swallowed it down. I didn't know exactly what was making him do this, but it wasn't about the kid.

When I felt the bridge of my nose burn, my eyes go a little sandy and dry, I knew I had to get the hell out of that vehicle that smelled like him and where we'd spent so much of our time together.

I clutched the purse tight in my hands and gave him one last look. "Whatever you find yourself doing next, Erik Wilder, I'm glad

I got to know you." I paused, trying to get my voice under control. "I can never thank you enough for what you've done."

His forehead wrinkled as he stared me down, and at the intensity shining in his eyes, I found my hand trembling in its haste to pull the handle on the car door.

I stood quickly, pulling in a deep breath. My eyes felt like they were holding back the fucking ocean, and it was a horrible realization when I noticed he'd climbed out of the car too. I met his gaze over the roof of the vehicle.

"I'm sorry," he said.

It was my turn to watch him quietly. I'd said all the nice things, I'd made my final goodbye, and maybe now it was his turn to let a few words tumble past his lips.

He shoved a hand through his dark hair, the first gesture that belied any frustration. "But you'll be just fine without me. You don't need anyone's help to face anything. You're strong enough on your own."

"I know I am." I gave him a sad smile, and one tear slid down my cheek. "But it doesn't hurt to have someone hold your hand once in a while either."

I inhaled through my nose, and with that fortifying breath, I turned and walked into my parents' house.

By the time I shut the door behind me and sank against the wood and glass, another tear had leaked out. I brushed it away quickly because how stupid did it make me feel? Crying over a guy I hardly knew, who'd hardly touched me.

But it didn't feel like I hardly knew him. Didn't feel like he'd hardly touched me.

It felt very much—at that moment—that Erik Wilder had carved his name straight into my heart.

"Lydia?" My mom came around the corner, concern etched on her beautiful face. "Are you okay?"

I sniffled, such a pitiful little sound, and she wrapped me tight in her arms.

"What happened?" she asked, smoothing a hand in circles on my back. She pulled back, using the edge of her thumb to dry my cheek where a second or third tear had decided to join the first.

Mom led us to the long couch that faced the wall of windows overlooking the lake. It was a nice day, warm and sunny, and the water sparkled like it was coated in diamonds. Shiny water, I used to call it when I was little. Today, though, that shiny water hurt my eyes, so I turned to the side, tucking my knees up against the couch.

"Erik just quit."

Her mouth fell open. She blinked, gathering her composure. "What happened?"

I sighed. "It's ... kind of a long story."

Recapping our outing—the superfan and the almost kiss included—didn't take very long, but I found myself going further back. The practice facility. Everything. By the time I was done, she'd mirrored my sitting position. She was still wearing a dress from work, but curled up on her side on the couch, my mom looked so much younger than she was.

These moments made me never want to leave. The quiet way our parents listened so well to the things we said and the things we didn't. They'd always had an uncanny knack for silent communication between the two of them, but they were just as good at reading Faith and me and knowing what we needed from them at any given moment.

Mom tucked her hand in mine while I finished my story, and I held onto her hands like a life preserver.

"My goodness," she said quietly. "You've been keeping some juicy stuff to yourself, my darling girl."

"A little." I sniffed again. "A lot, I guess. But it doesn't seem like an easy conversation with your parents to say you want to suck face with the guy they hired to protect you."

Not much fazed Alexandra Sutton-Pierson, the woman who commanded a billion-dollar enterprise every day in four-inch heels. And in my hurt-laden response, she did nothing but smile.

"Tell me about him," she said gently.

So I did. Sometimes, she laughed—at the coffee order and the battle over his music. But mostly, she just listened with a soft smile on her face. I laid my head on the couch and risked a glance out at the bright, sparkling lake. The sun had shifted behind a cloud, and it didn't hurt to look at anymore. "I think I expected him to be judgey, you know? Of who I am and how I've made my own money."

"He wasn't, though?"

I shook my head. "No. I told him about my master's degree."

Surprise lit my mom's blue eyes. "Isn't he the first non-family member to know?"

"Yeah. It felt stupid to hide it when I was with him so much." I smiled. "And he told me I was 'fucking amazing.'" I held up my hands. "His words, not mine."

"Good man," she murmured.

My fingers fiddled with the edge of the pillow.

"Can I ask you something?" Mom said.

"Of course."

She leaned her head on the couch, snuggling her legs up against mine. "When did you fall in love with him?"

My eyes watered again, and I fought very, very hard to keep that damn water right where it belonged.

"I didn't," I said weakly.

She shot me a look.

I sighed. "I don't know. Doesn't it sound so predictable if I say from the beginning?"

"Not predictable." She grinned. "I never would've pegged him as your type."

"He *isn't*. He's so big and grumpy, and he never answers my questions. He hates my music, and he thinks my plans are crazy."

She winced, and I smacked her hand, which made her laugh.

"They're not that crazy," I amended.

Mom laughed, cupping the side of my face. "You are so wonderful, Lydia. And I'm sorry that he felt like he needed to quit. Give him a few days and maybe reach out to see if you can figure out why." She got a sly look on her face. "Maybe you need to take him out for drinks or something."

"He'd say no," I said glumly. "Alcohol and Erik Wilder? Yeah, right. He'd never lower his inhibitions like that, especially around me."

As she was laughing, Dad swept in through the front door, eyes zeroing in on us laughing on the couch. In his hand was his cell phone.

"Why did Erik Wilder just call me and quit?" he barked.

Mom lifted her eyebrow imperiously. "How about you not yell at us about it?"

He softened, walking over to give her a sweet kiss. Then he set a hand on my hair. "You okay? Did something happen?"

"I'm fine," I assured him.

My mom's phone dinged on the coffee table, and she leaned over to pick it up. Her mouth dropped open. She snapped it shut.

"What?" my dad asked.

She gave me a look. "I think I know why."

She handed me the phone, and on the screen was a picture of Erik and me on the track. The grainy quality made it look like a screen grab from a video. It was just after he'd caught me. His biceps bulged as he braced his arms under my ass, my hands were in his hair, and our lips were inches apart.

I blew out a hard puff of air.

I'd read so many trash articles exactly like the one staring me in the face. And this had all the necessary components. A source—after seeing the video posted by the Wilder superfan—reached out to the magazine, claiming that I was working out my PTSD issues with the older, mysterious former player—because of course, they'd dug up who he was this time. Someone picked apart the past few months of my life, the accident, the subsequent hiding I'd gone into as a result, the loss of some of my big sponsorships, and the last-ditch effort to keep Dior on the hook. That same source told them that I was melting down—*"practically incoherent"*—anytime someone forced me into a car (Fuck you very much, Jill).

And it was after that little gem, they slid in the first of a series of pictures that had been pulled from the Dior event.

Me looking upset on the dance floor, his hand on my arm. Another sly mention of my anxiety and mental health problems.

Then another image from the track. Erik looking up at me, my face tilting down in his direction, and oh shit, what a face I'd given them. It looked like he'd just shoved his hand down the front of my pants for how dreamily I was gazing at him.

The caption under that shot was how we'd hardly been seen in public together since the Dior event because we spent all our time holed up in my downtown apartment. Nothing was known about where Erik lived, but the not-so-anonymous source questioned whether he was with me for my money and the … perks.

My face was fiery red hot because my dad was leaning over my shoulder, swearing up a blue streak underneath his breath.

At the end of the article, with its bullshit conjecture, only the slightest toe-hold on the truth, was the money shot.

Erik had one hand cupping my face, his thumb clearly touching my bottom lip. My hand was curled into his shirt. Whoever got the screen grab from the video the kid posted had excellent timing. Because we looked a split second away from doing it on the hood of that bright red car.

Yeah. They wrapped up with some pearls of absolute wisdom from their expert in body language, and I didn't even have to keep reading to know what they said.

The former player and the billionaire's daughter are DTF.

He might not have seen the picture yet, but the fact that it had been snapped on his watch explained exactly why Erik wanted far, far away from me. He was now front and center, where the vultures would have no problem finding things to pick apart.

They'd effectively painted me as the weakling rich girl, exorcising her issues on an older guy. And Erik? It was almost worse. The washed-up player was using me for more than one reason, and none of them looked good. Not from any angle.

I dropped my head into my hands and groaned. Maybe, just maybe, it hadn't been such a good plan after all.

Chapter
SIXTEEN

Erik

THE BED IN MY SISTER'S GUEST ROOM WAS FINE. IT SAGGED A bit in the middle, but it only bothered me when I slept for too long. When I got home from dropping off Lydia and calling an annoyed Luke Pierson, the apartment was blessedly quiet.

Adaline was hardly ever home because she spent most of her time at work anyway. Her apartment wasn't much more than an expensive holding spot for her clothes and furniture, which served me just fine.

I'd worked out in the gym on the first floor of the apartment building, angry music blaring in my ears so I could drown out a single thought of Lydia.

I pinched my eyes shut because if I started down that train of thought, I'd curse myself out something mighty.

Turning on the bed, I buried my face in the pillow and sighed. The sun still wasn't up, but my internal alarm clock had me unable to get back to sleep.

Sleep, I thought with an angry huff.

Even in my sleep, she'd plagued me.

Bare legs and black shorts. Blond hair against a naked back.

Nothing explicit had happened, but every second of the dream had been a whirring catalog of all her softest parts.

Pink lips, satin smooth against my thumb.

A stubborn chin and flashing blue eyes.

I rolled onto my back and stared up at the white ceiling. It was like a rotating list of why I'd had to walk away.

Noticing any of it was a huge fucking problem, even without that fucking kid watching us. The first—on its own—was cause for concern. Something I'd already been shoving down when we left the Wolves facility. But when my notice of the first distracted me from the presence of the second, I was no longer capable of doing my job.

Not well enough, at least. Not to my standards.

There was nothing about it that I could romanticize or justify. Yeah, Lydia had looked at me more than once with proverbial hearts in her eyes, but she was young. Too young for me.

At twenty-two, she thought she knew what she wanted, but if I thought about who I'd been at the same age, I'd find very little of that man left.

Resting my hand over my bare chest, I took a few deep breaths and tried to focus on something else. Anything else. Through the closed door of my bedroom, I heard my sister get up and start a pot of coffee. I'd have to explain what happened to her before she heard about it from Molly.

If Luke had been frustrated with me, then no doubt I'd have a line of women buried deep in the Wolves hierarchy who'd want my balls on a silver platter for walking away without notice.

From the nightstand, my phone buzzed. I rolled over and saw my mom's name, but it was too early, too soon to prep myself for whatever she wanted from me going into their anniversary celebration.

That was the other problem. Lydia had been such a perfect distraction from my slowly lengthening absence from home. Without that job, I had absolutely no excuse not to go back home. Possibly for good.

Unbidden, my mind went back to her.

I didn't want to worry about Lydia Pierson, didn't want to wonder how I'd made her feel by leaving, but fighting that was like fighting gravity.

Absolutely fucking pointless.

"Walking away again, Wilder?" Luke had asked me on the phone. His tone hadn't been unkind, but the ugly truth of it still smacked me across the face about as effectively as a punch to the nose. "This seems to be your pattern, and you might want to make a new one before it's too late."

That damn question was what had me working out until my muscles shook and my body screamed for relief the night before. Why I'd stood under a scalding hot shower until the water ran cold. Why I'd crawled into bed so early. Because if I stayed awake, or if I sat still for too long, I'd have to think about what he said.

Walking away was for her own good.

Just like staying away from home was for my family's own good.

Out in the kitchen, I heard Adaline's muffled voice in a conversation.

Mom had probably called her when I didn't answer.

Something dropped in the kitchen, followed quickly by a "Holy *shit*!". I sat up at the alarmed tone in my sister's voice, absently tugging on some gym shorts when I stood out of bed. Just as I opened the door, she shoved into my bedroom, eyes wide, phone wedged against her ear, and an iPad clutched in her hand.

"No, Mom, I hadn't seen it yet," she said, waving the screen frantically.

I snatched it with an annoyed huff because I couldn't see anything with her doing that. But the panicked look on Adaline's face had me holding my hands up in question.

"What's wrong?" I mouthed.

She jammed her finger at the iPad. "Mom, I'm sure he was going to tell you." She pinched her eyes shut. "Yeah, he's a real dick for keeping it a secret, isn't he?" When she opened them again, she was glaring like I'd just punched a kitten in front of her.

I gave her a look, finally tearing my gaze away from my sister and trying to focus on the brightly colored website displayed in front of me. All I could see at first was the headline.

*Lucky Lydia dips her toes into the pool of players! All the details on her steamy new relationship (He's older too! *fans face*)*

Dread was far, far too small and tame of a word for what happened in my body when the headline registered.

"Shit," I whispered, scrolling down on the screen until the first of the images appeared.

It was so, so much worse than I thought.

Even when I knew I needed to walk away, it wasn't because of this. There was no lingering fear that the photos would make any sort of ripple in my life because I never considered myself interesting enough to warrant tabloid gossip. It was the mere fact that I'd stopped paying attention to our surroundings because I couldn't pay attention to anything but her.

Only bits and pieces of the article itself registered, but I almost cracked the iPad screen when I saw the line that said I was with her because of her age—and her money.

The ice-cold wave of my first reaction gave way slowly—so, so slowly. I didn't get mad often, but when I did, it was terrifying. The intensity of my own frustration made me feel like I could rip down houses with my bare hands, snap a tree in half, or breathe fire at whoever painted my relationship with Lydia in such a light.

To them, it was so easy to call her a scared little girl who'd lap up attention from anyone if it made her feel better. That I was a user, some washed-up player trying to reclaim his glory days with a hot young piece of ass.

Everything went blurry around the edges of my vision because

I wanted to destroy anyone who'd say such things and demean her like that.

Adaline laid a cool hand on my arm, and I blinked up at her, my breath coming in harsh pants from my overworked lungs. Concern was etched all over her face, and I took a steadying breath. I wasn't even sure how much time had passed while I looked at the article.

Ten seconds.

Ten minutes.

All I knew was that if Lydia hadn't seen this yet, she would soon. I tossed the iPad on my bed and ripped a clean T-shirt out of my closet, snatching my wallet and car keys off the dresser.

"Hang on, Mom," Adaline said in a rush. "Let me see if he's up."

She punched the screen on the phone, muting the speaker.

"I cannot talk to her right now," I whispered harshly. "I have to go see Lydia."

"Is it true?" Adaline asked carefully.

"No!" I yelled. "What do you think? I'd never take advantage of anyone, and in what *universe* do you think I'd sleep with Lydia Pierson because she's young and rich?"

"Hey," she snapped, "don't lash out at me because you're getting your first taste of the celebrity limelight, you ass. I'm on your side, okay?"

I rubbed my forehead. "I'm sorry. I just … I quit yesterday because of what happened. We were, I don't know, caught up in the moment, but *nothing* happened."

"It doesn't look like nothing happened," she said quietly.

Mom spoke on the other end of the phone, calling my sister's name.

She took the call off mute. "Sorry, Mom, I was just … seeing if he was awake yet. I didn't have much luck getting through to him."

I shook my head.

Mom clucked her tongue. "Don't wake your brother if he's not ready. Don't you remember how grumpy he used to get when I had to get him up for school?"

They both laughed, and the sound of my mom's laughter sent a sharp pang through my chest. I missed her. I missed my whole family. But the last time I'd seen them … it was so awful. I'd ripped so much of their happiness away in one single conversation, and I couldn't bear the thought of ever doing that to her again. Not with Tim being sick.

"I'll leave him be," Adaline said, giving me some meaningful eye contact.

"Good," Mom said. "But when you talk to him, can you do me a favor?"

I swiped a hand over my mouth at how tentative she sounded, which was never a word I would've paired with our mom. She was a force of nature, always had been. And because I'd stayed away, she wasn't quite sure how to approach her eldest son.

"Of course," Adaline said. "What is it?"

She pulled in an audible breath. "Tell him I want him to bring Lydia home with him for the party."

Adaline's mouth fell open, and I clenched my teeth against the urge to swear and swear mightily.

"Mom," Adaline said slowly, "I don't know if—"

"If he's … dating this young woman," my mom interrupted, "then there's something special about her. I may not have seen my son in years, but …" She stopped, her voice wobbling dangerously. "I know him. I know his heart. And if he's let her in, then I want to meet her."

This was so, so much worse than anything I could've anticipated. A thousand excuses sprang to my head as reasons I'd give for why Lydia couldn't come home with me.

Until she spoke again, tears thickening her voice. "He owes me that, Adaline. He owes Tim and me this small glimpse into his life after cutting us out for so long."

I could hardly breathe through all the things coursing through my body.

She was wrong for asking.

But she was right about what I'd done. No matter what my reasons had been—the place of hurt and grief and betrayal that they'd come from in my own life—I had cut them out of my life.

I'd walked away because I thought I was protecting them. Just like Luke said.

Adaline looked about as panicked as I felt, and she gave me a helpless shrug. I nodded, setting my hand on her shoulder.

"*Really?*" she mouthed.

I shrugged right back.

"Yeah, Mom," she said. "I'll tell him. I'm sure he'll do his best."

They said their goodbyes, and I sank down onto the corner of the bed, my head in my hands, while I mulled over the absolute clusterfuck of the last twenty-four hours.

"What are you going to do?" Adaline asked. "Mom thinks you're coming home with a girlfriend that doesn't exist, Erik."

"Trust me, I heard."

"What if Lydia can't come with us?"

"Then her request is a moot point, and I'll deal with it." I shook my head. "In all the ways I imagined going back home, it wasn't like this."

Adaline lifted one imperious eyebrow. "So you did imagine going back home at some point? Fascinating."

Even my best big brother stare didn't faze her. "You know this hasn't been easy."

She moved toward the bed, tentatively lowering her weight next to me. "No, it hasn't. But ... what happened with Olivia, everything after"—her voice softened—"it didn't change how they looked at you."

She wasn't there, and she definitely didn't understand the

position I'd been in, so it was pointless to argue. I clenched my fists, and she gently laid her hand on top of them.

"I think it changed how you looked at yourself. Going home is a reminder of whatever failure you pinned on yourself. And you've been a little lost since then—"

"That's *not* what this is about," I interrupted.

"I disagree," my sister said in a firm but kind voice. "But I also love you enough to drop it."

Wise move on my sister's part. My head had too many other moving pieces to focus on that one irksome accusation.

I wasn't avoiding my home or my family because I felt like a failure. I was giving them space to grieve freely without me sitting in their front yard.

Adaline sighed. "What a morning. I did not have enough coffee yet for this."

"Is there enough for me? I think I need an IV at this point."

She nodded. "What are you going to do?"

"I'm going to go talk to Lydia."

"If she'll see you," Adaline pointed out.

"Thanks."

"Just saying. I wouldn't want to mess with any of the Pierson women." Her eyes got big and dramatic. "Like … at all. Allie stares down linebackers *all day* and eats them for breakfast."

I rubbed a hand over the back of my neck. "Do you feel like this is helpful? I know Allie and Luke, and yes, they love their daughters, but they'll be reasonable when I explain."

"Mmmkay." My sister clucked her tongue, patting me on the face just a bit harder than I would've liked. "When she shoves her stiletto up your ass, don't say I didn't warn you."

Chapter
SEVENTEEN

Erik

Me: I know you don't owe me any of your time, but can I stop over today? I'd like to talk to you about something.

Lydia: I'm studying all day, but yes, you can stop by.

Lydia: Can't guarantee my dad will let you in the door, but … he'll be gone midday for some college commentating gig.

Me: I'll be there around 1 then. Thanks.

THE CLOCK ON THE DASHBOARD OF MY CAR CLICKED TO ONE o'clock on the dot just as I turned into the curving driveway of the Pierson family home. I'd heard stories about how Luke and Allie met, living in neighboring houses overlooking the lake, just before she took the reins of leadership at Washington. I didn't remember details of it myself, but even decades later, their unconventional love story—the star quarterback and the unlikely team owner—was still talked about on *SportsCenter* and news sites.

Lydia, and her penchant for the spotlight, kept their love story at the forefront of people's minds.

And it was a good story for two really good people. But still, I knew those good people would do exactly what my sister threatened because of how I'd failed in the responsibility they'd given me.

It was an uncomfortable walk to the front door, which hadn't seemed too big and imposing the first time I arrived to meet Lydia. It was shaped in a graceful arch, double doors made of solid wood and waved glass with iron handles flanked by solid light sconces set into the home's stone exterior. Lydia was currently framed in that wavy glass behind the double doors. I could see her watching me as I approached, and I blew out a hard breath. She had every right to be furious, embarrassed … Insert any adjective in that space, and she'd be able to claim it.

The Lydia I'd known before might've opened the door before I had a chance to knock, greet me with a smile and an eye roll that I was hesitating, but this Lydia made me walk all the way up. About five feet away from the door is where she stood, arms crossed over her middle, and even though her facial features were indistinct, hurt rolled off her in palpable waves. Even though she could see me, and I could see her, I knocked quietly, tucking my hands behind my back while I waited.

She waited only a few seconds before she approached the door, pulling it open without so much as making eye contact with me. Neither one of us spoke as she led me into the two-story foyer and into the family room, flanked by their kitchen and casual dining area. It was a relatively small, circular wooden table, the kind with dings and scratches in the top, and I knew it was a place they gathered often.

We bypassed it, though, and I followed her into the main seating area.

Lydia picked a spot in the corner of the long couch, tucking her legs up against her chest as she burrowed comfortably into the spot. Next to her on the couch were a few textbooks, her laptop coated with colorful stickers, and a notebook filled with her neat handwriting.

Because of where she sat, I chose one of the leather armchairs that faced the couch, sliding my hands down my thighs. Her quiet made me unaccountably nervous because I wasn't used to it from her. She wore very little expression on her face as we sat there in our respective seats, but her blue eyes were expectant. She looked so different than when I'd seen her the day before, happy and smiling and flushed, vibrating with the energy that I now associated with being near her.

The quiet between us allowed a thought to slip in—without my permission.

I missed her.

In twenty-four hours, having to shove down the thought of not seeing her again because my brain didn't want to acknowledge it, I had missed her. I closed my eyes and gave a brief shake of my head like I could somehow dislodge the thought.

"I'm assuming you came here to, I don't know, speak at some point?" Lydia said.

When I opened my eyes, she had a tiny smile on her lips. It conjured one of my own.

"I'm so sorry about the picture," I said. "And the article."

"You can't control what they write, Erik. Just like you can't control that the kid posted something innocently, unaware of what would happen as a result. You don't owe me an apology for anything they choose to do."

That she meant the words was clear in her eyes, but I could see hints of dark circles that spoke of a sleepless night.

No, she might not hold any of it against me, but it affected her all the same. And it lit a dangerous, slow-burning fire in my gut that there wasn't anything I could do about it. I wish I could've used that fire to burn all those words away.

I nodded. "All the same. I wish I'd thought it through. That someone might be watching. And I didn't. I owe you an apology for that. I wasn't doing my job."

Lydia licked her lips. "That's why you quit."

There was no question there because she knew me well enough now. I nodded again.

"That's not why you're *here,* though," she said. Those eyes were steady on my face, and something in them had a thin line of sweat breaking out along the back of my neck. She'd never unsettled me so much, but this calm, assured side of her had me feeling very much at a disadvantage. She reminded me of her mother, the way Allie effectively maneuvered rooms full of men without breaking a sweat. Made me feel even crazier for asking her what I was about to ask.

"Yes and no," I answered. "I should have explained myself better yesterday when I left, and it is about the pictures but not in the way you might think."

"Okay," she said carefully.

"It's not a quick story." The idea of sharing it with her—even a cleaned-up version—was uncomfortable. More than that. My feet dangled off the edge of an unseen cliff, and there was no way for me to know what waited at the bottom.

"I've got time." Her answer was simple, and I wished that what I was about to ask could be classified as the same.

With my hands clasped loosely in front of me, and a pretty girl sitting tucked against a couch while I spoke, I told her about my mom, how she raised my sisters and me after my dad left, moving us to Sisters, Oregon, to live closer to my grandparents. How, in that small town, she met Tim and his three kids. Through their unexpected love, an entirely new family came into our life when I was still in elementary school. How about two years after they got married, they added Poppy into the completely wonderful chaos of our life.

The careful expression on her face faded as I spoke, and she looked a bit more like herself. The Lydia I'd gotten to know, the one who smiled easily, who wanted nothing more than to know more of me than I'd been willing to give her.

"So you have … six younger siblings?"

I nodded, conceding a small smile. "I do."

A dimple popped in the side of her cheek when she grinned. "I *knew* it."

"You did," I murmured.

Her smile faded. "What's next in the story?"

I closed my eyes and took a deep breath. She'd only get a skeleton version of my past, but even that felt like someone was plucking my ribs out, the thing that held me upright.

"All I wanted as I grew up was the same kind of family that my mom and Tim had. I'd never be my father, someone who walked away from his responsibilities. In high school, I was the guy who couldn't wait to start that family. Get married, make my mark on the world, create the kind of life that I was fortunate enough to have after my dad left."

Her forehead creased. "That's admirable."

I hummed. "If you marry the right person, it is."

Lydia's mouth fell open into a gentle O. "You were …"

"Married," I finished. "Olivia was a friend. I had a crush on her, and she had one on me. We started dating junior year. Got married right after high school. My mom told me there was no rush, and maybe we should wait. But … no one could tell me I was making the wrong decision. Back then, I could be a little … stubborn," I conceded.

A ghost of a smile graced her face.

The words of my past, the truth of it, got stuck in my throat. Roughly, I swallowed, but I couldn't dislodge them.

"When did you get divorced?" she asked quietly.

I locked my gaze with hers. "Right after my injury."

"Oh," she said on a shocked burst of air. "She left you?"

With a tilt of my head, I made a gentle adjustment to her guess.

The words sounded remarkably calm coming out of my mouth, probably because I stayed clear of all the details that might make me bleed if I tried to say them. "Not because of my knee. Because of the man she'd been sleeping with while I was here playing. The injury just … forced the issue when I came back home."

Lydia's mouth hung open. "That *bitch*."

I laughed under my breath.

"She was a part of our family for a long time," I said, choosing my words carefully. It was the most pivotal chapter of my life, condensed beyond recognition. "And the fallout of what happened between us, it … made it hard to go back home."

Lydia searched my face. "And you'd … you'd already decided to walk away from football."

Instead of answering the question the way she deserved, the way I knew she wanted, all I did was nod.

Lydia took in a deep breath. "Wow," she breathed. Her gaze never left mine.

"It's a lot, I know."

She smiled. "It is, but … I just didn't know you could string together that many words in a row." At my shocked expression, her smile widened. "So you have a past that's kept you away from home. You thought I'd hold that against you?"

I rubbed the back of my neck. "No, but … it doesn't exactly make me sound good either."

Lydia unfolded her legs and mimicked my posture. Her hair, tangled and hardly holding together in a messy bun, slid over her bare shoulder. "It explains a lot, actually."

I didn't intend for it to be "figure out Erik Wilder hour." I just needed a couple of days of her time. It didn't change anything between us. But she was looking at me like she wanted to dissect me under a spotlight, pluck my deep-seated issues from somewhere hidden and untangle them from the knotted mess that I'd let them become.

"That's not ..." I said, pausing when I wasn't exactly sure what I wanted to say next. "I just wanted to give you some background is all. Before I ask you what I'm about to ask you."

Surprise had her eyebrows lifting slightly. "And this is about the article?"

I held her gaze just long enough before I said anything that her cheeks turned a pale shade of pink. "My mom saw it," I told her.

In the next moment, the pink disappeared, along with all the blood in her face. "Oh," she whispered weakly. "Oh, dear."

"Yeah." I swallowed, thinking of the words I'd practiced on my drive over. Logical, rational explanations as to why her presence was required. And as she watched me, all those words fled, my request boiling down to the most basic way I could say it. "I need your help, Lydia."

Her mouth fell open. "Mine?"

I told her about the anniversary party, and my mom's phone call that morning to Adaline. She listened quietly, a hand covering her mouth now.

My voice should've been raw, split open from all the things I was admitting to her, but it came out sure and steady. "I know you don't owe me anything. Not a single second of your time after what happened yesterday. But if I can give my mom this, just one weekend when she thinks that I'm okay and happy, then I'll feel like I've replaced some of what she's lost."

Lydia sucked in a breath, holding it for a moment before she blew it out with puffed cheeks. "When is this party?"

I wiped a hand over my tired face. "We'd need to leave in two days. Spend a few nights there."

Lydia thought quietly, rearranging her hair into something only slightly less messy. "Is this like a, *whoops, we have to share a bed in the parents' house* kind of deal?"

Again, her cheeks went a little pink as she asked, and I had a sudden vision of the absolute fucking torment it would be if that were the case. Sharing a bed with her would be hell in the most exquisite way. Because I knew if she agreed to this, I would not touch her. No matter how she'd slipped silently under my skin, Lydia Pierson would be safe from whatever thoughts had taken root in my head.

"No," I told her with a gentle smile. "I have a small place on the family property. It's not much, but we'll have some privacy. And our own space to sleep," I added meaningfully.

She nodded.

"If you're willing, I only have one condition," I told her.

"What's that?"

"You have to be careful with my family."

Lydia tilted her head. "What do you mean?"

This was the part I'd practiced, and I knew it was as important as anything I'd ask of her. "My sisters will interrogate you like the best journalists in the world because they'll want to know everything. My brothers will have a massive crush on you almost immediately." Lydia smiled but didn't interrupt. "And my parents—my mom and Tim—they will love you."

"Well, I am very lovable. It's not like I can help it."

Despite myself, I laughed quietly under my breath. "I mean … no meddling in their lives. No trying to become their best friend or making plans with them outside of this weekend. You can't … you can't make them think you'll be around forever. Because I don't want them to lose anything else important."

For a moment, I worried that she would push me on why this was so important. That the bare-bones version of my story didn't match up with the seriousness of what I was asking her. Her curiosity was stamped all over her face—in the way she bit her lip and the slight furrow to her forehead. But Lydia must have seen something in my own expression that kept her from pushing because after a moment, she nodded.

"I have a condition too," she said.

I sat back in the seat and regarded her warily. "What?"

"If I do this, you don't get to quit." She tilted her chin up and dared me to argue.

"Lydia," I started, "it's not a good—"

"Do not tell me it's not a good idea," she interrupted, eyes flashing. "Don't tell me you failed or some other bullshit excuse for why you're running away."

I clenched my jaw and stared down at the ground. She had no idea what she was asking of me. And even if she did, Lydia didn't need me to follow her around anymore. And I had a feeling she knew it. But even if she didn't, my feelings toward Lydia weren't appropriate for anyone tasked with her safety.

But still … I needed her this weekend. I wouldn't beg, but I knew that facing my past would go more smoothly if she was there. There was still a gnawing sense of unease in my gut at what her presence within my family would do, but it was still a start. A way to step back into that place without all of their attention on me.

When my gaze rose from the ground, she was bracing herself for me to say no. To take back the invitation or argue with what she'd said.

And I hated how similar her words were to what my sister had accused me of a few hours earlier.

"I can't promise that, Lydia," I said quietly. "Or I shouldn't."

"Why not?"

I let out a slow breath. If we weren't facing such a pivotal stretch of days at my parents', maybe I'd be more honest with her. Give one of the many reasons why working for her was no longer viable. I couldn't be objective. I couldn't be impartial. And my focus—it was a struggle to pull it away from her.

"I already told you why."

There was a stubborn set to her jaw that I recognized well, and I braced for an argument. But something passed behind her eyes, and her expression softened.

"I know I can't force you," Lydia said. "But promise me one little thing?"

I gave her a look.

She huffed out a laugh. "Just … think about not quitting."

Sure. I could think about not quitting. For five seconds, before my aforementioned list of reasons snuck right back to the rational part of my brain.

But could I *think* about taking it back? Yes.

"That's all you want?" I asked, suspicion clear in my tone.

Her big blue eyes were guileless as she nodded, and that should've been my clue that she'd conceded far, far too easily.

"I'll consider not quitting," I agreed. Her face split into a relieved smile, and I held up a hand. "I don't think you need me, Lydia. Maybe you can't see that yet, but I think you will."

"Maybe," she answered with a sphinx-like smile on her face. The fact that she didn't argue should've scared me, but somewhere deep inside, somewhere dusty and hidden, I was relieved to know I didn't have to say goodbye yet. That the thing I'd gained was more time with her, even if it was only this weekend.

And I'd never let her know it.

Lydia stood and held out her hand to me. Like we'd done the first day we met.

I stood as well, and without shoes, her forehead barely cleared my chest. I could've tucked her against my body and hardly be able to rest my chin on the top of her head. If I held her, I thought, she'd fit so tidily in my arms.

Slowly, I slid my palm against hers, and when her cool, strong fingers curled around mine, my traitor heart did a jangling, off-rhythm beat somewhere deep in my chest.

"I agree to your plan, Erik Wilder," she said. Her eyes glowed such a bright, vivid blue, it was hard to hold her gaze. "And after this, we're even. Fresh start."

"Even," I said in a rough voice. As I said it, I heard that same whisper of caution plaguing me, like it had at the Wolves practice facility. But this time, I knew my reasons, and I knew that I'd be able to rein in whatever irresponsible feelings were unfolding. I could give my family this, and when we were done, I knew it was only a matter of time before Lydia realized she would be just fine without me.

It was better that way.

Chapter
EIGHTEEN

Lydia

H ANDS PROPPED ON MY HIPS, I TRIED VERY, VERY HARD NOT to look at my worried sister as I shoved the last "just in case" outfit into my suitcase. It was my seventh outfit in that particular category, but one should always be prepared for a weekend trip when the man you're traveling with was sparse on the details.

I don't know, Lydia, family stuff, he'd said. Like it was helpful in any way, shape, or form in terms of planning outfits.

"And you're sure this is a good idea," Faith said for the forty-seventh time in the past two days.

I sighed. "It's not a bad idea if that's what you're getting at. Which is different than it being a good idea."

Her dark eyebrows bent into a concerned V. "You like him, Lydia. I believe your exact words were, 'I more than like him.'"

Ugh. Eye contact could no longer be avoided. I sat on my bed and gave her a beseeching look. "It's fine. I can more than like someone and still be mentally capable of helping him out for the weekend."

"You could get hurt. I don't like the idea that he'd take advantage of your big heart in a situation of his own making."

"Like Erik has any idea how I feel." I pulled the zipper on the suitcase, tucking the edge of a sleep shirt in when it stuck out too far.

Faith scoffed. "Lydia, I saw the video. You were looking at him like you could picture your future babies with that man. You are not the most conspicuous in these types of situations."

I folded my hands primly in my lap. "I'm well aware that he doesn't feel the same way that I do, and it's fine."

She raised her eyebrows. Because she knew me. And knew me better than anyone.

"And?" she prompted.

My jaw set mulishly.

"Lydia. I saw the black lace."

"I have to sleep in something."

Faith threw up her hands. "You are impossible. Just admit it."

"Fine. If we accidentally fall into bed and *oops*! I sleep with Erik ten times this weekend and he realizes how great we are together, then so be it."

She shook her head slowly. "This has disaster written all over it."

"How? *Technically*, he's not my bodyguard right now, so he's not wading into some ethically gray area. And I'm going with him of my own free will, so Dad doesn't have to freak out about abuse of power or all the things he told us to be careful for."

Faith sat next to me on the bed, which somehow made it easier. I didn't want to hear her logic or her warnings that I was stepping straight into a situation where I was the most obvious candidate for a broken heart. I'd thought it through and decided that Erik—and the way he made me feel—was worth the risk.

"I don't mean the sex," Faith said carefully. "You're both adults, and if that's the decision you make—and you're safe—you know I am not someone who'd judge."

I stayed quiet because my older-by-seven-years sister didn't do the big serious talks with me often. So when she did, I respected her enough to listen. "Then what do you mean if it's not the sex?"

Faith chose her words before she said anything out loud. "You may not admit it to very many people, but you have the biggest, most tender heart of anyone I know, Lydia. And whatever relationships you've had in the past, you have never given them a piece of it." She slid her hand over mine and tangled our fingers. "Because you want the same thing that Mom and Dad have. You want a big, overwhelming, wreck-your-world kind of love. And I think … I think Erik is different than anyone you've ever been with. Just be careful. Because even if he's never touched you, I think he could still damage that heart of yours. I don't want to hate him if he does." She glanced at me, eyes a little shiny. "And I would. I'd hate anyone who ruins your ability to love the way you do."

I so badly wanted to argue with her—get defensive of my right to choose who I slept with—but I also knew she wasn't wrong. Erik was different, and even if I steadfastly refused to think about what it might be like to have him—then part ways—it was a possibility that I had to accept.

And it would suck.

Because now I had a face to go with all the things I once dreamed of in fuzzy images. A face and a stern mouth and dark eyes, and a heart that he couldn't hide.

I set my head on Faith's shoulder and sighed. "I love you. You always believe the best of me."

She wrapped an arm around my shoulder. "That's what love is, isn't it?"

"I suppose," I murmured.

"Even if I'm not at my best," she told me, "Dominic gives me the benefit of the doubt. And when he's not at his best, I love him enough to do the same."

I smiled. "Like almost picking fights because he's trying to be protective of your little sister."

"Exactly like that." She sighed. "You're my sister, and even if your plans are crazy and impulsive and put you right in the cross-hairs of any fallout, I'll still always think the best of you."

It was always like that with the really profound moments in life, at least for me. They popped the hell out of nowhere, and suddenly, you couldn't look away from a simply stated truth that should guide every facet of your life.

How would I navigate this weekend with Erik if I assumed the best in him and his intentions.

He didn't strike me as a man who'd cross lines without thinking of the consequences, and if anything, what he'd told me about his background—his marriage—only proved that he was a man who valued love and commitment and the responsibility that came with it. And the distance from his family, I saw his face when he spoke of them.

If I was falling in love with Erik, then believing the best in him was what I'd do.

I didn't want to view him through the lens of cynicism or distrust, even if that might offer me a bit more protection. If my time with him taught me anything, it was that I could trust myself—and my instincts—more than that.

A text dinged on my phone, and Erik's name appeared on the screen.

Erik: Be there in five. Adaline said you get shotgun, and you're not allowed to argue with her.

"So romantic," I drawled. "Maybe the black lace was a little presumptuous, huh?"

Faith laughed. "I don't think presumptuous is the right word. Unnecessary is probably better."

I cut her a look. "Gee, thanks."

She nudged me with her shoulder. "Don't misunderstand me.

If Erik Wilder can actually resist you after all this, then you won't have time to put it on, little sister. But be careful all the same, okay?"

I nodded in assent, but even as she left my room, and I finished gathering my things, I tried to picture how the next days of my life would pan out, and no matter what my sister said in warning ... all I could see was possibility.

Erik

After just five minutes on the road, I was ready to turn back around and drop Lydia back off at her house. Her and her excessive amount of luggage. Who brought a duffel and a large suitcase for a two-night trip? My hands tightened on the steering wheel because I refused to allow myself to wonder what was tucked neatly into those two spaces.

She'd have her own bed.

And a door—with a lock—would separate us.

It would be fine.

As long as she stopped doing everything she was doing that was making my brain spin like a top. Current example—she was sitting backward in the passenger seat to talk to Adaline more easily, which put her profile directly in my sight line. And when she thought I wasn't looking, she'd sneak her hand into the bag of trail mix I'd brought, only picking out the chocolate candies.

"Whoa," Adaline breathed, flipping through the stack of brightly colored Post-it notes that Lydia produced from her giant leather bag of mystery. "This is intense."

Lydia laughed. "Test me."

Adaline flipped a notecard so the front of it faced Lydia. I could see her neat writing in thick black ink, just one word visible.

Greer.

Lydia cleared her throat delicately. "Greer Wilder. Biological sibling to Erik and Adaline, twenty-two years old. She's an interior designer for the family construction business, Wilder Homes, which was started by your stepdad, Tim Wilder. She got her degree at the Heritage School of Interior Design in Portland. She's allergic to cats, bunnies, and players with dark hair and blue eyes."

I gaped at the woman in my passenger seat. "How do you *know* all that?"

Lydia shrugged. "Social media is a goldmine. All I had to do was write a notecard for every member of your family—based on what I could find in their posting—and the rest is easy. Repetition, repetition, repetition."

Adaline hooted with laughter at my expression. "You are a secret genius, Lydia Pierson." She glanced at Greer's postcard again. "Allergic to players with black hair and blue eyes." She wiped a fake tear from under her eyes. "Oh, how I wish Greer could see this."

The two chatted back and forth as I settled in for the four-hour trip back home. Even if a part of me knew what a massive fucking mistake it was to bring Lydia back with me, I couldn't deny that she was a welcome distraction from what was facing me at the end of the drive.

In the two years that Adaline had worked for Molly Ward, she'd crossed paths with Lydia and Faith a handful of times—not just at Wolves games or family events, but simply because Coach Ward's wife and Allie were best friends. As they laughed about something she'd written on Poppy's card, I knew it was the only way this whole stupid plan felt doable.

And it wasn't like my siblings hated me for staying away—to varying degrees, they understood why.

Except Ian. He thought I was a giant prick who did nothing but prove him right about what kind of guy I really was in the end.

Adaline flipped to a new card. "Okay, let's see how well you know Parker."

Lydia shifted her legs, bare and tan and smooth, tucking them against her chest as she lounged back against the dashboard.

It made the V of her shirt tug down, and the edge of a light purple lace appeared. The skin next to it was lighter than the skin on her chest, full and round. I shifted irritably.

"You shouldn't sit like that," I barked. "It's dangerous."

She gave me an amused look. "Did we leave our manners back in Seattle?"

I cut her a look.

"Touchy, touchy," she mumbled, turning around to sit correctly in the seat. As I suspected she would, Lydia wedged her bare feet on the dashboard. Her toes were purple, just like the glimpse of her bra I'd seen. Suddenly, I couldn't help but think about all the varying shades I'd seen on her toes in the weeks earlier, and I hated myself for wondering whether they always matched.

It made me think about when they were black. I pinched my eyes shut for a moment because all I could imagine was Lydia covered in black lace, and I was pretty sure the pits of hell just lit in preparation for my arrival. If I tried hard enough, I could smell the sulfur all around me.

Adaline met my gaze in the mirror, and at the sight of her shit-eating grin, I scratched the side of my face with my middle finger.

"Where were we?" Lydia asked.

"Parker," Adaline answered.

"Hmm." Lydia tapped her feet along with the God-awful shit she'd pulled up on her phone. "Parker Wilder is the biological son of Tim. He's twenty-one and plays tight end at Portland State University." She paused, chewing on her bottom lip as she thought. "He loves pasta, and he has a tendency to get very embarrassed by his roommates, who also play football. Their names are Dante and Mitch. He doesn't post many selfies, which tells me he's not vain, and he seems very serious about his classes."

Adaline nodded. "Super serious. He's a total brain. If he wasn't so good at football, I could see him ending up as a professor or a doctor or something."

Lydia shook her head. "He's good. He's got great speed off the line, and if he worked on his social media, I bet he could get some solid draft interest if he doesn't have it already."

"No."

The two women in the car gaped at my harshly spoken interjection.

"We made a deal," I told Lydia. "No meddling."

She folded her arms over her chest, setting her chin mulishly. "I'm not meddling. I'm just saying that he's good enough to be drafted, but he could get real top-tier interest if he creates a better brand image of himself. He has no highlight reels on his social media, no workouts, nothing that talks about who he is as a person."

My hands tightened on the steering wheel. The mountains stood steady in the distance even as the tall, green trees whipped past as we drove down the highway. This was exactly what I was afraid of. She'd come in and see what they needed, what they wanted, and every single one of them would see her as some missing piece. A savior in the sad story of how my relationship past had played out.

But there was nothing to be done about it now. According to Adaline, my mom had cried happy tears when she knew Lydia was coming with us. Still, I'd been enough of a coward to let my sister handle it, rather than stack lie upon lie to my mom before I could face her.

"Just don't." I paused, letting the frustration ebb from my voice before I spoke again. "Don't fill his head with promises you can't deliver, okay?"

Adaline was quiet, but I could feel her eyes on me. And in the passenger seat, Lydia watched the scenery pass for a moment, just as I had.

"You're afraid I'm going to hurt them, aren't you?" she asked quietly.

I glanced at her, nodding slowly in answer. "My family's been hurt enough over the years. They deserve peace."

Lydia let out a slow breath, then gave me a sweet smile. "Then that's what we'll give them."

Her words didn't make me feel better. Because I had the terrible suspicion that giving something like that to my family would only end in the complete absence of it for me.

Chapter
NINETEEN

Erik

MY PARENTS LIVED FAR ENOUGH OUT THAT WE WEREN'T required to drive through the small downtown area of Sisters in order to get to their property. Adaline, sensing the shift in my mood as we got closer to home, took over the role of tour guide for Lydia.

"They have about fifteen acres," she explained, as the trees became more familiar, the landmarks heralding the approaching entrance to the place I hadn't been in so long. "The main house used to be my grandpa's, but he gave it to Mom and Tim shortly after they got married. Poppy still lives at home. Parker is away at school. Greer has an apartment in town. Cameron has his own place on the back of the property, like Erik."

"Cameron, the builder who took over the family business from Tim when he retired," Lydia said immediately. "He posts maybe once a year and has a favorite drill bit and loves his leather tool belt."

Adaline laughed. "Yes."

For whatever they were worth, Lydia knew enough from her little notecards to fool my family.

She just didn't know the ugly stuff, the things no one would ever post on their cyber highlight reel. And if I was lucky, I'd escape the next few days without her ever knowing them.

I'd drop her off on her parents' front porch, and if I was lucky, I'd never have to see her again. All she needed was a few more days to realize she was just fine without me. That I was doing her no favors.

The thought of it should've filled me with relief, but instead, it sank like a rock, heavy and hard and uncomfortable.

Through the passenger window, Lydia snapped a quick video on her phone, then gave me a questioning look. "Would you prefer I don't post anything about your family's property?" At my momentary hesitation, she gave me a quick smile. "Later, I mean. No locations posted while I'm there, I promise."

I grunted. "Not really too worried about photographers being out here, but thank you for checking. As long as you don't post my parents' faces, it's fine with me."

Adaline rolled her eyes. "Greer puts them on the Wilder Homes account all the time. They won't care." My little sister patted my shoulder condescendingly. "You and Ian are the only social media haters in the family. Funny how similar you are for how little you get along."

Lydia sat up. "Yeah, what's the deal with Ian? I couldn't find anything about him."

I shifted in my seat and kept my mouth firmly glued shut. Even Adaline hesitated because she loved both of her brothers. The one she shared a parent with, and the one she didn't.

"Ian has been working in Europe for the past two years," she said. "He designs custom furniture. And when some bigwig home design company in London started buying his pieces, it was worth relocating. He usually only makes it home for Christmas."

More than I'd done.

Lydia's blue eyes met mine when I glanced sideways to gauge her reaction. "And you two don't get along?"

I frowned, but instead of denying it, I just gave her a terse shake of my head.

Adaline had no issue answering now that we were less than ten minutes from being faced with all the Wilder family dynamics. "It's a birth order thing if you ask me."

"What do you mean?" Lydia asked.

"They're both the firstborn in their families," Adaline explained. "And with our dad leaving when Greer and I were just babies, Erik really ... felt like he was *the man of the house,* ya know? Even though he was little, he was always taking care of us. Taking care of Mom. Ian did the same thing in his family even though they lost their mom from sickness. So you put two bossy big brothers in one family, both with younger siblings to take care of, and things didn't always go well."

"He's just a stubborn know-it-all who can never admit when he was wrong," I mumbled. "He'd be easier to get along with if he was capable of admitting someone else is right once in a while."

Lydia rolled her lips between her teeth, and behind me, Adaline sighed obnoxiously, shifting so she could set her chin on the edge of the driver's seat. "Now who does that sound like?" she mused.

I gave her a look in the mirror.

"It must've been so hard," Lydia said quietly.

My head snapped in her direction because I thought she'd been trying not to laugh, but somehow—Lydia was looking at me all shiny-eyed and sad.

She sniffed, waving a hand in front of her face. "Ignore me. I think doing all this Wilder family studying is getting to me. When I think about you guys as little kids, it's just heartbreaking to imagine everything you've been through."

"We had a good life," Adaline said quietly. "Even though it came with some rough patches."

Lydia sat quietly, and suddenly, I had a frantic need to know what she'd say next. We were so close to my parents' house, so close to shifting the dynamic between us, and because she'd taken me by surprise—again—I was desperate to know what my relationship with Ian uncovered to her.

It was one more thing that I wanted to deny, wanted to ignore, but I couldn't.

That was when she turned and set those big blue eyes on me. There was something soft and sweet in them, something I wanted to erase with a swipe of my hand, but I knew I couldn't.

"No wonder you feel like you have to be perfect," she said. "It was your job to make sure that everyone else was taken care of. There was no time for you to stumble over anything."

Something sharp and quiet pierced through my chest, a secret place between my ribs that I didn't realize I'd left unprotected.

I'd stumbled. In my singular focus on a certain type of future, I'd married the wrong person, leaving me and my family's hearts broken in the process.

And because of that stumble, I'd convinced myself it was better to stay away.

Just like Adaline said.

For the rest of the ride to my parents'—down the long gravel driveway flanked by towering Douglas fir trees on either side—I couldn't say a word. Everything in my brain was fuzzy white noise because I wasn't actually sure I could face all the people I'd let down. The ones I'd been completely un-perfect for.

The cabin that served as our family home appeared at the end of the drive, exactly as I remembered it. The thick hand-hewn wood columns held up the house-length front porch and black metal roof. The chimney stretched up through the middle, where smoke billowed out when my mom lit the two-sided fireplace that dominated the center of the living space.

I had missed it. And until I saw each log, each tree in the front yard, I'd forgotten how much.

But I had to get myself under control before I could face them.

"Adaline, we'll be back to the house in a few, okay?"

Her dark eyebrows rose slowly as I brought the vehicle to a stop by the front entrance. "You're not coming in?"

Ignoring Lydia's curious look, I shook my head at my sister. "Tell Mom we're going to drop our bags off at my place, so Lydia can freshen up before she meets the family."

"Oh, I'm fine—" she started. I clenched my teeth and met her gaze. Her voice trailed off, and she nodded, understanding in her eyes. "Yeah, I could use ten minutes or so, I guess."

Adaline opened her mouth to speak but thought better of it. Because her duffel bag was on the seat next to her, she hiked it into her lap with a resigned huff. "Okay. But don't take too long. You keep putting this off, and it won't get any easier, Erik."

Once Adaline was clear of the car, I made a sharp turn with the steering wheel and accelerated back down the driveway.

Lydia stayed quiet, her body language relaxed, and in turn, it made me relax that I wasn't creating any discomfort between us. About a hundred feet to the right, I saw the slight fork in the road. If you weren't looking for it, it was invisible to the naked eye. Beyond a grove of more Douglas fir trees was the small house I'd moved into after my wife left.

"It's so cute," Lydia exclaimed, sitting up with a wide smile on her face.

It was. I'd painted the siding a deep charcoal gray—it looked almost black when the sun went down—and the trim a crisp white. The front stoop was just big enough for a rocking chair and a planter that someone had recently filled with bright orange mums. Oh yes, it was a small house with a lot of beauty. And it held some of the ugliest memories of my life.

And at that moment, I was so thankful I didn't have to walk into it alone.

My heart raced hard in my chest, and my hands tingled at the tips.

What would it look like inside?

Through the windows, there was warm light.

We parked, and Lydia wandered with unabashed interest. She touched everything like she could absorb the details through her fingers. I didn't want to take anything in from this place. I wasn't even sure I'd be able to sleep in those walls.

"It's, uh, it's pretty simple inside," I hedged. "I wasn't here long enough to decorate much."

She shrugged. "As long as I've got a bed and a shower, I'm good."

Right. Lydia and a bed and a shower. Images of her in both places were not the kind of distraction I needed. Not with the mood I was in. Because as we walked through the front door and into the living area, and I finally saw what my mom had done in preparation for my arrival, I knew very few things on earth would serve as a healthy outlet for what raged inside me.

It didn't smell musty and unused.

It wasn't empty and soulless. She'd placed warm, cozy-looking furniture in it, and it smelled clean and crisp. On the square island in the small kitchen was another pot of mums, yellow this time.

"When were you here last?" Lydia asked. This time, she touched the pads of her fingers to the soft line of the brown leather couch that I'd never seen before.

My voice was rusty and unrecognizable when I spoke. "One year, three hundred days."

One year, three hundred and three days ago, I'd assembled a crib in the second bedroom. A white one with curved edges and light yellow sheets on the mattress.

Someone removed it while I was gone.

In its place was a reading chair and a lamp, a bookshelf that my mother had filled. My hands tingled, an omen that I couldn't ignore. It was a mistake to come to this place first. And I hadn't known it until I walked in the door and saw it transformed. As I'd left it, it was half-empty and hardly decorated, but it'd held promise for a future I was still hanging onto by a frayed thread.

A future for which I'd given up my career. To be the dad that mine wasn't.

My mom had made it a home, something I'd never managed to do. Because she loved me, and missed me, and wanted me to know I was always, always welcome here. And it was almost enough to send me spiraling dark and angry, somewhere clouded and black. Ink stained my thoughts, and my heart churned in my chest.

It was the kind of angry I didn't let my past access anymore. This was why I'd stayed away. Because I was never sure what to do with it or how to get it under control. If I thought too hard about what I'd lost, it was always simmering.

It wasn't my mom's gesture that made me angry, *that* broke my fucking heart. It was what I'd lost, what I'd hardly allowed myself to mourn until I stood in the cheery, happy space.

"Was this a place to start over?" Lydia asked quietly. She'd stopped touching, stopped wandering, and was watching me with a sort of silky soft curiosity in her beautiful face and beautiful eyes. "It must be hard to come back."

There was no morbid reason to ask, nothing she wanted to pick apart. She asked because she cared. She asked because she simply wanted to know me.

And if I stared at her too long, I'd do something stupid.

If Lydia had reacted flippantly, tried to downplay it, or chastise me for staying away, I could've boxed her into that first version of her that I'd thought she'd be.

But as usual, she did none of the things I anticipated.

The walls started closing in on me, my chest tightening as I tried to take a deep breath. I shouldn't have brought her here. I should have told my mom no and let the disappointment continue.

"I can't do this," I growled, and I strode from the house, the front door banging against the siding as I shoved it open. I speared my hands into my hair as I paced the gravel in front of the house.

It wasn't too late. I could say Lydia got sick or had a family emergency and take her back. Because if I had to stay there in that small house with one bathroom and her eyes and all the parts of her that kept me on my toes, I'd crumble. I'd crumble simply because losing myself in her was a better alternative to facing what I'd left behind.

Lydia's footsteps came down the steps, and I braced my hands on the roof of my car and hung my head, sucking in air like I just finished a marathon.

"Lydia," I warned, "go back inside."

But she didn't. Of course she fucking didn't.

"Turn around," she commanded.

At her steel tone, I actually straightened and glanced at her incredulously over my shoulder.

"I need you to take a deep breath for me." Her eyes held mine, and she took a few steps closer.

I'd said something similar to her once, and I swiped a hand down my face. "I'm fine."

Then Lydia Pierson narrowed her eyes and marched the remaining distance. She planted two hands on my chest and pushed me back against my car. "Erik Wilder, you *will* take a deep breath for me."

My eyebrows shot up, and I was too stunned not to comply. Her hands stayed on my chest, and I could feel every single inch of where her body came into contact with mine.

Her eyes softened. "Good. Another one."

No. I was not in the mood to be handled, so I swatted her hands away. "I don't need another one."

My reaction had the desired effect because the softness was gone in a flash. That was what I couldn't withstand. Not from her.

I didn't want to know that side of her, and if I had to be the world's biggest prick to keep it off her face and out of her eyes, then I'd do it.

"You're such a hypocrite," she hissed. "You tell me to do it all the time. *Take another one*," she mimicked my voice. And my skin … oh, it went hot. "Can't you ever let someone help you?"

"No!" I shouted. "I shouldn't need help."

Her mouth fell open at my naked honesty, then snapped shut. She blinked. "Well … tough shit."

"Excuse me?"

She poked my chest. "Tough. Shit." Lydia spread her arms open. "What do you think I'm doing here, Erik? I'm helping you. Because that's what people do for someone they care about."

Her words had my chest heaving dangerously.

"It doesn't make you weak." She moved closer. There wasn't even room for her to do it, but somehow, her chest brushed mine. "It doesn't mean you failed. It makes you human."

My blood hummed hot, so very, very hot. And if Lydia moved a single inch closer, she'd feel between us exactly how human I was. Because this strange little outburst had me as hard as fucking concrete.

I leaned in. "I don't need your help. I didn't even want you here. You're here because my mom begged."

Wrong choice of words. The words hung between us, and Lydia's gaze flickered down to my mouth. My gaze flickered down to hers.

Her hand moved slowly, and I could've stopped it, but I didn't. She slid it up my chest, lightly, delicately, until she reached the collar on my shirt.

"You have no idea what you're doing, little girl," I whispered. "I'm not in the mood to play games."

"Perfect." Her fingers curled into the material of my shirt. "Neither am I."

Lydia licked her lips, a delicate touch of her pink tongue to the curve of her mouth, and that was it. Whatever single thread held me back snapped—a clean, sharp, audible break—and I speared my hands into her hair, slanting my mouth furiously over hers.

My tongue dove between her soft, soft lips, and she let out a delirious sound of whimpered relief. With my hands, I angled her face so I could take the kiss deeper, winding her hot, slick tongue around mine until I was able to suck the tip into my mouth. She sucked in a breath through her nose, her hands digging into the back of my neck as I turned us.

Finally, the glorious weight of her hair tangled in my fingers. All that fucking blond hair, the way it fell around her face and down her back, I'd hardly been able to admit how insane it drove me. There was so much of it, and when I tightened my fingers in the thick, soft mass of it, Lydia moaned.

Her lips met mine, push and pull, in a perfect furious rhythm. I wasn't in control of this kiss any longer because she was right there, battling for dominance. And it had lit a fire under my skin because she'd be able to handle anything I could give. There was no passive acceptance of my kiss. Lydia was right fucking there with me. Of course, the only woman who dared to push me out of my strictly defined comfort zone would be there every step of the way as we descended into lust-fueled madness.

She licked into my mouth, a slow slide of her tongue against mine, and I growled.

With one hand under her ass, I boosted Lydia up against the side of my car. Her legs split around my hips, and she moved sinuously, slowly in a maddening rhythm. She tugged at my bottom lip with the sharp edges of her teeth, and I groaned.

Nothing had felt this good … ever.

Nothing had tasted so sweet.

And I wanted her sweetness on my tongue in all the spots I could find.

The relief after the weeks of holding myself back was heady. She met me kiss for kiss, and I pressed my hips hard against that sweet warmth she rolled against my stomach. Lydia whimpered, and the sound of it sent a slick rush of power through my veins.

All the tension I'd held tight in my arms wrapped into her lithe frame, and if we'd been in a bed, I'd have torn half our clothes off by now. Just to have a release. Just to find a place that could bear the brunt of everything that had built between us.

There might have been other reasons I'd finally crossed the line, why she'd finally pushed me further than normal, but this was just about us. And I knew it as I tilted my face to deepen the kiss.

The sweet sounds she made in the back of her throat were the most delicious payoff to waiting, and the strength in her hands as she clutched me to her had my heart thundering.

Like I was going anywhere. Not now. Not now that I knew she tasted like candy. Not now that I knew the sound of the wet pop of her lip after I dragged it into my mouth.

Lydia tore her mouth away, gasping up to the blue, blue sky, and I sucked at the sensitive skin on her neck until she moaned. Maybe I'd mark her skin, and the thought of it had me sucking harder. She tried to scramble higher, tighter, closer, but there was nowhere to go. I pressed my hips against her, and she whispered a tortured, "Oh *please*, Erik."

Something animal prowled beneath the surface of my skin at the begging and pleading tone in her voice. I wanted to stamp this moment into my skin, remember exactly how wild and perfect it was when I was ready to take what we both wanted against the side of my car.

I slid my hand up the side of her waist, memorizing the curve of her body while our tongues tangled and our teeth clashed. The warm, heavy weight of her breast filled my big palm, and she clenched her thighs tight around my waist.

This was the thing we'd been waiting for, the explosion that kindled dangerously underneath every single interaction we'd had since the moment we met.

"Holy *shit*, Erik. Could you not?" my sister Greer yelled.

Lydia and I froze. Her breath came in heavy pants against my mouth.

"Gawd, Mom sends me out to get you for dinner, and I find a *porno* in the front yard."

I set my forehead against Lydia's and muttered a curse. She breathed out a laugh.

Amazing how quickly my body could turn into a giant block of ice.

Carefully, I helped Lydia find her footing, and her cheeks were flame red with embarrassment. And I ... I just wanted to light my skin on fire as a reminder of what could happen when Lydia Pierson pushed me just a touch too far.

Lydia smoothed her shirt, hardly able to meet my eyes, as we turned to Greer. My little sister had her arms crossed over her chest, and a shit-eating grin on her pretty face.

"Quite the welcome, big brother," she said. "Reminds me just how much I've missed your ass."

I rubbed the back of my neck. "Sorry. Didn't, uh ... I didn't know you were there."

She raised an eyebrow. "Obviously."

I sighed, holding my arms open. She grinned, walking toward me for a hug. I lifted her off the ground, and she laughed. "Good to see you," I murmured by her ear. She squeezed.

"Wish I hadn't seen *that*, but it's good to see you too." When I set her down, she smiled at Lydia. "Since my brother has forgotten his manners in the sexual mauling against his car, I'm Greer Wilder."

Lydia took her outstretched hand with an embarrassed grin. "Lydia Pierson. I really, really wish we hadn't met this way. Like ... *really.*"

Greer laughed.

Lydia cocked an eyebrow at me. "Maybe this will teach you to control yourself, mister."

I narrowed my eyes, which made her laugh.

Greer slung an arm around Lydia's shoulders. "Oh, yes. I like you just fine. Come on, Mom's got dinner ready, and if Erik makes her wait any longer, she'll be the one coming out here."

The color leeched from my face at the thought of that. "Let's get this over with then."

And as I followed my sister and the woman who I would never, ever touch again if I knew what was good for me, I felt the full weight of what I'd gotten myself into.

Chapter
TWENTY

Lydia

ON THE SHORT WALK TO THE MAIN HOUSE, I HAD TWO PRETTY important revelations.

1- My legs still worked, which I'd doubted entirely.

2- Erik Wilder could angry-kiss like it was his singular and divine purpose on this earth.

The surprise addition of Greer was a double-edged sword. I couldn't help but marvel at the palpable thing unleashed between Erik and me, and because of her friendly chatter with a brother she clearly missed, I was able to do exactly that as we walked through the woods.

And holy shit, did I *marvel*.

I'd never been kissed like that, not even by half. None of the sex I'd had came close to that kiss, and boy, wasn't that a revelation. Because if kissing him made my head spin like a top, then sex with Erik Wilder would probably topple my world off its axis.

And I wanted axis-knocking activities with him. Immediately.

Not just because of how he kissed and how his hands felt tangled tightly in my hair, but because of everything leading up to it too. There was *stuff* stewing underneath that quiet exterior, and it just made him even more appealing. Made me even more sure about him.

How was that even possible, right?

But that was where I found myself. Surrounded by Wilders and big tall trees that stretched up to the sky and the existence of a kiss that changed everything.

Only once did his dark eyes cut toward me, and I couldn't read much of anything in them when they did. But I smiled because if I knew him at all, he'd be berating the absolute bejeezus out of himself for allowing such a thing to happen. The man was even harder on himself than I realized.

He'd quit because—in his mind—he'd ignored his duty to me by allowing a single moment, a single opportunity for a stranger to take a picture that could be misconstrued the way it was.

He'd stayed away from his family because his marriage had failed, and they'd lost, I don't know, the greatest daughter-in-law ever or something? She must have been Mother friggin' Teresa, by the way he was acting. But by the same token, he seemed to be over her. Nothing he'd said had been about his ex-wife. And I could only assume that was also tied into why he didn't return to Washington. Even though his injury was a big one … it would hardly end a career.

For as much as he'd given me the benefit of the doubt, Erik did not extend himself the same grace. And it only made him even more endearing to me.

Endearing and something much, much less innocent in nature. I wanted him to break a bed with me in it. I wanted him to slide a ring on my finger. Put a baby inside me. Stand alongside me no matter what the future brought to our lives.

"And you heard about the bid Cameron just won, right?" Greer asked.

I blinked out of my little daydream. Erik and babies and rings, oh my.

Erik nodded. "Good for him. I'm just glad Tim ended up with a couple of kids who wanted to keep it going."

Greer nudged him. "I have much bigger plans than just *keeping it going,* if I can get my brothers on board."

He gave her a look. "What does that mean?"

Greer turned her attention toward me. "It means I'm going to pester your girlfriend endlessly this weekend while I have the chance."

"Me? I don't know anything about building houses."

Like her brother and Adaline, Greer was tall and lanky with the same dark hair and dark eyes. And even though she was a solid five inches taller than me, she hooked her arm through mine. "Because the plans I have require total social media domination."

I laughed. "What kind of plans are those?"

"I want to turn Wilder Homes into a premier lifestyle brand out in the Pacific Northwest. A line of high-end furniture—courtesy of Ian, gorgeous custom homes—thanks to Cameron, and interior design—from yours truly."

My mind started spinning immediately, and I gauged her bone structure with a skilled eye. "And if your brothers are even half as gorgeous as you, why not pitch a reality show?"

She raised a fist in the air. "Exactly what I was thinking! Gawd, Erik, you picked a good one. She gets me."

"Nope." Erik's voice cut straight through her infectious enthusiasm. "Absolutely not."

Oh, yes. His single caveat in bringing me along for the weekend. No meddling.

Greer sighed. "You don't actually get to tell us no on this, Erik. It's not your business that's going to explode into the stratosphere if it works."

"No, but Lydia didn't come here for you to milk her for her connections either," he said.

I looked down at the ground when Greer's face took on an

embarrassed expression. "That's not what I meant," she said quietly. "I just … wanted some of your expertise on content creation and how to pitch something like this."

"I know that." I patted her arm. "I'm … changing up my own social media brand at the moment, but I'd be happy to bounce around some ideas if that would help."

"I noticed," Greer said, but not unkindly. "You do such a good job of seeming approachable, even if your life is wildly different than the average person. That whole week where you took us through your different pajama pants and grading them based on length of binge-watching comfort was so funny."

My face went a little warm at Erik's curious look. "Ahh. Yeah. That was about a month after I broke my arm."

"Well, you made it work, regardless of what brought it about."

Erik mumbled something under his breath that sounded like, "I fucking knew this would happen."

Greer laughed when I rolled my eyes.

"He's just grumpy," I said, patting Erik on the back. "It's a constant state of being for him."

"Oh, I like you, Lydia." She gestured at the house, the windows lit with warm yellow light and smoke that now curled from the chimney. "And they will too, but I'll warn you, we're an intimidating bunch at first."

I eyed the house. "Why? Do I need to worry about anyone in particular?"

"Ian," they answered in tandem.

My immediate laughter faded when I realized they were serious. "He's that bad?"

Erik answered first. "Yes."

"No," Greer amended. "He's just … hard to get to know. A little wary of newcomers."

As we approached the front porch, running the entire width of the house, I felt an ease about the entire space. It was so warm and welcoming with small seating areas and a massive swing bed dotting the covered area. This was a home. It was full of love, full of comfort, and I couldn't help but give Erik a sideways look, wondering how much it had changed since he'd been back, wondering how much he must have missed it.

Through the glass in the double front doors, I saw bodies milling around the space, centered around a sunny yellow kitchen. An older woman—a mirror image of Greer and Adaline, but with liberal silver streaked through her dark hair—caught a glimpse of us and smiled widely, clasping a towel to her chest as she rushed over.

I set my hand on Erik's arm. "Your mom?"

His gaze was locked on her, completely unreadable, but he managed a short nod.

Like he'd done for me on the night of the Dior party, I slid my hand into Erik's and twined my fingers through his.

His head turned sharply in my direction, and I would've given anything to know what this mysterious, impenetrable man might be thinking. Touching him now was different—after our kiss—because even that simple connection of his fingers surrounding mine left me a little breathless.

The door opened, snapping the moment cleanly in two, and I couldn't even be mad when Erik pulled his hand from mine. He didn't have much of a choice. Because Erik's mom, tears already visible on her face, threw herself into her son's waiting embrace.

My eyes prickled at the sight because she was so small in his big arms. Where her face was pressed against his shoulder, I heard a telltale sniffle, and Erik closed his eyes, releasing an audible sigh of relief.

Greer gently touched my back and motioned that she was going into the house. I watched her head in, a little unsure of what I was supposed to do. I turned toward the house, thinking I'd give him some privacy, but he reached out and touched my elbow.

Wait, he mouthed. I smiled, giving him a nod.

His mom released a watery laugh. "You're such an ass for making me wait this long, Erik."

He smiled, and oh my dear sweet baby Gucci, when he did, I caught the tiniest glimpse of a dimple buried in that dark stubble.

A *dimple*, for fuck's sake.

"I love you too, Mom," he said quietly. "I'm sorry I was gone so long."

She pulled back and cupped the side of his face. "You know I forgave you a long time ago. That's what family does. But don't ever do it again, or I'll cut you out of my will, and you don't want that because it's a good one."

Erik exhaled a quiet puff of laughter. "Got it."

His mom—Sheila Wilder, age sixty-one, loved gardening, canning, homemade bread, and her kids—swiped at her pretty face and gave me a sheepish smile. "Goodness, my manners fly out the window when he shows his face. You must be Lydia."

I'd never done a meet the boyfriend's family thing, and whether it was legitimate or not didn't matter at all because you still had to navigate carefully. Was she a hugger? A handshaker? The wrong move right off the bat was something I'd lost sleep over the night before.

My family was definitely full of huggers, but gawd, I had nightmares of opening my arms at the exact moment she held her hand out for a polite handshake.

But Sheila held her arms out, and I smiled. "Thank you so much for inviting me," I said as she gave me a warm squeeze.

"Oh honey, the more, the merrier in this house." She eyed my face, and I wondered if my lips were still pink and flushed from her son's kiss. "I can't wait to chat with you, but it won't be tonight. There's a house full of hungry people who I haven't fed at the same time in … well … a long time. Maybe you can come over and have breakfast with the girls and me in the morning?"

"I'd love to."

Erik set a hand on my back. Right in the middle, a warm weight that made me imagine my heart as a soft pink glowy light in my chest. "I don't get breakfast too?" he asked.

His mom hardly spared him a glance. "Nope. I may have forgiven you, and I'd take a bullet for you in a heartbeat, but that doesn't mean you've earned my cinnamon rolls just yet."

I laughed, and Erik's mouth softened into a smile.

"Fair enough." He looked into the house. "Everyone here?"

"Almost," his mom said. "Just missing Parker and Ian."

"Parker is the one who plays at Portland State, right?" I asked.

She smiled. "He is. He's picking up Ian from the airport on his way off campus, but Ian's flight got delayed out of Chicago."

"Park doesn't have a game this weekend?" Erik asked.

Sheila shook her head. "We lucked out. Their bye week lined up with our anniversary, if you can imagine that. Not even college football dared to mess with my twentieth-anniversary party." As she said it, she mimicked her daughter and hooked her arm through mine to lead us into the boisterous house. "Now I'll warn you, Lydia … when Parker gets here, he'll pick that brain of yours about Washington. He's always dreamed of playing there even though his father is a diehard Niners fan."

"Well, there's no accounting for taste," I demurred.

Sheila laughed loudly, drawing the attention of every single freaking person in the room. Every eye zeroed in on Erik and me. Some were curious. Some, like Adaline, were encouraging. But even in the curiosity, I felt the stunning weight of what I'd signed up for.

This wasn't just a weekend when I could see what might develop between Erik and me. This was the mending of a family—a really great one, from what I could see. And knowing that, he'd still trusted me with it.

Even if I wanted to reach for his hand, for that single innocent tether, he'd moved toward his stepdad, who was sitting in a recliner under a big, colorful quilt. The two men embraced after Erik helped

Tim stand, and I remembered Adaline mentioning something about Tim's health when we first got in the car.

Everyone was so friendly, and after a few minutes of introductions—and more hugs—my head was swimming with names and faces and who went with who. My notecards had not prepared me for half of the people present at this dinner. Sheila handed me a plate loaded down with lasagna and garlic bread, and shoved a cousin down the table so I could have a seat. Someone else—Greer maybe—set a glass of red wine in front of me.

Erik still spoke quietly with his stepdad while I took my first few bites of the delicious dinner, and even as people chattered around me, I watched him openly. There was occasional nodding, some back-patting, and then a handshake.

His stepdad looked tired, the kind of tired that only someone really sick can wear. And when he turned his face in my direction, I gave him a friendly smile and waved. Again, Erik's eyes were unreadable. He helped his stepdad back into the worn leather recliner and then made his way to where I was sitting at the long dining table.

There was no room for him to sit, but he settled a hand on my shoulder when I tried to rise.

Erik leaned down until he could speak into my ear. "Enjoy your dinner. I'm going to go help my mom in the kitchen." His mouth was so close to my ear that I fought a shiver. I nodded, unable to turn my head to look at him without risking my mouth brushing his again.

And I wasn't sure anyone wanted us to start that again, not in the middle of the dining room table, at least.

Erik's broad back disappeared into the kitchen, where his mom gave him a grateful smile and wrapped her arm around his waist.

The weekend had already changed something between him and me, but I was just starting to see how changing *something* was the least of it.

It could change everything.

Chapter
TWENTY-ONE

Lydia

ERIK WILDER SLEEPING ON A NORMAL-PERSON-SIZED COUCH was a sight I would not miss, even if it meant setting my alarm for pre-sunrise hours. The room was still dark, and I wasn't due at the main house for another couple of hours, but when he'd insisted on giving me the bed the night before, I vowed to myself that I would get up early enough just once to see his long legs hanging off the edge.

And … maybe satisfy my curiosity as to the state of undress that Erik slept in.

Knowing him, he'd zip up in a parka if he thought I was going to take a curious peek. Everything was dark when I cracked the bedroom door open. The only soft light shining came from the vicinity of the tidy little kitchen. I'd hardly had time to register the details of the home the day before. By the time the family dinner wrapped up and we walked back in silence, Erik had fully committed to his "I will not touch or talk, and I definitely won't bring up the kiss because if we don't bring it up, then it didn't happen" plan.

He'd opened the door for me, bodily hustled me into the

bedroom, brooking absolutely no argument about who was sleeping where. Then he shut the door in my face, leaving me to pout quietly in the bedroom.

I mean, I hadn't expected him to like, sweep me off my feet and carry me over the threshold or anything, but a simple conversation about what had happened might've been nice.

Enter my current plan to put him at a disadvantage. Erik was always the one in control, and when he didn't feel in control, that was when those impressive walls of his lowered a bit.

From my vantage point, no big man feet were hanging off the edge of the couch. With a furrowed brow, I tightened the cotton robe around my body and tiptoed closer.

But even when I cleared the edge of the couch, it was empty. Hands propped on my hips, I stared down at that empty couch and tried not to pout.

His voice came from a darkened corner. "Looking for someone?"

With a shriek that would make a mouse proud, I whirled to find him sprawled comfortably in the armchair on the opposite side of the room. He was in a T-shirt and dark sleep pants, a coffee mug resting comfortably in one hand.

"N-No, I was just …" I yanked on the tie of my robe, clearing my throat primly. "I was just making sure you could fit okay on the couch. I felt bad."

Even though the sun was barely rising in the sky, I could see enough of his face that one brow rose slowly.

"I'm not lying."

"You putting words in my mouth now, Pierson?"

I did some eyebrow rising of my own. "We're going by last names now, Wilder? Excellent plan if you want your mother to believe we're *dating*." I went a bit heavy on the enunciation of that last word just because I wanted to see him squirm. And he did. Sort of. He took a sip of coffee and averted his eyes.

When I glanced down, there was nothing on display. My robe covered all the good bits, skimming my upper thighs.

"Not that you did much to sell it last night," I said breezily.

"Excuse me?"

I shrugged. "You hardly talked to me all night."

"Yeah, my family kept you pretty busy with that, if you didn't notice. I would've had to knock someone over if I wanted to wedge myself into those conversations." He took a sip of his coffee, eyes trained on me in the dark.

"Everyone was so nice." I smiled. "Your uncle Albert had funny stories about his days playing football back in college."

"I bet."

"He probably loves talking to you about your years at Washington," I said. The fact that I asked was shameless, really. Albert—who was actually his great-uncle—told me that when Erik was home after his injury, he never wanted to talk about football. Too painful, I guess, he'd said in his sweet little old man voice. You lost so much of what you loved in one year, and it'd crush even the strongest man.

It made me think about how much had changed in the past six months of my life because most people would think that losing sponsorships, losing contracts, would be a death knell for my career. But all it felt like was opportunity, sweet and fresh and exactly what I'd needed. And it was awful to think about Erik experiencing the opposite, going through something so bad that it kept him away from such a wonderful place for so long.

"Uncle Albert would line up right now if anyone would have him," Erik answered, a wry smile in his voice. I wanted to see that smile. Something about the rarity of them was scarily addictive. A game I could play with myself, just to see how often they could be wrung out of his serious face.

Wary of the short hem on my robe, I perched on the arm of the couch and crossed my legs. His eyes flicked down, then back up to my face. "Well, I could think of a couple of teams that could use him on their O-line, and it might be an improvement. Probably shouldn't tell your stepdad that I'd consider the Niners one of them."

And damn if that coffee mug didn't hide his answering smile. I knew he did too because his eyes crinkled attractively at the edges.

There was a soft kind of comfort between us in this place, and I knew it wouldn't take me long to crave it, miss it when it was gone, and find ways to recreate it now that he'd strong-armed us back into more firmly drawn lines.

"What's he sick with?" I asked quietly. "That wasn't something I got on my notecards."

Erik set the coffee down onto a small end table and unfolded his body from the chair. When he passed, I got a tantalizing whiff of his crisp, clean scent. My arms dotted with goose bumps because when his arms had been tight around my body, I'd inhaled it greedily.

Because I was learning his silences, I waited patiently while he fiddled with something in the kitchen. And when he appeared in front of me with a steaming mug in his hand, my eyebrows rose in pleasant surprise. Judging by the color, he'd added exactly the amount of creamer that I liked.

I took it carefully. Our fingers brushed, and this time, my toes curled up helplessly.

"Thank you."

He grunted in response and took his seat again. "Cancer. It's his second time."

"Where?"

Erik sighed heavily. "Lungs. This time, at least. He had prostate cancer about four years ago."

My heart broke, thinking about how sweetly Tim and Sheila had interacted the night before. After everyone was fed, I'd watched her perch on his lap so they could look at old photo albums together while her family cleaned up in the kitchen. There was a wordless ease between them, something I noticed with my own parents.

"The chemo," Erik said, "wipes him out. He started treatment again last month."

"I didn't want to ask and ruin the mood last night, but I could tell he wasn't feeling well."

He leaned back in the chair, and it was finally light enough in the room that I could see the slight shadows beneath his eyes.

Erik fidgeted at my naked perusal. I wasn't trying to hide the way I watched him anymore. The man could accurately guess the weight of my boob from up-close and personal study, so I figured we were past that point now.

"What?" he asked.

I pointed at the skin beneath my own eyes. "You look tired. That couch can't make for a good night's sleep."

His gaze stayed locked on mine. "It doesn't."

"The bed would be more comfortable," I answered silkily.

Erik stayed quiet, but his eyes … they blazed so hot, I could practically feel the heat from across the room. "You volunteering to sleep out here?"

I quirked an eyebrow. "No."

He dropped his head back and let out a controlled breath as he stared up at the ceiling. "It can't happen, Lydia."

"Why not? You were there yesterday too. Don't even lie to me that that wasn't the hottest fucking kiss of your entire life, Erik."

Erik's chest heaved on a massive inhale, and it took a moment before he lifted his head again. He didn't say a word at first.

"It wasn't."

Under any other circumstances, I would've frowned. Or felt a sharp, hollow pang of disappointment.

Except his voice sounded like he'd chewed glass in order to get those words out. So it was going to be like *that* for the hours we had left together. I tilted my head and studied him, then set my coffee down. When my hand went to the tie on my robe, he started shaking his head.

"Lydia," he warned.

But did he look away?

Oh no, his eyes were locked on the gentle plucking motions of my fingers as I pulled the bow free. The robe fell open with a whisper, and a quiet look of relief filled his voice when he saw the shirt underneath.

But then I shrugged off the robe, and his jaw clenched.

"What are you doing?" he asked, his voice a hoarse, tortured whisper.

"I need to take a shower before I have breakfast at the house." I tugged the nightshirt up over my thighs, and I heard his sharp exhale when the pink lace covering my hips appeared.

"We have a bathroom, you know," he ground out. "Most people get undressed in there."

"Hmm, most people probably do." I tossed the shirt down and shook my hair out. If he thought I was even remotely embarrassed to strut naked around the entire house to prove a point, he didn't know me very well. The small lace triangles covering my breasts were completely transparent, and I had to give Erik credit. Because those devilishly black eyes never strayed from my face as I padded quietly across the floor. I braced my hands on the back of the chair he sat in like a throne.

It would be so easy to slide my knees on either side of his hips, stretch my legs over the width of his lap and see how long it took him to break. And I'd never have dared without the way he ate at my mouth a mere handful of hours earlier. This man—now so contained—sucked at my tongue like it was made of vanilla ice cream and coated in chocolate.

Maybe I'd shown up to help him, and maybe I was walking a tightrope lined in dynamite for how spectacularly this could explode in my face, but I'd go to my grave disappointed if I didn't take this chance with him.

He and I, we were past the point of making choices that would later stink of regret. I just needed him to admit it because it was there in his eyes.

Erik Wilder wanted me. And if he let himself go, I'd be the happy recipient of all that pent-up sexual tension, all that strength he kept so carefully leashed.

His hands tightened into fists on the tops of his big thighs, and he kept his gaze locked tight onto my face. I leaned in and considered what he might do if I licked at the seam of his lips.

He'd kiss me. Maybe he'd put his hands up the back of my thighs and dip between my legs, rip the lace until it disappeared. But no, that wasn't the way past his reserve.

So I slid my mouth along his cheekbone and felt the tremor under the hot surface of his skin until my lips brushed against the shell of his ear.

"Liar," I whispered. I pulled back and met his eyes.

He looked drugged as his gaze dropped to my lips.

"I'll leave the bathroom door unlocked," I told him as I straightened.

Erik remained stubbornly silent. It wouldn't matter if the door was locked or not. He wasn't ready to concede this particular battle line.

Because I couldn't *not*, I glanced down at his lap. Admitting my victory was pointless because Erik Wilder couldn't hide jack shit when he was wearing cotton sleep pants.

And when I raised my eyes, the man made my heart bubble with tender happiness because his cheeks held the slightest flush of pink.

I took two slow steps backward to see if he'd stand and join me, but he stayed locked in that seat like he was chained to it. With a resigned sigh, I leaned down to swipe my discarded clothes from the floor and twirled them at my side as I disappeared into the home's single bathroom.

As I showered, my hands sliding over my soap-slick body, I

imagined what it would be like if he yanked open the curtain and stepped under the hot spray of water. This time, my sister wasn't there to interrupt the fantasy as it played out.

And only a few minutes later, I couldn't think clearly enough to know whether I moaned loudly enough for him to hear.

The front door slammed. Quite angrily too.

I laughed.

There was nothing—not one single thing—keeping him from exploring it with me, other than barriers of his own creation.

When I left the steamy bathroom, the house was empty, and I got ready for breakfast with a bounce in my step and a grin on my face.

I slipped on black joggers and a Wolves shirt, tied neatly at the waist. When I stepped out of the front door, I took a deep, grateful inhale of the tree-scented air.

The walk to the main house gave me enough time to wonder what I might be walking into, this sweet invitation to get to know the Wilder women better. Adaline was the only one who knew why I was there, but there were moments on the drive down when I caught her watching our interactions speculatively.

I knocked on the front door, and Sheila waved me in from the kitchen. Letting myself in, I took another deep inhale of cinnamon and coffee and warm bread.

"Oh my gosh, it smells like heaven," I told her.

She handed me a mug filled with coffee and wrapped an arm around my shoulders in a quick hug. "You're the first one here, sweetie. But the girls will be down shortly. Poppy never wakes very easily, so naturally, her sisters are up there torturing her."

I took a seat at one of the stools lining the long butcher block-topped island. "Poppy was telling me last night how much she loves having everyone home."

Sheila hummed, sliding another pan of bubbling cinnamon rolls from the oven. There was enough laid out to feed a football team, and I couldn't help but think that she fully expected all her sons to appear, despite her threats from the night before. "She was *everyone's* baby when she came along, even though Greer and Parker were only four when she was born. Moments like this, she may say she hates having her big sisters pile into her bed to wake her up, but she's still not used to them being gone."

"Erik was how old when she was born?" I pulled apart the first cinnamon roll, moaning when the spices and sugar hit my tongue.

Sheila sipped from her coffee, memories sliding briefly over her face at my question. "Twelve. He took everything so seriously when Tim and I got married. Like there weren't two whole parents around to watch over everyone else." She smiled sadly. "It hit Poppy the hardest when he didn't come back for so long. She loves all her siblings, but she just idolized Erik."

A derisive snort came from the opposite end of the kitchen. "As usual, I pick the wrong time to enter a conversation."

I turned, eyebrows high in shock, at the tall, dark-haired guy striding into the kitchen. He looked like a thundercloud and a grumpy bear had a hot lumberjack baby. "Morning, Sheila."

She gave him a look but offered up her cheek for a kiss. "Morning, Ian. Be nice in front of Lydia, okay? She actually likes our family so far, and we don't need you scaring her off."

He stopped, assessing me with a single, unimpressed glance. His eyes dropped to my shirt, and he could hardly stifle the eye roll. "I'm guessing they already warned you about me?"

I smiled sweetly. "A little. It's nice to meet you, Ian."

He did not smile back.

Sheila elbowed her stepson. "Good Lord, Ian, don't be a dick." She gave me an exasperated smile. "I'm sorry, Lydia. Normally, he has some manners."

"Do I?" he asked dryly. "Just trying to figure this whole thing out. You're not Erik's usual type."

I set my chin in my hand and stared him down. "It sounded to me like his usual type needed a bit of a change."

Sheila smothered a smile.

Ian narrowed his eyes. "Well … we all know that the Golden Boy can do no wrong. So at least he traded up, if not in looks then in net worth."

I whistled at the impressive dig. Before Sheila could muzzle him, I waved away her horrified gasp. "It's fine, Sheila. I've practically got a PhD in dealing with judgmental assholes." I stood and breezed past him to snatch another cinnamon roll. I licked the frosting off the edge as I stared him down. "And the unimpressive ones are easier to handle. If the best you've got is to insult my looks and my bank account, then you've got to sharpen your skills, buddy. I won't even break a sweat at this rate."

Sheila laughed.

Ian didn't, but I caught the slightest flash of begrudging surprise in his bearded face.

The whole family, gawd, they were blessed with good genes. Because every single one of them was gorgeous so far, and Ian—with his prickly attitude—was no exception.

Ian broke the stare first, and his stepmom pinched his stomach, earning a hissed exclamation.

"Be nice," she commanded.

He rolled his eyes but nodded. After filling his mug, he gave me one last unreadable glance and left the kitchen.

"Goodness," I mumbled. "They weren't kidding about him."

Sheila sank into a stool and sighed, weariness covering her pretty face. "He'll never admit it, but he idolized Erik right along with the rest of them. And they've been like oil and water since day one. It was the biggest struggle we had in combining our families." She gave me a look. "I mean, that and when Erik left."

I ate some more of my cinnamon roll and caught the sound of happy, feminine laughter coming from the bedrooms down the hall.

Looked like my alone time with Sheila wouldn't last much longer. I considered my words as I swallowed the delicious roll.

"She really did a number on him, didn't she?"

Sheila nodded slowly. "The affair was bad, the timing of it … but the fallout was worse." She paused, assessing my face. "How much did he tell you?"

I liked her too much to lie, more than I already was, at least. And it definitely wouldn't help us get through the weekend if I did. "A little. He doesn't like to talk about it."

She hummed. "No, that he doesn't." Then Sheila pasted a slightly forced smile onto her face, and I knew Erik wasn't the only one who didn't like this particular topic of discussion. "I think the girls are coming. Want me to refill your coffee before they take it all?"

I shook my head. "No thanks. Erik made me a cup this morning before I walked over, so I've had enough."

That had the smile on her face softening into something far more real. She set her hand on mine. "I can't tell you what it does for us to see him happy with someone."

I laughed under my breath. "I think I drive him insane more than I make him happy."

She winked. "All the good relationships are like that, sweetie. That's what keeps things interesting."

"Well … then we've got the most interesting relationship in the world."

Chapter
TWENTY-TWO

Erik

PLAYING FOOTBALL TAUGHT ME A VALUABLE LESSON, BUT I didn't realize at the time that it could extend into every facet of your life. Not until the weekend at my parents' with Lydia walking around half-naked in front of me, practically daring me to take her in the shower.

The lesson was simple—in even the staunchest defense, there was a weakness.

They could be the best defense in the world, with players and coaches that were the prototype of physicality and intuition. And there would be a chink built in, a flaw that could be exploited.

Lydia found mine.

Somehow, in the weeks of quiet car rides, unanswered questions, and a steadfast determination not to let her get under my skin, she was there nonetheless. And what was so much worse was that now she knew it.

And I knew what she tasted like.

I knew what she felt like under my hands.

And I knew—in a way that I'd never ever be able to forget—how she reacted when I was touching and tasting her.

If I'd followed her into that bathroom, we'd rip fixtures from the wall, we'd break bed frames and scratch over the delicate skin that covered our bodies. I'd never recover from her, and now, I was avoiding my own space at my parents' because I was scared shitless of what she'd try next.

I was terrified at how easy it would be to take this thing I wanted. Because she wanted it too.

Everyone reacted to fear differently, and the level at which Lydia scared me had me hiding. Like a coward.

And even spending the day hiding from her, I couldn't escape.

A hike in the woods while she showered ended in me imagining her tugging me behind a thick tree. Hearing her cries bounce around the open air, the branches of the trees the only witness to what I wanted to do to her.

Coming back to the house once she'd gone to breakfast ended in a brisk, ice-cold shower where I could still smell her in the small tiled room. I'd kept my hands braced on the wall because this was the punishment I deserved for being stupid enough to bring her in the first place.

I probably could've held out. I probably could've ignored the remaining handful of nights we had in that small house, knowing only a thin wall separated her and me.

And it was through the thin walls of that bathroom that I heard her come back home, humming off-key to a tune I couldn't recognize. I stood in the bathroom, toweling off my chest, trying not to study the sound of her moving around my house.

I finished drying off, and with the towel clutched in my hand, I realized I'd forgotten to grab a shirt.

Yes. My fear of the electricity between Lydia Pierson and me ran so deep that I'd reverted to middle school, where I worried about showing my upper body to a girl I liked.

"Shit," I said, tugging on my boxer briefs and black shorts with a rough jerk. I set my hands on my hips and stared in the mirror before I left the bathroom. "This is ridiculous," I muttered.

And with as much bravado as I could muster—as a man who had absolutely no faith in my ability to resist one woman—I yanked open the bathroom door. She was snuggled into the couch, reading a book that my mom had left on the coffee table.

A football book. Of course.

She was wearing black leggings now, her feet covered in expensive-looking athletic shoes. Her Wolves shirt was tight to her body, and her hair was slicked back in a high ponytail. And her eyes, they traced my chest, shoulders, and abs like she wanted to lick me from top to bottom.

Lydia sighed happily, setting the book down on her stomach.

"What?" I barked.

"Look at you," she purred. "You're perfect."

I laughed dryly. "If you say so."

She stood from the couch and approached with slow, deliberate steps. I eyed her warily, snagging a T-shirt out of my bag. Before I could tug it over my head, Lydia snatched one end. "So this football game"—she locked her gaze on my stomach—"it's not a shirts versus skins thing?"

"You think my sisters would go for that?"

"Sports bra counts as skin," she said.

The sudden image of Lydia stretching to catch a ball, only wearing a sports bra and leggings had me frowning. "No."

She grinned at my terse answer. "Didn't think so, but ..." She hummed, finally conceding my shirt when I tugged again. "A girl can dream."

I sighed heavily. "You ready to go?"

Lydia nodded. "I have a couple of water bottles in my bag for us. Your sister said they'd bring the ball."

Once my shirt was on, I breathed a bit more easily. "The field we play on is only about five minutes away."

"How do we split teams?" she asked once we'd left the house.

"Depends on how many cousins and neighbors show up, but usually Ian and I pick."

She climbed into the passenger seat, buckling her seat belt while I started the car. "You two are always the captains?"

I nodded, breathing more easily now that we were fully clothed and nowhere in range of a bed. Or a shower. It was amazing how much I relaxed when I didn't feel like I needed to worry about the sexual blitzkrieg she wanted to unleash on me.

"Oldest," I said by way of explanation.

"You guys keep track of who wins?"

Behind us on the winding dirt road that led to the field, I saw Cameron's truck turn out from a side road on the property. "Nah. We used to when we were all home and played more, but …" I shifted in my seat. "I haven't played as much in recent years."

She hummed, but nothing beyond that.

Now I was less relaxed. What was she thinking when she hummed like that?

It was such a blatantly sexual sound that I could imagine her making it for so many reasons. And even worse, I wanted to know what was going through her head when she did it in a non-sexual way. Now that I was giving her this glimpse into my life—which was what she always wanted—what did she see?

She sat forward in her seat, letting out a happy *ooh* sound when she saw the field. "It's like … legit!"

I smiled at her excitement over the painted white lines and the uprights on either end. "It is."

I'd hardly put the car in park, and Lydia was hopping out of her side, practically skipping over to the side where there were stacks of orange cones, flag belts that we'd each wear, and a small bin of soccer balls for when Poppy came out to practice. My sisters were stretching on the sideline, joined by some younger cousins who'd grown like weeds since I'd last been home.

Parker waved from where he talked to them, and he jogged over to wrap me in a huge hug.

I laughed. "Holy shit, Park, you gained fifty pounds of muscle since the last time I saw you."

My little brother, who was no longer littler than me, grinned. "Maybe not fifty, but I did a lot of work in the weight room since last season."

Lydia was talking to Poppy, who had pulled a soccer ball from the bin and started dribbling between her feet. Parker nudged me, laughing under his breath when I realized I'd been staring.

"I met her at breakfast this morning," he said.

"Yeah?" My eyes found their way back to her. She got a ball of her own, gesturing wildly as she talked to my youngest sister, who laughed loudly.

"I like her."

I blew out a hard breath. Whether Parker liked her or not was irrelevant, I reminded myself. But I gave him a quick smile. "Good."

His eyebrows rose. "Damn."

When I looked back at Lydia and Poppy, Lydia was dribbling a ball like she was a blond reincarnation of Mia Hamm, bouncing it off each foot so that it didn't hit the ground. If the ball went too high, she'd adjust, push the ball off her chest so that she'd snap it back up into the air with her raised knees.

She leaned forward, catching the ball on her back, and Poppy whooped.

Something frustrating and hot climbed up the back of my neck. Was there *anything* she couldn't do? And for reasons I refused to name, it made me uncomfortable that my family was seeing this new facet to Lydia alongside me.

I wanted to know her.

And I wanted to run.

When she was near me, I felt edgy and restless, unable to stem the flow of energy she brought pulsing into the room. When she was standing across the room, I found myself coming up with excuses to be near her.

"I better tell her she'll be on my team," I mumbled. "No fucking way I'm letting Ian get near her."

Parker shoved me with a laugh, and I strode over to Lydia.

Poppy was doing something fancy with her feet, snapping the ball neatly between them when I approached, and she smiled happily at the sight of me. "Hi. I love her."

Lydia smothered a smile, and I ruffled my little sister's hair. "Yeah, well, now I can see that you two can never be on the same team if we play soccer because you'll kick our asses."

Poppy laughed. "I had no idea Lydia played in college."

I slid my gaze over to Lydia. "She's full of surprises."

She shrugged. "Only my freshman and sophomore year. After I got two concussions, my dad put a nix on anything more. We do not mess around with head injuries in our house."

I grunted. "You're on my team," I told her. Her eyes glowed when she nodded.

Parker and Cameron approached with Greer and Adaline.

"How do we decide the QB?" Lydia asked.

My siblings traded loaded looks, which I ignored. "Ian and I always play quarterback."

Lydia set her hands on her hips. "What if someone else is better?"

Parker's eyes got wide. Cameron choked on a laugh.

I gave her a level look. "It's just how we do things."

Her chin rose a notch. "And you don't think it's wise to adjust based on roster changes?"

Parker whistled.

"Meaning?" I asked, crossing my arms over my chest.

"You've never had me on your team. Why can't I try?"

"You can be a receiver," I told her. "With Parker and Adaline. Cameron and my cousin Adam are the running backs. Everyone takes turns blocking depending on the play."

My siblings' eyes bounced between Lydia and me like ping pong balls, and my skin started to feel itchy when I saw her eyes narrow. "Is it a woman thing?"

"No!" I shouted. "Of course, it's not a woman thing. I can just … throw it the farthest."

Her head tilted. "What about accuracy? A big arm is pointless if you can't get the ball on target."

Adaline wheezed with laughter, bracing her hands on her knees. Cameron smacked her on the back like she couldn't breathe.

"For fuck's sake," I said on a rough exhale. "What do you want, a tryout before the game?"

"Yes." She motioned to Parker. "Have the other team line up. We each get to call an audible at the line, and whoever completes their play call better… they're the QB."

"Holy shit," I breathed. "Why did I bring you home again?"

Lydia aimed a sunny smile at me, tightening her ponytail while she did. "You afraid, Wilder?"

"Terrified. I played professional football for five years, *Pierson*."

She leaned in, winding her fist into my shirt and tugging me closer. "As a defensive end, *babe*." She nipped at my chin.

I clenched my jaw and leaned down by her ear. "You trying to distract me?"

Lydia pushed back, stretching her arms out over her head. "Is it working?"

My eyes tracked down her body, and I shook my head. "I don't want to disappoint you, Pierson, but you're not winning this one."

"We'll see." She tossed me a football. "Oldest first," she said.

We huddled up, and I fought to clear my head, but she had it spinning, the little witch. "Cameron, you block left, give Parker room to run. Park, run a slant route, and I'll hit you around the thirty-yard mark."

He nodded.

We lined up, and I called for the snap. Adaline and Greer pushed against each other, laughing when Greer tripped head over feet, Poppy somehow snuck past our cousin Adam, but as I dropped back and settled my feet, Lydia blocked my littlest sister before she could snatch the flag off my waist.

Parker cut to the center of the field, and I stepped big into the throw, adrenaline surging through my veins after the entire day without an outlet. Ian ran almost step for step with Parker, and as the ball started dropping, I swore. Because it was going to be about five yards ahead of him.

I slicked my tongue over my teeth when he stretched but couldn't pull it in.

Lydia approached, patting me consolingly on my back. "Pretty throw," she said. "Just a touch too much power behind it."

I glanced sideways. "I wouldn't start bragging too early."

"No?" She snagged the ball when Parker tossed it to her on his way back to line up. "Which one of us was raised by a Superbowl-winning quarterback again? Just because my dad had girls doesn't mean he didn't have us throwing a perfect spiral before we hit double-digit birthdays."

Lydia spun the ball in her hand and then set it on her hip to face my siblings. Every single one of them was watching with unconcealed glee.

"This is the best game ever," Cameron breathed.

I flipped him off, and Adaline cackled.

Lydia motioned us into the huddle. "Okay, we're running a naked bootleg."

My eyebrows rose. "There's no way you're fast enough if Ian is staying up front to rush the passer. Which he will."

"That's the point," she said calmly. "They'll expect me to get rid of the ball as quickly as possible on a screen pass or something less than ten yards out. So when I fake the handoff to Cameron—you blocking in front of him—and then run to the opposite direction, they'll follow the receiver." She motioned to Parker. "Meanwhile, our tight end here will run a skinny post route, and I'll catch him on the sideline."

Parker nodded excitedly. "Love it."

"It won't work," I insisted. "You'll have no one to block you because we've all pulled in the other direction."

She leaned in, her face inches from mine, and our eyes locked. For a split second, I forgot we were surrounded by my family, and we were the best entertainment they'd ever seen.

All I saw was her.

"When are you going to figure this out, Erik?" she said quietly. "The fact that people underestimate me is my superpower. They never see me coming."

Then she placed a feather-light kiss on my mouth, eyes dancing while I growled behind closed lips.

She strolled to the pocket, wiggling her ass back and forth while we got into position.

"Ready," she called. "Set, hut!"

Lydia spun to the right, extending her arm to fake a handoff to Cameron, who cradled his arms and took off even though the ball never left Lydia's hands. I shoved at my cousin Adam, like I was making room for Cameron, and Parker sprinted down the line.

Lydia swung back from the pocket, sprinting away from where the rest of the line was pulling.

Ian noticed the ball in her hand first. "Shit!" he yelled. "She's got it."

She danced back, eyes determined and laser sharp. Lydia set her feet and snapped her arm forward like she was Tom friggin' Brady.

A perfect spiral, it sailed in the air without a single bobble, landing perfectly into Parker's waiting hands.

She jumped, arms raised over her head, as he strolled easily into the end zone.

I set my hands on my hips, chest heaving, while my brothers and sisters surrounded her, all high-fiving and fist-bumping like she'd just won the Super Bowl.

Lydia was flushed and happy as she pulled from the circle of my family and strolled in my direction.

She held out her hand. "No hard feelings?"

I snagged her hand and tugged her in. "You better not lose us this game, Pierson," I said into her ear. "I hate losing."

She curled a fist into my shirt and stared up at me with heavy, want-drenched eyes. I was probably looking at her the same fucking way. "We have that in common, Wilder. I have no intention of losing anything this weekend."

Before I could do something stupid, like shove my tongue into her sassy little mouth, I stepped back. "All right. Looks like we've got ourselves a new QB. Let's get this game started."

Parker tossed her the ball, and she did a little victory dance that even had me smiling.

That was how I knew it would be a freaking miracle if I survived the weekend without Lydia barreling through every single ounce of my restraint.

Chapter
TWENTY-THREE

Erik

W E WON THE GAME. HANDILY.

To Lydia's credit, she didn't brag, simply accepted my family's praise with a wide smile and flushed cheeks.

I drove her home, where she—to my utter surprise—didn't tempt or tease and try to undress me with her eyes.

She said she was still amped up and was going for a walk if I wanted to join her.

I shook my head and watched her with curious eyes as she took off at a steady jog down the dirt road away from my house.

I showered. Again.

This time, the water was even colder than my first shower of the day, and when she still wasn't back, I decided to read outside on the front porch.

I'd only flipped through a few pages when I heard feminine laughter coming from the trees. I walked down the steps, tucking my hands into my pockets when I caught sight of my sisters.

Showered and changed after our game, Greer and Poppy were taking pictures down the main driveway. Poppy was telling her to smize and laugh naturally and keep moving, and it honestly just looked like someone was practicing interpretive dance or something. Even though it was warm and sunny out, Greer was wearing a fuzzy sweater and tall boots lined with sherpa. I'd never been more confused by what my sisters were doing.

Which was impressive because they confused me a lot over the years.

I scratched the side of my face as Greer skipped and danced back down the driveway, Poppy crouching about ten feet from where I stood, snapping away.

"What the hell are you two doing?" I asked.

Poppy grinned up at me. "Shooting content for Greer."

"Uh-huh."

Greer hugged a tree, and Poppy snapped that too.

"Oh, that's so cute. You should use that one on Earth Day."

"Earth Day is in April," I said slowly. "It's the fall."

"Yeah. We know."

Greer paused in her weird posing and jogged over to us. "Gawd, it's so hot in this sweater." She peeled it off and then motioned for the phone. As she flipped through the shots, Poppy stood and slung her arm around my waist.

"Whatcha doing, big brother?" she asked.

I ruffled her hair. "I was reading, but I might go find Parker and Cameron. I didn't get much of a chance to talk with Parker before the game."

"They're working out. They built a gym in the back barn about a year and a half ago."

"Park can never take a break, can he?"

"You should join them." She patted my stomach.

"Excuse me?"

She winced. "Just sayin'. You haven't seen Parker on the weights lately. He might have you beat."

"He's a kid," I barked. "I can lift three times as much as him."

Greer snorted. "You should go see what he's doing with Lydia then. She's having him shoot some workouts."

My jaw went tight. Greer gave me a sideways look. "Whose idea was that?" I managed.

"Parker asked her for advice, and she told him to start posting some of his workouts and a highlight reel. I mean, the NFL might eat him alive because he's just a bit too pure-hearted for this world, but the kid is good."

"Why didn't he ask me? I played in the NFL. Did everyone in this family forget that?"

Poppy glanced up at me, eyes big and guileless. "Did *you* forget it? Because it kinda seems like you have."

Greer whistled.

I cursed under my breath, and it had both of my sisters laughing. Even though my reentry had been a little rough, it was good to be around them. Poppy was an adult, not the gangly little kid who shadowed me for years. Parker was old enough, talented enough, to think about how he could gain the notice of the professional scouts. It was an uphill battle, playing at a smaller Division One school, but not impossible.

And of course, he was asking Lydia for help.

"Have I mentioned that I fucking love Lydia?" Poppy said.

"You're old enough to swear now?"

She rolled her eyes.

Greer laughed. "She's as bad as Ian."

"I hope not."

"He's in the gym too," she said casually. "You might not want to leave him unsupervised with Lydia, you know."

"Why? They hardly talked at the game."

"I think they had a little exchange at breakfast," she said.

"What did he say?"

At my tone, Greer laughed. "Chill, Lydia not only survived

unscathed but I'm also pretty sure she ran Ian off in about three minutes flat."

I thought of how she handled Jill. "She has that effect on certain people."

"Come on," Poppy said to Greer. "You heard Lydia. You need enough shots to be set for a few months if creativity runs dry."

My sisters didn't hear my annoyed sigh. As they walked away, trying to find new places to shoot and easy ways to switch up her outfit, I heard sprinkled comments about how smart Lydia was. How much they loved her. How maybe I'd come around more often now that I had her.

Now that I had her.

Frustration boiled over into my veins dangerously. I didn't have her. But there I was, stomping over to the converted gym with thoughts of exactly that coursing like a flashing bulb through my brain.

Jealous thoughts of her sweating in some tiny workout getup in front of my stupid brothers who'd drool all over her. They might not do anything because she'd come with me, but holy shit, they'd look. Because they had working eyes, and Lydia was an eleven on a scale of one to ten.

That had me lengthening my strides, and when I flung the door open, the scene in front of me didn't compute.

Lydia—looking like a fucking badass ninja with her lithe muscles wrapped in a black spandex number—was doing some sort of … competition with my brothers.

To the beat of the awful song she had blaring over the speakers, they were trading off with push-ups, tapping their shoulders in a plank, then switching to plank jacks. Parker finished, and damn if his chest wasn't about twice the size as the last time I saw him. Cameron went next, knocking out the same rotation, and with a sunny laugh and a sweaty braid hanging over her shoulder, Lydia finished at exactly the same rate that the much bigger guys next to her were managing. Then she popped up and bounced with excitement.

"That was *perfect.* Now go do some squats, and I'll film." She bent over to take her phone off some complicated-looking stand, and I caught a glimpse down the front of her sports bra.

The T-shirt from earlier was gone. And I really, really wanted to find it.

My mouth watered at the sheen on her ripe curves on display. Parker stood next to Lydia while they watched whatever they'd just filmed, and the sight of them was enough to distract me from … her. He looked like a man. Tall and broad shouldered, his golden brown hair was a bit shaggier than the last time I'd watched one of his games. Together, they looked like an advertisement for some young, good-looking cult that would transform you into an air-brushed "after" photo.

No one had noticed me yet because Lydia had the music so loud. It was amazing they could hear themselves think.

"Why squats?" Parker asked, squinting at her phone.

She tapped on the screen as she answered. "Well, you've got to think of your social media content as an elevator speech, right? Stats are important, and so is game-day film, but teams want hard work-ers *and* good guys, you know? Especially if they're taking a chance on a guy from a smaller D1 school. If you're not showing them that you're the entire package, you'll disappear in a sea of *SportsCenter* top ten clips from flashier schools."

My youngest brother nodded earnestly because that was how he did everything. Parker was the serious one. The one who'd work his skin to the bone to achieve whatever was set in front of him. And I'd had no idea that he was still looking at the spring draft like there was a chance for him.

He was good, and I knew that. But I'd made myself so unavail-able to my family that he was seeking out the assistance of the fake girlfriend I'd brought home because she was raised in the world he wanted to step into.

Cameron did a double take when he saw me standing in the open doorway, and when he realized what I was staring at, he smothered a shit-eating grin.

The song changed to something even more awful than the song before it, and Lydia started bobbing her head to the driving beat and unintelligible lyrics. She tilted her phone toward my brother, pointing at something on the screen.

"See how he's got this clip of game highlights one day, and for the next two, he posts his workouts. Scouts don't have to search out anything on YouTube. They go right to the source, and it shows everything they need to know about him." She tilted her head, a considering look in her eyes. "And right between it all, you see all the other stuff he values. His little sisters. A dog shelter where he volunteers. Teams don't just want assholes who can play well. Or at least Washington doesn't."

Parker's eyes shone with excitement as he listened to her. There was nothing for me to be jealous of.

Nothing I should've envied.

But all I could see as I watched them was how disappointed they'd be when she was gone. They'd look at me and wonder what happened, wonder what I did.

Because here she was, stepping into all these places they valued and showing them exactly how to get what they wanted. Filling a void in everyone's life, something they'd miss without her.

Filling a void in mine, before I'd been able to recognize what she was doing.

Cameron came to stand next to me while Parker lined up to do some squats with an unholy amount of weight lined up on the bar. "He's a beast, isn't he?"

"How'd I let it go this long, Cameron?" I asked quietly.

He snorted. "Because you're a stubborn piece of shit."

Parker dropped his weight, steady and even, the bar across his back, his muscles popping as he straightened back up.

Lydia moved around him in a smooth circle and encouraged him to do a few more reps. The moment she got her toe into the Wolves organization, she'd fill her mom's shoes seamlessly. No one intimidated her. Nothing about the scope of that scared her, and even if it did, I knew her well enough now that she'd just learn more about it until she could channel that fear into something productive.

"I like her," Cameron mused. "She's young, though."

I made a grunt of acknowledgment. "Everyone seems young compared to me."

That earned me a grin. "True enough." He slapped my back. "I've missed your grumpy ass around here. Hope you come back for Christmas."

He spoke during a break in the song, and Lydia turned her head toward us, happy surprise lighting her eyes when she caught sight of me.

That happiness did dangerous things underneath the surface of my skin. Because it wasn't fake. Not much about her was, no matter what version of herself she showed to the world. They were all her.

Sweet and thoughtful.

Intuitive.

Savvy and sexy.

Hopelessly, dangerously romantic.

It was dangerous because as she made her way over to us, I knew she'd climb over hot coals to reach some unattainable version of happiness that she thought was waiting out there.

My hands tingled as she came close. My mouth watered. She tilted her head, studying whatever she was seeing in my face. "Hi."

The black strappy contraption around her chest looked terribly complicated, and I couldn't quite figure out how it was holding up the absolute perfection of Lydia's chest. It should be illegal.

She should be illegal. Classified with drugs or narcotics or equally addictive substances. A man could lose his head with a woman like her looking at him like that, and I was close to snapping.

And because I had to find something to break that tension, I grasped at the very first thing that came to mind. "You're breaking the rules."

Her lips curled into a devious smile. "Am I?"

I took a step closer and stared down at her. "You know you are."

Lydia's hand lifted slowly, a test to see if I'd back down because my brother was next to us, but I was feeling far too volatile, far too unstable. But instead of laying it on my chest like I thought she might, it slid onto my side and moved down until she toyed with the hem of my cotton shirt. Her fingers brushed the skin above my shorts.

Cameron blew out a slow breath. "I'm just gonna ... go because I feel like I just walked in on you two naked, and it's really, really uncomfortable."

Lydia exhaled a shaky laugh. Her pupils were black and huge because she was so turned on. And mine must've looked the same.

"What are you trying to do?" I said in a low, rough voice. "With my sisters, with Parker. You promised you wouldn't interfere."

Her fingers, clever and nimble and too quick for my liking, curled into the waistband of my gym shorts, and I struggled to breathe evenly. She tugged me an inch closer. My head curled over hers, and I inhaled deeply. She smelled like salt and clean sweat, something soft underneath it.

"I just want to help. You can't expect me to ignore them when they ask." Lydia looked up at me. "Is that what you want me to do?"

What did I want her to do?

My thoughts were foggy, and I couldn't find anything to ground them. The only thing in front of me to grab onto was her. And if I set my hands on her, even once, I was taking her to bed. And by the look on her face, that was what she was hoping for.

"Uh, should we leave?" Parker asked.

I blinked, backing away from her. Her hand fell to her thighs, and she looked just as shaken. It was gratifying that I wasn't alone in how quickly we seemed to ignite now.

When I looked over at my younger brother, he was grinning widely. "Welcome back to earth, Erik."

Him, the guy I'd gone looking for because I'd hardly seen him the last couple of years. And all it took was Lydia crooking one little manicured finger in my direction for all my intentions to go up in smoke.

Just as I was about to say something, the door opened up behind me and in walked Ian.

His eyebrows shot up at the sight of Lydia and me. His gaze locked onto mine. "Am I interrupting?"

"Nah," Cameron said, settling onto one of the weight benches. "Erik and Lydia are just making everyone twitchy with their animal sex vibes. Join the party. It's fun."

Parker laughed while Lydia's face flushed a fetching shade of pink. And then Ian snorted derisively. "Why am I not surprised? You bring someone like her home to meet Mom and Dad, what did you all expect?"

I whirled on him, hands tightened into fists. "Someone like her?" I roared.

"Erik," Lydia said, stepping between my shit-head stepbrother and me, settling her hand on my chest to stop my forward progress. I could hardly wrench my eyes from Ian, but when I did, she was calm and collected. "Don't."

Less than a minute in his presence reduced me to this version of myself that I hated. I still loved Ian, he was my brother, and most of the time, I could think of him as the skinny kid with the mop of dark hair who showed up that first day. But at moments like this, I didn't care why he had such a chip on his shoulder. Or why he was so mad at me all the time.

If I'd had less frantic, pent-up energy coursing through my

veins, I might have taken a moment to try to ask. Ask how it got to this point, ask why I seemed to be the target of all his piss-poor attitude.

It was never anyone else in our family, just me.

And I hated that he now found a new person to zero in on, who'd never done anything to him. The only thing she'd done was come home with me.

It was enough to have me giving her an apologetic look, and I brushed past Ian and stormed right back out through the doors.

Chapter
TWENTY-FOUR

Lydia

THERE WERE HARDLY WORDS FOR WHAT MY HEART DID WHEN he walked out.

No flowery descriptions of hammering or thrashing or erratic beats would cover it. Because honestly, it was an aching that I'd never experienced before. Something poignant and tender, all because of the look on his face when Ian pushed his jerky little finger right onto Erik's biggest trigger.

It broke his heart, even if he hid it behind anger. Behind a protective instinct that he'd never be able to fake.

In turn, it broke mine, just a little.

"Aren't you going after him?" Parker asked.

Ian ignored me, striding toward one of the empty weight machines. I was glad for it because I could've scratched his eyeballs out without the slightest bit of hesitation.

"Nope," I said. "Why would I chase after the angry bear?" And look! I sounded so calm and collected. When in reality, I knew that not going after him was a massive gamble. Erik needed to be the one to take all the next steps if there was any chance for us. I chewed on my lip and rolled the dice, turning the volume higher on my phone. The door was still cracked open, and unless he had his hands jammed over his ears, he could hear it as he walked away.

And if I was right, he'd be back before I could finish counting to fifteen.

Cameron chuckled.

Ian shook his head. He couldn't see me, but I glared at his wide back. The song hit a particularly energetic refrain, one that when I played it in his car made Erik punch the stereo power button so fiercely that he almost popped the button off.

I gathered my water bottle, slung my discarded Wolves T-shirt over my shoulder, and moved toward the doors.

All three of his brothers watched me with undisguised interest. Even the prick with the beard and a bad attitude.

"Four, three, two, one," I whispered.

Nothing.

I sucked in a slow breath and fought a wave of disappointment, but then the door swung in again on a violent shove. Erik stormed toward me, fire in his eyes, and before I took another breath, he bent at the knees and scooped me up over his shoulder.

I laughed breathlessly as his hand clamped over the back of my thighs.

Parker waved, a crooked grin on his face. Cameron was shaking his head, and Ian rolled his eyes.

With a sunny smile, I flipped him off behind Erik's back, and his face darkened even further. Parker shoved him with a laugh, and they disappeared from view as Erik walked us through the woods. Only the sound of his boots crunching on the ground punctuated the silence.

Now my heart was doing all the things.

The thrashing and the jumping and the excited tumbling over each beat. My poor ribs could hardly contain it.

"I can walk, you know," I said, but I didn't fight because why would I? Instead, I tucked my hands into the waistband of his shorts again, relishing the hot, smooth skin underneath my fingertips. He didn't stop me, didn't make me pull them out, and when his hand tightened on the back of my thigh, I had to bite down on my lip.

"Yeah, but then I'd have to stop and listen to why my family is obsessed with you, and I'd have to admit that bringing you here was the worst idea I've ever had in my entire life," he snapped.

I laughed. "To be fair, not everyone in your family is obsessed with me."

He grunted, taking the steps up to his house in a single bound. When we were in the family room and he'd kicked the door shut behind us, Erik bent again, setting my feet down on the ground.

The room spun slightly, and I only *sort of* needed to set my hands on his waist while I regained my balance.

He jabbed a finger in the air. "I knew this would happen."

"Did you?" I wanted to curl my arms around him and nuzzle into his great heaving chest like a cat. And I wanted to strip his clothes off, shove him back on the couch, and ride him like a pony. A little bit of both, and the warring desires were actually quite enjoyable. I'd never felt either so strongly, not even by half.

Erik raked a hand through his dark hair. "Yes," he barked. "I knew you'd come in and be exactly what they wanted, some … fairy godmother in a Wolves shirt that would make everything right again."

I tilted my head. "Make everything right for who?"

He spread his arms out. "Everyone."

The idea of it tortured him so much that he was actually angry about it. It was fascinating. Erik wanted me so badly because all I had to do was casually glance down, and oh my, was the proof of that desire impressive. The man must've been in pain, hiding what looked like a baseball bat in his shorts, but still, he kept his hands off. He just needed … he needed to know that it was okay to let the walls down, even for a moment.

He was so concerned with following the rules he'd laid out for himself, even if they no longer applied. Deviating from that path would take some gentle nudging, but once he crossed the line, I knew he'd feel what I was feeling.

That this wildly out-of-control thing between us needed to be indulged, not caged up and ignored.

"How do I make things right for *you*?" I whispered, my hands hovering in the space just over his chest.

He clenched his jaw tight, staring down at me with turbulent, unsteady eyes.

"You can't."

At his terse, bitten-off response, I smiled because he took a step closer.

I licked my lips, and his eyes tracked that single tiny motion—my tongue wetting my lips—like I'd just stripped naked. "This weekend," I clarified. "Right now. There has to be something that will … make you feel better."

To my own ears, I sounded breathy and impossibly turned on because I was. We straddled a tightrope over an endless canyon that I desperately wanted to topple into. But only if he was the one who tugged us over the edge.

"Make me feel better," he mused quietly.

My chin went up a notch. The air between us pulsed hungry and hot, and I pressed my thighs together in a weak attempt to ease the building ache.

"I'm not sure it will," he continued. "If I do to you what we both want." Something about his voice was so velvety smooth that it had me swaying unsteadily on my feet, a long lick of his tongue around the words like he was savoring them as they left his mouth. A dark chuckle passed his lips when he saw me blink, slow and drowsy.

"What do you want to do?" I asked. My fingers curled up helplessly because I couldn't—wouldn't—push him any further than I already had. I wanted him to take this last step, initiate the last touch, and ignite this smolder into a sky-high blaze.

Erik prowled closer, forcing me backwards until I hit the door. I arched my back and stared up at him, waiting for his hands to settle somewhere, to touch and tease and taste.

"So many things," he whispered, dropping his head so his mouth ghosted over my cheekbone like mine had done to him just that morning. "And if I only have this weekend, maybe I should pick my favorites, hmm?"

"*Please,*" I mouthed. The word hardly made a sound, but he chuckled dark and dangerous.

His thumb, just that one thick finger, traced the sweat-soaked edge of my bra, and the gentle touch had my eyelids falling shut. It was the only place he touched me, the evil, evil man. He knew it, too. Another fingertip curled the edge of one exposed rib underneath my skin, circled the belly button over the edge of my leggings. Erik was determined to drive me out of my mind with want, one small innocent touch at a time.

My thighs squeezed again.

He tugged the edge of my leggings away from my waist and then let it snap against my skin. I gasped, ready to mount him like a freaking tree.

"This is pretty high on the list," he said at the edge of my jaw. "You're so turned on that I hardly have to touch you, and you're ready to do whatever I want."

My hands couldn't stay off him any longer, and I curled them tightly into his shirt, tugging ineffectually when he wouldn't come closer. When he laughed again, I glared up at him.

"Are you going to tease me all day or actually do something about it?" I asked. "Because my fantasies have a lot less talking."

Erik snatched my hands from his shirt and slammed them above my head on the door, swooping down to devour my mouth in the next breath.

At the onslaught, a delicious lick of his tongue, a suck of my bottom lip between his teeth, I whimpered helplessly into his mouth. He breathed me in, pulled my body against his until there wasn't a single inch of space between us. My hands, pinned under his, tugged uselessly to get away. He had one free, and with that hand, he wrenched the strap of my bra down my shoulder.

The kiss was an assault on my entire existence in the very best way. Because there was no coming back from this.

No erasing what I knew about Erik Wilder and how he made me feel.

No erasing the way he ravaged my mouth, burning down any memory of anyone who came before him.

No erasing this insatiable, writhing creature he turned me into by the touch of his strong hands.

I fought against his grip again because not touching him was torture, even though his body fully blanketed mine against the door. He groaned a low, scraping sound that had my skin vibrating restlessly.

He relented, curling his hands down the arched bend of my back until his palms dug underneath the tight fabric of my leggings. The shock of his hot skin against mine and his greedy hands palming the flesh of my backside had me tearing my mouth away to swear.

"More," I begged.

Erik's answering chuckle against my skin was dark and dangerous, and didn't help temper my feverish need for him, the edginess that hadn't quite gone away since the day we met. Because I knew—had known all along—he'd be like this. That no matter if he felt exactly the same, he'd pull this moment out, slow and stretched to some unseen breaking point.

"You're always so impatient," he whispered. "Can't you just enjoy the ride?"

He sucked my earlobe into his mouth, his big thigh wedged between my legs. Locked into place, I sought relief with a dragging swivel of my hips, my hands slipping eagerly under his shirt. I raked my nails down his back, and he tore at the other strap of my bra until my chest was exposed.

Before I could blink, he'd boosted me up against the door, pinning me in place with the hard strength of his hips and one thigh between my legs. His mouth slid down my throat, my shoulder, and with one flat tongued lick against my sensitive, peaked skin, I dropped my head back against the door.

"Oh shit," I breathed. My hands curled into his thick hair, holding tight when he sucked my skin until it hurt. Erik lifted his head, where he'd marked the hot aching flesh of my chest, and locked his gaze onto mine. Nothing about his expression was dazed. No, this was clear-eyed, about to crack my body in half lust, and he walked us easily toward the bedroom.

Clear of the doorway, he let me drop onto the bed and ripped his shirt off in the next breath.

Was I purring? I think I was, based on the cocky-ass grin that ghosted his lips. I got up on my knees and ran my tongue up the groove of his flat, muscular stomach. I ran my nose along the dusting of hair across his massive pecs. This was a *man,* and my whole body trembled from my desire for him.

I tugged my bra off, taking a moment to preen—just a little— at the way his pupils dilated from the sight of me topless on his bed. I lay back, slowly peeling the leggings from my hips, then I braced my feet up on his chest. He curled his hands into the tops where they were bound tight against my knees, and he yanked until my legs were free.

I rolled over, gratified by the hiss of air that left Erik at the sight of me on my hands and knees. But if he thought that was the way our first time was going, oh he had another thing coming because I was going to watch every blessed inch of what he was about to do to me. I yanked a small foil packet out of the side of my suitcase and stretched luxuriously onto my back while he shucked his shorts off.

Oh, yes. Yes, please.

Future me was already sore, looking at what he'd been hiding this entire time. And when he stretched the long length of his big, hot body over me, I sighed in relief.

"Too heavy?" he whispered, his hands sliding up my thigh, my hip, onto my chest where he had me writhing in helpless arches of my back.

"No, oh, don't you dare move," I told him, sucking his bottom lip into my mouth. I let it go with a dirty, wet pop, and I wanted to hear that sound on repeat for the rest of my life.

The weight of him, the sheer mass of Erik Wilder, was everything I'd imagined. I'd die here happily, if it came down to it, if it meant I'd finally feel him press me into the mattress.

Our kisses slid smoothly from hot and wet, deep and sweet, and my hands traced all the muscles along his back, memorizing the way they shifted and bunched as he curled himself over my body.

His hand spread wide over my stomach and pushed down between my legs, and I helped, guiding him exactly where I wanted.

He grinned in surprise as my fingers adjusted his speed, the pressure that had me breathing in choppy exhales and soft moans.

"Someone knows what they want," he spoke against my greedy mouth.

"I-I told you," I moaned, "I had some fantasies of my own."

My words were disjointed, unsteady.

Erik whispered some of his own in my ear, and at the rough whispered words, my body unraveled, slow and sweet in warm, rolling waves. Everything melted, long, impossibly long—coming down as I caught my breath. Erik kissed me through it, his hand weaving into my hair as he held my head still. Every noise that came out of my mouth, he breathed in, seemingly absorbing into his body because each one caused a tightening of his hands, a rough edge to his kisses that had my head spinning like a top.

He'd be able to wind me back up so fast—a simple flick of his fingers, a twist of his tongue, and I'd be going round and round.

But before I could catch my breath, before I could fully soak up the sweet relief he'd brought me, Erik pressed one of my thighs up against his side.

"My turn," he ground out.

I arched my back, my breasts against his chest, my palms bracing on the headboard as he pushed himself forward, forward, forward, pausing halfway to drop his forehead against mine.

"More," I begged.

Erik stopped where he was, eyes flashing with something formidable and dangerous. His body was perfectly frozen, and my toes curled up, my back arching in a helpless curve, but I couldn't get him to move.

"Erik," I whined.

"I thought you were trying to make me feel better," he said. "I'm not trying to rush this, sweetheart."

Even with the tenderly spoken endearment, he'd lit the match under my skin, and an edgy, clawing sort of pleasure snaked up my spine at his impossible restraint.

How was he just … not moving? He held himself so still that I wiggled my hips, and he hissed. Oh, yes. He could stay just like that, and I'd be able to roll myself against him and feel that sweet, slow build again.

So I tried it again, moving my body in a tight, rolling circle, and he swore.

"I would make you feel better if you just … let me." I nipped his chin. "Erik, *please.*"

His gaze stayed locked on mine. "I just wanted to hear you beg."

Snap.

His hips shot forward in one unyielding, endless motion, and it tore a scream from my throat. That was all it took to topple me over the edge again.

This pleasure was razor-sharp, glass clear, and instead of warm, rolling waves, it wracked my body with pulsing tremors that could hardly be contained by my skin and bones.

I cried out when he did it again, unable to do anything but hold on tight while Erik Wilder unleashed himself on me. The room filled quickly with the sounds of our bodies, shouted curses from him, and curling, aching moans from me.

He was relentless in his rhythm, slow, slow, then *fast, fast, fast.* Slow again, his thighs held him in that position with impressive strength.

Then Erik sat back on his haunches and tugged me forward, my hips held in the strong grip of his big hands. He moved again at a different angle, a different speed, and his dark, fathomless eyes locked onto mine.

He slid his spread hand up my quivering stomach, ghosting over my chest in a way that had me arching my back.

When I did, he spread out over me again in tight, short movements of his sweat-soaked body over mine.

By the time he called my name in a glorious roar of satisfaction, I had tears streaking down my temples, sweat soaking my back, and muscles wrung dry from any single ounce of tension.

I curled my arms around him as he slumped the full weight of his body onto mine and kept my thighs locked tight on his sides. Left up to me, we'd sleep that way, sticky and sweaty and immediately able to do more, feel more, push ourselves into exhaustion for the rest of the night.

He lifted his head, staring down at me in awe.

I laughed at his expression, smoothing the hair off his forehead. "What?"

"You knew, didn't you? That it would be like this."

Humming, I kissed him softly, hissing when he pulled away and tugged me with him as he settled on his back.

"Of course I did."

He chuckled when my hand started wandering down his stomach. "Have mercy," he begged. "I need a bit more recovery than you do."

"Oh, I'll go easy on you," I promised. My fingers danced across the stacked squares of his abdomen, and he snatched them up, pressing a kiss to the tips.

"Liar," he said around a yawn. "Let me rest, devil woman."

I curled my body into his, a wide smile on my face that might never go away. We napped like that, and I knew that one weekend would never be enough. I just had to hope he felt the same.

Chapter
TWENTY-FIVE

Erik

THERE WAS A CERTAIN DECADENCE ABOUT TAKING A NAP. IT was an indulgence that I rarely allowed myself. And that … it was absolutely nothing compared to a nap fueled by middle-of-the-day sex.

And not just sex.

Sex with Lydia.

To my utter dismay, it was a fucking revelation. Something I could never forget, never un-know.

The sun was high in the sky, filtering through the half-closed shades in the bedroom when I slowly opened my eyes.

"Wake up," a voice whispered gently. Lips followed the voice. They hit along my rib cage in soft puffs of air against my skin. Her hair brushed against my chest, and I tangled my fingers into the sheer mass of it as she nibbled the skin on my stomach.

All I allowed for an answer was a disgruntled sigh, which made Lydia laugh. It always did. In a twisted corner of my mind, maybe that was why I'd always done it. Except now, I'd picture her laughing as she sat above me at that moment.

Naked as a jaybird and so beautiful that it hurt.

With no shame of her own nudity, I watched through drowsy eyes as she worked her way around my body, tasting and licking and sucking on anything that struck her fancy.

When I ran my hand up her thigh, she tutted disapprovingly. "Hands off, Wilder."

Again, I frowned. And again, as I was coming to expect, she smiled. But like an absolute chump, I obeyed, tucking my hands behind my head and letting her have her way with me.

Occasionally, I'd tilt my chin up to the ceiling and mutter her name like a curse, which filled her with great delight. Whenever I did that, she'd pull her hand away to light teasing touches and change the motion of her mouth to something set to drive me insane.

She slid her body over top of mine, catlike in her movements and filled with such innate sexuality that I had the brief worry that the house might need to start on fire to get us out of that bed anytime soon.

Her body was lush, wonderfully curved in places, trim and toned in others, and it was a testament to my exhaustion that I could lay on that bed and not fill my hands with what was on display in front of me. No matter what she'd asked of me, I knew I'd *always* want to touch her, given the opportunity.

For a fleeting moment, I had to claw up the reminder that this was—that it had to be—temporary. That no matter what I wanted, after I dropped her off at home, there'd be no more of these opportunities.

This weekend at home was a brief pause in both of our lives, and the collision we'd been heading toward since the moment we met. And she seemed just as determined as I was to make the most of every second.

With her hands braced on my chest, and her eyes on fire, Lydia tugged her knees on either side of my legs and rolled her hips.

My hands fisted into the comforter on either side of my head, and she chuckled low in her throat.

"I had no idea you'd follow instruction so well," she teased, leaning over me to snag my lips in a slow, decadent kiss. Her tongue rolled in tandem with the motion of her hips. My muscles locked up tight, my hands fisting under my head at how badly I needed to touch, grab, feel. When she pulled away, my mouth followed hers.

"I don't," I growled.

After another roll of her hips, I almost blacked out. The muscles in my arms shook from the effort to hold them in place, and that was before Lydia decided to take her cowgirl act one step further.

By the time she took me in hand and sank down over me, I'd lost any ability to hold myself in place. I sat up, her chest flush against mine, and snapped her wrists together behind her back. She gasped into my mouth as I took another kiss, and another, one hand binding hers, and one hand guiding her into the rhythm that had sweat bead slowly down her temple. I licked at it, then sucked her earlobe into my mouth.

We were messy and sweaty, raw sounds and dirty, delicious kisses by the time I flipped us over, her on her back so I could push us into a punishing pace.

This will never be enough, a voice whispered through the roar of what our bodies were capable of. I wanted to chase it away, destroy it with a swipe of my hand because I knew it was true. Nothing good and right could feel this sinful, feel like I was chasing an impossible high.

There was such a small window of time that I'd allow myself this with her, to take and take and take, and let her do the same in return. Lydia keened underneath me, almost mindless with what I was wringing from her body. And still, I couldn't banish the thoughts that I'd made a colossal mistake in kissing her even a single time. Touching her once was enough to damn me into this space, where I'd always want her.

My hands were desperate, my mouth brutal as I feasted on hers. But as always, Lydia was here with me, the same edge to the way her nails dug in my back, the way she bit down on the curve of my bicep when I curled my arms around her head to hold her in place.

Her eyes locked onto mine, pupils big and gaze searing.

A wisp of a memory tugged at the back of my head as I felt an uneven gallop to my heart.

About locked eye contact, chemicals in your blood that made you feel passion. And love.

Back then, I'd scoffed.

But now, with her body wrapped around mine and a silvery-hot pleasure pushing up from my legs and my back, I believed her. Which was why I closed my eyes, broke that locking of her gaze, and kissed her again, swallowing her moans as she toppled over the edge of her own pleasure, and with the tight clench of her body around mine, I chased right after her.

We had no time to lay in bed any longer than we already had, but still, I ignored the ticking clock and curled myself around her as we caught our breath.

Lydia's arms flopped out onto the bed, and she let out a dramatic, happy-sounding sigh.

"This should be your full-time job," she said drowsily. "You're so good at it. It's stupid."

I laughed into her skin, and my lips brushed against her shoulder. Not quite a kiss, but I didn't move away either. Her hand slid through my hair, and I fought the impulse to push into that sweet contact.

Easy affection had been gone from my life for so long, and she was so free with it.

So giving.

But then, I'd always known that about her, hadn't I? She was like this with everyone she loved.

Again, Lydia sighed, but this wasn't the happy sigh from earlier. Lifting my head, I searched her face. "What is it?"

She smiled, trailing her fingers along my jaw until I nipped at the tips when they touched my mouth. "We need to get ready for tonight."

With a groan, I rolled to my back to check the time on the clock mounted to the opposite wall. "Shit."

Lydia propped up on her elbow. "We could always stay here longer," she said lightly. Her eyes didn't meet mine. They stayed locked onto her fingers, still moving softly over the skin on my chest. I captured her hand and pressed a kiss to the knuckles.

It was so tempting. To press at the barriers of time and allow for another day like this with her.

"Let's just take it one day at a time, okay?"

She nodded.

"Do you need to shower again?" I tugged on my gym shorts, not bothering with anything underneath it. She was biting down on her bottom lip as I did. When I cleared my throat, she blinked up guiltily.

"Yeah, I should." Lydia stood too but didn't cover a single inch of her body as she strolled past me toward the bathroom. "I'll go first since it'll take me longer to get ready."

I nodded, eyes lingering on her backside. If I lived to a hundred, I'd remember the curves of her ass on my deathbed.

Because I was staring, I missed that she'd glanced over her shoulder.

"Unless you want to join me this time." Her lips curled in a smile. "You wash my back, and I'll wash yours?"

As I shucked the shorts off and walked her backward into the bathroom, I gave her a stern look. "That's all. We don't have time for anything else, Pierson."

She gave me a mock salute. "Yes, sir. I'll be on my best behavior."

I cracked after two minutes under the hot water, making a liar out of us both when I pressed her hands against the tile and curled myself around her back.

After that, we kept our hands to ourselves while we got ready for dinner and strolled to the main house with her fingers lightly tangled in mine. I glanced down at her bare legs as we walked, the lines of her elegant pink dress falling gently around her thighs. The ribbon around her waist, black and thin, made her look like a present that I'd get to unwrap later.

And somehow, walking into my parents' house with her this time, it felt less like a lie. We didn't separate that evening. She stayed by my side while we chatted with Parker and Cameron.

"Have a productive afternoon?" Cameron asked, one eyebrow lifted.

I stared him down until Lydia elbowed me lightly in the side.

"Very," she said. "So kind of you to ask."

He laughed.

Parker had a faint tinge of red on his cheeks when he watched Lydia curl her arm around my waist. "I posted the thing you told me to."

She perked up. "Yeah? And?"

"A few Wolves players shared it, so I'm glad I listened to you and tagged them."

I watched my younger brother's face carefully as he talked to Lydia. The serious kid who'd grown into a serious man didn't need Lydia to achieve the things he wanted out of life, but she helped him because it was just her nature to do so. He was stepping into the world she loved, and it didn't bother me like I thought it would.

The only thing that bothered me now was trying to imagine navigating my life without her presence in it. But if my past had taught me anything, it was that I was capable of it. Watching her move forward when I still wasn't sure of my own future would hurt. For her, though, it was the best thing.

Across the room, my mom and Tim held court at a small table

for two that Greer had set up with tall tapered candles and a spray of wildflowers. She winked when she caught me staring. And when her gaze settled on Lydia tucked into my side, she blinked a few times, a telltale sign that she was fighting tears.

Discomfort resonated through me like someone plucked the string of an out-of-tune guitar.

Lydia broke into my thoughts with a burst of bright, sunny laughter at something Cameron was describing to her.

"She didn't," she said, covering her mouth when a few people turned to look.

Cameron nodded. "She did. We had to demo the entire kitchen for a second time. All the built-ins we'd designed, the weeks of work, and all that material, gone."

Lydia moaned. "I would've cried."

"I almost did," Cameron answered with all seriousness.

A gentle tapping against a glass pulled everyone's attention to the front of the room.

My mom was standing with Tim, and even though he was bracing most of his weight onto the back of his chair, it was good to see him at full height. He'd lost weight, and he looked pale, but his eyes sparkled happily in his face while my mom tried to quiet the crowd gathered in their home.

"Thank you so much for coming," she said. She curled a hand around Tim's elbow. "I've been appointed the speech maker this year, and Tim and I are so honored to have all of you here to celebrate our twenty years of marriage."

Claps and whistles filled the air, and I couldn't help but smile at the blush that stole across my mom's face.

"We've had two decades filled with so much love and laughter and fights and tears and chaos," she said. "And that was just from the boys under the roof." Tim barked with laughter, and my mom waited for him to compose himself before she continued. "Tim and I found love at the most inconvenient time, and it's given us both a life of happiness that cannot possibly be explained." Her voice wobbled slightly, and Tim stepped closer, sliding his arm around her shoulder. "So for being by our side these last twenty years, we thank you. No matter how many years we have left, we're so grateful for every single day, and we can never repay everyone here for taking a role in that amazing life."

Next to me, Poppy sniffed noisily, and Greer curled her arms around our youngest sister while she quietly cried. The weight of Tim's sickness fell like a heavy blanket over the joyous atmosphere, but instead of crying, the man who raised me smiled out at the crowd—clear-eyed and happy. My jaw clenched tight together as I tried to imagine our family or my mom without him.

He was the rock when we needed one, a father that I'd never experienced before he stepped into the role. Every single one of us in our family owed him a debt that we'd never be able to repay, and as I glanced at the red-eyed faces of all of my siblings, Ian included, we were all thinking the same thing.

My stepbrothers had lost a mom when they were young—Ian was the only one old enough to remember her—and now they stared down the loss of their father. It might be years, or months, or weeks, but even the knowledge of it put the present into a slightly melancholy perspective.

Because she always seemed to sense my shifting mood, Lydia tucked her arm through mine and set her head on my shoulder. At her innocent gesture, I fought against the warm swell that accompanied it. All of it with her felt so right. But I couldn't understand, couldn't make sense of how it could be right when so many pieces of it didn't fit into the picture in my head.

At a time in my life when the future was fuzzy and indistinct, Lydia grounded me.

She challenged everything. What I'd thought was true about her. And even scarier, about myself.

It was such an unlikely role for a woman that I'd

underestimated—her superpower, as she called it—that she could be an anchor, something safe and comforting, and at the same time, be the most dangerous person I'd ever met.

Because I didn't know what came next. Didn't know how to picture the future, not without her as a part of it. Or be able to see what place made sense for me.

Soft chatter filled the room once my mom lifted her glass in a toast that we all joined, and I had to expel a quiet breath at the quickly shifting tone of my thoughts.

Avoiding my family hadn't changed anything, really. All it had done was keep me on the outside while life continued marching on. But the thought of sliding back into the rhythm of this place still felt slightly unnatural because I'd convinced myself for so long that I was doing the right thing.

Soft music started playing, a crooning voice singing about love in unlikely places, and Tim held his hand out to my mom. She laughed as she took it, and even though they simply swayed back and forth, it was enough to shift the tone of the evening.

A few more couples joined them, and the cleared-out middle of their family room became an impromptu dance floor. Ian, to my surprise, held out his hand to Poppy, wiping away what was left of her tears before they clasped hands and turned in a gentle waltz.

Lydia tilted her chin up and whispered in my ear, "That's surprisingly nice of him."

I hummed. "He has his moments."

Poppy said something that made him laugh, and for a moment, he looked like the punk kid he was when our parents first got married. Even then, he'd walked around like he was mad at the world. But when he was happy, when he smiled, everyone around him felt it.

"Your brothers are good dancers," Lydia said quietly. "It must feel awful to be the only one in the family with two left feet."

I gave her a look that had her laughing under her breath.

My sigh was heavy and made her eyes sparkle happily.

What a sucker I was.

"Oooh, that was a good one," she whispered. "Almost a ten."

"You rate my sighs?"

Lydia bit down on her bottom lip and nodded.

"Is that why you always did things to piss me off?" I slid my arm tighter around her waist, my fingers lightly tracing the shape of her hip.

She hummed, eyes locked on my mouth. "Maybe."

It was the only way I could explain why I turned and held out my hand to Lydia. Her eyebrows rose in gentle surprise, but her lips curled up in a pleased smile.

"People can see us, you know," she said in a stage whisper.

I sighed. Again.

She laughed, a light sound of delight as she slid her fingers around mine. "Just checking."

Whether I'd regret the dance wasn't even a question because there was no escaping it when she curled herself against my chest. My hand slid up her back while our joined hands were tucked against my heart. When I set my chin on the top of her head, there was a subtle movement somewhere under my ribs when my heart finally seemed to make peace with the reaction to her nearness.

It wasn't as simple as acceptance because I'd never know how to accept that anyone could make me feel what Lydia Pierson did. It wasn't calm or quiet because she didn't have it in her nature. It was like facing down a tornado, feeling the wind whip over your skin and knowing you should take cover but still being unable to tear your eyes away.

There was a furious beauty inside her, and I understood why she drew people to her so effortlessly.

She wasn't hiding who she was as she hummed along to the song, just slightly off-key, and she didn't even attempt to conceal her pleased expression that I was willing to do something so simple as dance with her.

It was hard to imagine what it must be like to live in that state of being. She immersed herself in every moment, and as her frame expanded on a deep, contented inhale, I realized that she'd brought that out in me too.

Before, I would've been trapped in my own thoughts of why I should or shouldn't do something. The details, small but no less significant, would've been completely overlooked. And now, I noticed everything. The silk of her hair against my face. The warmth in her fingers as they curled through mine. The steady beat of her heart where she pressed against me.

Instead of worrying about whether it was right or wrong, instead of turning it over in my head of what fallout there might be, I closed my eyes and just … held her.

And to my amazement, it was letting myself stay anchored in those small details about Lydia that kept the cold, snapping feel of fear at bay. There was nothing to be afraid of in this dance because it was just her and me.

Much like sex with her had been, everything about it would be stamped indelibly into my brain. It was a memory I'd never erase, tucked safely away where I'd keep it, in the moments when I inevitably missed her.

Lydia looked up and searched my face. "You're thinking very hard."

"How do you know that?" I murmured. I cupped the side of her face, brushing my thumb across the silk of her cheek.

Her blue eyes saw everything, and in turn, let me do the same. She'd love me if I'd let her.

But instead of saying it because Lydia seemed to know exactly what I needed, she simply watched me with a sweet smile playing along her perfect lips. "Because I know you."

I didn't think about who might be watching or what the

consequences might be. I slid my hand into her hair and kissed her. Her lips gave immediately, opening so that I could touch my tongue to hers. The kiss stayed gentle and slow while I sipped on her top and then bottom lip. Lydia pushed up on the balls of her feet and made a tiny whimpering sound when I didn't pull away.

Maybe she didn't know me quite so well because pulling away was what she'd expected.

It was what I expected too.

Everything about it, about the night, made it seem like a giant hourglass had been tipped over. If I watched it too closely, I'd see the sands slip noiselessly through to the other side. But I didn't want to watch that, didn't want to think about the result.

For the first time in my life, I wanted to feel whatever she was feeling, even if it was just this once.

That night, hours later, when I slid my body over hers between the cool sheets on the bed, I didn't think about the next day. Or the day after that. I didn't worry about how she could sneak past every barrier I'd erected over the past few years.

We hardly traded a word once we'd stripped off the clothes covering our bodies, and the moonlight shining outside of the windows played over her naked body in the dark of the room. I kissed the soft, quivering skin on her stomach while she clutched my hair with a gasp, and I dragged my teeth over the insides of her thighs while she whispered my name in a pleading tone.

Only after I pulled her under once, with my tongue and hands, did I climb back up over her body and press myself back between her legs. It was all soft sighs from her pink lips, puffs of air from my mouth against her neck while I rolled against her in a steady, painfully slow rhythm. Lydia clutched me so tight, and my hands found their way curved around her back, gripping her shoulders so she could hardly move.

We were locked against each other, our mouths slipping,

sliding, and sucking until I was able to fall over the edge right along with her.

She was sweet and drowsy against my side as I settled onto my back, and as we fell asleep holding each other, I kept my mind trained firmly on every part of her that I could feel, instead of the dwindling hours we had left until the sun rose.

Chapter
TWENTY-SIX

Erik

Mom: Can I have breakfast with my son before he leaves? Just the two of us.

THE TEXT WOKE ME IN THE DARK ROOM. LYDIA WAS STILL plastered to my side, and I eased my arm out from underneath where it was curled around her shoulder. Leaning up on one elbow, I tapped out a quick response saying I'd be there shortly. Phone set back down on the nightstand, I let my eyes study the sleeping woman curled up next to me.

Gently, I brushed a tangle of her hair away from her face, smiling when she buried further into the pillow.

I'd never see her wake again, and the cold, uncomfortable truth of it coiled through me. Instead of feeling uncomfortable sharing a bed with her, knowing the feel of her from the inside, where she was a perfect fit for every part of me, I had to face the discomfort of walking away because it was best.

For both of us.

She had a future, sure and steady, well within her grasp. It was bright and limitless. She was young and had years to find someone better matched for that path.

It was so tempting to wake her with my mouth, indulge one last time when she was sleepy and soft and drowsy. But it wouldn't help, wouldn't make anything easier.

Which was why I slid silently out of bed and pulled the covers up over her bare shoulder so she didn't get cold.

And I still battled that instinct to do whatever was necessary to make her feel safe and taken care of.

When I slipped out of the front door, dressed and slightly more awake, she was still sound asleep. The walk to my parents' house was still and quiet. Only the sound of crunching sticks and leaves under my boots punctuated the silence.

I'd need to figure out how to let them know that Lydia and I separated because with Tim's sickness and my job with Lydia at an end, I had no real reason to go back to Seattle. I could move back into the small house and help my mom wherever she needed it.

I tucked my hands in my pockets, blowing out a slow breath. The same question had plagued me since my injury and decision not to play. Where did I belong?

For years, I'd avoided the place called home because I thought I was making it easier on them. And as much as I'd missed it—missed them—I still wasn't entirely sure that I belonged there either.

When I approached the house, a few soft lights were on in the kitchen, and I opened the front door without knocking. My mom was in her favorite chair, a worn brown leather recliner that had seen better days. She held a cup of coffee in her hands and a far-off look in her eyes.

"Morning," I told her.

She blinked out of her thoughts, smiling softly as I leaned down to kiss her cheek. "Good morning, my firstborn."

Mom watched while I filled a mug with steaming coffee and plopped a warm cinnamon roll onto a waiting plate.

"Want one?" I asked her.

"In a minute, I will."

I took a seat opposite her. "You usually up this early?"

"No." She gave me a sly look. "Knew this was my best shot of getting some time alone with you. You disappeared for quite a while yesterday."

My face burned hot, and I pulled on the edge of the steaming hot roll.

Mom laughed. "Haven't seen you blush since high school."

"Enjoy the party last night?"

At my subject change, she smothered a knowing smile. "It was perfect. Tim will be exhausted today, but it was worth it."

"It was nice seeing everyone," I admitted. "Even Ian played nice."

"He's dealt with a lot of loss in a very short life, and not everyone knows how to deal with that well."

She'd always had his back, something that used to drive me crazy. But the truth was I was in no position to judge. My own loss hadn't brought out my best side either.

Slowly, I chewed the sweet, fragrant roll and thought about all the ways I'd probably reacted worse than Ian. But no one, not a single member of my family besides him, held it against me.

"Do you think you can come back for Christmas?" she asked. "We'd love to have you two here."

There it was again. The thing I couldn't avoid. I'd taken the first step back into their life, and that one wouldn't be enough. Not anymore. But her question wasn't just about me.

At my silence, I felt the weight of her gaze on my face. Finally, I looked up and met it straight on. "I may come back to Oregon for a while, actually."

Surprise lit her face. "Really?"

I nodded. "I'm between jobs right now, and I think I've overstayed my welcome at Adaline's."

"What about Lydia? Would she be okay with you four hours away?"

"I think Lydia understands that my family needs me," I answered carefully.

That was enough to satisfy her. "She's wonderful," she said. "I wasn't sure how I'd feel about someone so much younger than you, but …"

Her voice trailed off, and I felt a pinch in my chest at her words. It was everything I was prepared for, but somehow, my body hadn't quite braced for impact. And there was impact, all right, as she finished her sentence.

"She's perfect for you, Erik." My mom's eyes glossed over. "And you know I don't say things like that flippantly."

I blew out a harsh breath. My hands started tingling because only a short walk away, she slept peacefully in my bed. Somewhere I never should've joined her. Never should've opened Pandora's box.

"She's a great girl," I said gruffly. "But, uh, we haven't talked much about the future."

My mom stood, settling her hand on my shoulder. "She's more than that, and don't you try to fool me, son. I've never seen you look at anyone the way you looked at her last night."

An elephant settled nicely onto my chest, the crushing weight making it hard to pull in a full breath.

"Mom—" I started, but she held up a hand.

"I know you, Erik." Her eyes were firm. "I understand that she might seem like a surprising choice, and how people react will weigh on you, but I have prayed for someone to bring life back into your eyes after Olivia left."

Her name on my mom's mouth had something splintering inside me, and tension spread like a vine across my back and shoulder blades.

She cupped my face, and I struggled to hold her gaze. "You have more than life in your eyes right now, son." Her voice wobbled. "I see your heart. And you never let people see that if you can help it."

I stood before I could stop myself, and her hands fell limply by her sides.

"Please don't run away from that," she begged. "Not even to come back home."

Swiping a hand down my face, I struggled to keep my panic in check. I'd failed at this one thing, a simple bridge in allowing me to come back, to mend the broken pieces I'd left behind, and now everything was worse.

She walked into the kitchen and opened a drawer. When she didn't immediately remove something, my interest sharpened, a brief distraction from the mess in my head.

But when she did withdraw her hand, I sank back into the chair underneath me.

With a careful look on her face, she approached with a black ring box in her hand. I knew what was in it, and I was immediately shaking my head.

A tear slid down her cheek unchecked as she crouched in front of me.

"Mom," I whispered.

She set the box onto the table next to me. It was worn on the edges, the gold design looping over the frame smudged from being handled over the decades. "Grandma gave me this when I married Tim because she knew that he was the man who'd cherish my heart. She *knew* your father wasn't the one." She gripped my hand and holding her teary gaze had my heart shattering into a million pieces. I couldn't do this to her again, yet it's exactly what I was about to do. "Olivia was a good girl with a misguided heart, and she was not for you. I know how badly you wanted what Tim and I had, and I hate that she cost you so much of what you wanted. But you are not done yet, Erik Wilder."

I dropped my chin to my chest. Words crowded my

throat—explanations and ugly truths, but somehow, I swallowed them down.

The tears flowing freely down her face didn't stop her in the slightest. "Do not run away from this chance at happiness because I can see you ready to do it. Don't use us as an excuse because she scares you."

My head snapped up. It was almost word for word what Lydia had told me.

"You have no idea what you're talking about, Mom," I said. "She doesn't … we're not …" My voice halted because admitting it felt impossible.

"You are in love with her," she interjected. "And nothing you say will convince me otherwise. It's the only reason you'd fight this so hard. You saw what happened to me with your dad. And then what happened to you with Olivia." She emitted a small sob. "And you see Tim sick, and I know you will do anything in your power to avoid feeling like that again. But she makes you happy, and that makes her incredibly precious to me."

Hearing the words snapped something loose, and before I could stop myself, I shoved the chair backward with a clatter and paced away from the table.

The box sat on the edge of that table, and I knew exactly what was inside it. I'd seen it on my mom's finger for twenty years. The diamond was an oval, a delicate ivy pattern wound around the band, dotted with smaller diamonds. And for a moment, I closed my eyes and imagined it on Lydia's finger.

The corresponding burst of emotion under my ribs was so bright, it almost brought me to my knees.

If I knew what it was like to *really* have her, to give her my heart, and she ever left, I'd never recover.

"Oh, Erik," she whispered.

"It was a lie," I heard myself say. Where the words came from, what finally released them, I wasn't quite sure. All I knew was that image, that future, it wasn't meant for me. I'd always known that. And it was time to stop pretending anything different.

"Wh-What was?"

I opened my eyes. "All of it. The pictures, they weren't … real. We were never together."

Mom's mouth popped open.

In an emotionless voice, I told her about her car accident. Luke hiring me. The anxiety she'd worked through during our time together. The photograph. How I'd quit. Why I'd asked for her help.

Her chest was heaving as she listened, her mouth covered with one hand.

"I don't believe it," she whispered. "I don't believe that it was fake."

I clenched my jaw, fought the unfair wave of anger that rose dangerously. My anger didn't need to be aimed at her. Only the person I stared down in the mirror was a worthy target. "Well, it's the truth. It was a stupid plan because I didn't know how to tell you no when you begged me to bring her home."

Now, it was her eyes flashing. "And the *truth* never occurred to you? I didn't raise you to deceive your entire family."

"Of course it occurred to me," I shouted. "But that's not always so easy to face, is it?"

Mom's face softened. "No, it's not. And you've had your fair share of ugly truths, Erik. But I raised you better than this."

An incredulous laugh fell harshly from my lips.

"You involved that sweet girl in this, and if you have fooled yourself into thinking she doesn't have feelings for you, then you are dumber than I ever thought."

My chest went tight again, but denial was an ugly, cold coating on my tongue that I couldn't quite fight. I didn't want to admit that she was right. I didn't want to admit how the past couple of days had felt, indulging in whatever bloomed between Lydia and me.

"She'll get over it," I said, words biting and hard. They came out like knives dragging against my throat.

The disappointment in her face was something I could hardly look at. "Oh, Erik."

"What?" I spread my arms out. Self-loathing had horrifying truths bubbling from my mouth, truths that I didn't want to believe spewing out of me because if I said them out loud, maybe I'd convince myself that I hadn't fucked everything up. "She will. She's twenty-two. She doesn't know what she wants."

"This isn't you," she said sadly.

"She's a kid, Mom. She'll find something else to distract her a month from now, trust me. If Lydia has one strength, it's that."

A shocked exhale came from the direction of the door, and I had to pinch my eyes shut before turning to look.

Because I *knew*.

I knew what I'd see, and I was so disgusted with myself for saying it, so horrified that she heard it, that I could hardly stomach the image of her face.

"Oh, sweetie," my mom said, rushing over to the door. "He doesn't believe that."

When I opened my eyes, she was holding a hand out to my mom's advances, her wounded eyes locked onto me. Unlike me, Lydia had enough spine to look at that discomfort head-on. And she made no attempt to hide the tear that slid down her face.

"Yeah, he does," she whispered.

"Lydia," I started, moving in her direction. "I didn't mean it—"

She tilted her head. "Didn't you?"

"No, I didn't," I said. "I was angry and frustrated, and sometimes people say stupid shit when they're angry."

"Is *that* your way of apologizing?"

My mom glanced back and forth between us. "I'm going to give you two some privacy."

Lydia shook her head. "There's no need, Sheila. But thank you.

And thank you for all the hospitality you've shown me this weekend." Her voice wobbled dangerously, but she dashed a knuckle under her eye and took a deep fortifying breath. "It was a pleasure to meet you and your family."

My mom's face ... it was pure misery. "The pleasure was all mine, sweetheart."

Lydia lifted her chin, stepping back out of the house and storming down the steps with a swish of blond hair.

"Dammit!" I yelled. This was all wrong. Nothing played out the way I'd thought, yet everything was so horrifyingly familiar.

My mom standing in her kitchen heartbroken because of my choices. Because I thought I had everything figured out.

"I'll be right back," I told my mom.

She was unimpressed, arms crossed over her middle and mouth flat. Nothing I'd ever done in my entire life had ever made my mom look at me like that, and suddenly, I couldn't get out of that kitchen fast enough.

I brushed past my mom and jogged after Lydia's retreating back. "Lydia, wait."

She didn't.

"Lydia."

The amount of speed she was able to produce, considering she was in flip-flops, was impressive. The sun was filtering weakly through the woods, obscured by hazy clouds over the mountains, and it gave the woods surrounding us an eerie feel. Or maybe it was the complete and utter disaster that I'd brought upon myself that made it feel that way.

I caught up with her, sliding my hand gently around her elbow to turn her toward me.

With a strength I hadn't anticipated, Lydia wrenched it from my grasp. "Don't touch me," she hissed.

I stepped back, hands raised. "Okay. I just ... I want to talk to you."

"What are you going to say, Erik?" She jabbed a finger into my chest. "That you're exactly like all those people I've learned to ignore?"

"I'm not," I said miserably. "You know I'm not."

"How do you figure? I just listened to you tell your mother that I'm an easily distracted kid." Her voice broke on the end. "You're worse than the rest of them because you pretended you were different."

It was too much. And all of it was my fault.

"I am so sorry," I told her. "I let my temper get the best of me, and it was at your expense."

Lydia studied me, her eyes watchful, her face flushed. Then she shook her head. "Your *temper*," she said quietly. "I actually think you believe that."

"What's that supposed to mean?"

"You weren't angry. You were scared. And I never thought you'd unleash that fear on someone who lo—" She paused, searching my eyes. Then she swallowed. "I thought you were better than that, Erik."

"You don't know what you're saying." I shook my head. "Lydia, I know you mean well, but … it's not as simple as being scared or not scared. It's bigger than that."

I didn't want to hurt her, but in her rosy-colored view, all of this was so easy. And it was the furthest thing from the truth.

"What is?" She curled her arms around her waist. "Not like you'll tell me. You don't tell me anything."

I steeled myself because the desire to touch her face was so strong. But it wouldn't help anything. It was better for her to know now that I was not the guy she should be romanticizing. "Do you think it would help if I unloaded all the worst parts of my past? The things I hate talking about?" Images crowded my head. Half assembled cribs and soft yellow sheets, a baby blanket and soft, tender things that I never wanted to look at again. Things I'd lost that she'd never possibly be able to understand. "It wouldn't help *anything*. Knowing those things doesn't give you some black and white playbook of how to handle me because this wasn't a relationship, Lydia."

Her chin wobbled. "You're full of shit."

"No, I'm not."

Lydia pointed back at my house. The one I'd never step foot into again without thinking of her. "Then what do you call that? Huh?"

My jaw was so tight, I could hardly force the words out. "Scratching an itch."

Lydia emitted a shocked gasp. Her face went pale, but she never—not even for a moment—dropped her gaze. "I take it back. You're not full of shit."

"Good."

She took a step closer. "You're a coward."

I rocked back on my heels at the ice in her tone. Not even just the ice, but how sure she was. My voice was rough and angry when I spoke. "You have no fucking idea what I've been through. What I've lost. If you knew even half—"

She interrupted me. "What I *know* is that you're punishing me for someone else's sins, and it's not fair."

She was right.

And she wasn't.

I wasn't punishing her. If anyone was on the receiving end of that word, it was me. But there was no reason to try to explain that to her. The sooner she walked away from this—from me—the better off she'd be.

"Life isn't fair, Lydia. You want to slap a bow on this and make it into some big romantic drama? Go ahead if that makes you feel better."

I could hardly feel my heartbeat anymore. All I could hear was the rush of blood in my ears. I didn't even recognize my own voice, but the words came all the same.

"What I know is that you're telling your mom that I'm some

kid who'll find a new shiny toy in another month, but I'm the only one of the two of us who's actually working toward a future I want. You are doing *nothing* but running."

No one had dared to say it to my face. Probably because I'd never given them the chance. And to hear it from her mouth, words formed from lips that I'd tasted, carved a hole straight in my chest. I could hardly breathe through it because if she'd reached forward, Lydia Pierson could've plucked my heart right out of my body.

"I know what you want me to do, Erik Wilder," she continued. There was no wobble in her voice, no tears streaking down her face anymore. And for that, I was grateful. "You want me to curse you out? Slap you and call you an asshole?"

I slicked my tongue over my teeth.

She shook her head. "Of course you do. Because it would make it so much easier on you if I did. Then maybe you could watch me walk away and pat yourself on the back for doing what's best for me. Because isn't that what you always do? You decide what's best for everyone when the only thing you're accomplishing is setting your own life on fire."

So I clenched my jaw and stared down at the ground.

"Don't follow me into the house," she said. "I'm packing my bags, and I'm going home."

My head snapped up. "How?"

Her smile was stretched thin at the edges. "Oh, I'm a resource-ful girl. I'll figure it out."

This cold, unhappy version of her was all wrong. Because I knew on the inside, she was vibrating dangerously with the impulse to make this better for me. To help me understand why I wanted to run—and run fast—from any semblance of happiness.

Watching her pivot sharply toward the house, the one I'd only been able to come back to because of her, it was physically painful to let her go.

Only one moment in my life had hurt more than this one, and

I almost sank to my knees in the woods when she slammed the door behind her.

I could've ignored her and pushed through the door. I could've kissed her or done all the things that would temporarily make her forget exactly how painful my words had been. Because no matter what I said, not for a single second did I think Lydia was a kid who didn't understand her own mind.

I didn't think she'd easily find a distraction and forget me.

I had the power to crush her heart as I'd already shown. And because of that, I watched from a distance as she got into a rented black car that arrived about an hour later and left.

All weekend, I'd thought fleetingly about how it would feel when she wasn't in my life.

And like a fool, there was an assumption that it would be easier to lose something good and pure the second time. Something that altered the shape of my heart and the way I looked at the future.

I was wrong.

This time, losing that good thing wasn't a result of someone else's choices or someone else's actions.

It was because of me. And I wasn't sure I could ever make peace with that.

Chapter
TWENTY-SEVEN

Lydia

THE BIGGEST THING I LEARNED ABOUT HAVING YOUR HEART broken was that the immediate aftermath—the days spent crying and drinking and vilifying—weren't actually the hardest part at all.

That came slowly. Because the worst part was the passage of time.

When the first week faded, and I picked myself back up, diving headfirst into school, the second week turned into a different sort of hard.

A silent phone becomes the saddest thing you'd ever seen. Most days, I left it sitting untouched on the end table in my bedroom.

Yes, the bedroom at my parents'.

Upon my early arrival back home from Oregon, with a tear-puffy face and a bright red nose, my parents stopped asking if I was going to move out. My dad brought me pancakes in bed the next morning, and I told myself that I'd probably never leave at that rate. And I couldn't find it in me to be embarrassed about it.

The pancakes in bed lasted the first week until I told him he was allowed to stop because my legs still worked—even if my heart was a bit bruised.

When I shuffled upstairs week two, and he was waiting in the kitchen with a patient smile and a steaming mug of coffee, I fought the prick of tears in my eyes as I accepted it.

He already had the TV on, and I curled up into my corner on the couch, dragging a chunky white blanket over my legs as he turned the volume up.

"Want me to make you breakfast this morning?" he asked, eyes on the screen. "Maybe you're sick of my pancakes by now."

"Never." I smiled. "But I am capable of feeding myself, you know."

He stretched an arm out and ruffled my hair. "I know, kiddo. Sometimes I like to pretend you can't, though. Makes me feel useful."

We watched in silence for a while as they transitioned from baseball news to football. Dad hummed in acknowledgment at a few things they said, and still, I found myself watching him.

Useful. What an interesting word when he seemed so ... integral to how our entire life worked.

"What is it?" he asked.

"Was it hard for you when you retired?"

Dad lowered the volume on the TV and shifted on the couch to face me. "Yes and no."

"But you had options, right?"

"Sure." He took a sip of coffee, then tilted his mug toward the talking heads on the screen. "A handful of commentating jobs came in the quickest, but sitting in front of the camera isn't for me. I didn't rush to find the thing that worked best for me."

"How come?"

He flashed a quick grin. "I had you."

My eyebrows rose slowly. "What do you mean?"

"Your mom was pregnant with you when we won that last championship, and there was nothing I wanted to do more than be able to help your mom after she had you. I traded early practices and film rooms for diaper duty and midnight feedings. Best choice I've ever made."

My eyes misted again. "I don't think I knew that."

"You and your sister have always been my first priority. Even when I played. If anything about my job had come at the expense of you two, I would've quit in a heartbeat if I hadn't already wanted to retire."

My fingers picked at the edge of the blanket. As it always did, my mind wandered back to Erik. The look on his face when I told him he was doing nothing but setting his life on fire. In hindsight, the comment didn't make me feel quite as good as it had at the moment. I knew, better than anyone, how hard it was for professional athletes to transition to something else after football.

I worried my bottom lip. "So when did you know what you wanted to do, like … for the team?"

"Well, I'm a bit spoiled there, you know. Married to the owner and all, I could take my time to figure out exactly how I wanted to stay part of the game. Your mom knows that I'd rather help with scouting for the combine, help mold the new talent." He tilted his head. "Speaking of which, you can stop sending me highlights of Erik's stepbrother. He's on our radar now. You made sure of that."

My pleased smile broke free before I could stop it. For the first time in two weeks, I felt all warm and fuzzy inside. "Really? You didn't say anything."

"I had to make sure I was bragging my kid's find for the right reasons." When I laughed, he nudged me with his elbow. "He's good. And he's the kind of solid player that can get overlooked really easily unless someone with a keen eye and really good instincts knows what they're seeing."

"I'm glad," I said. "He's got a really good head on his shoulders. But keep him away from the WAGS if you draft him, they will *eat him alive.* They'll all want to adopt him, and I don't know if he could handle their crazy."

My dad laughed. "Fair enough. I'll see if Paige can do the adopting. If Parker is used to being in a big family, then the Wards would be a good fit if Washington drafts him."

The warm and fuzzy was gone because now I was thinking about the Wilders. Thinking about what Adaline had told me when we texted a few days earlier. I'd read her text so many times, it was burned in my brain, but knowing me, I'd read it a few more times just to make sure I didn't miss a subtext.

Adaline: I am SO SORRY that my big brother is such a raging asshole, Lydia. I wish we could've said goodbye, but I understand why you had to leave right away.

Me: Thanks, Adaline. I wanted to say goodbye to you guys too. I really liked your family.

Adaline: I can't even look at his stupid face without wanting to punch him in the nutsack, so it's probably good he's back in Sisters again.

Me: Is he?

Adaline: Yeah. He's helping Mom and Tim around the property. From what I've heard, he just chops down trees and snarls at anything that breathes too loudly. So … he's basically dethroned Ian as the biggest prick in the family. I think he misses you. Which I know I shouldn't say, but I can't NOT.

Adaline: I promised myself I wouldn't interfere, but he is so full of idiot-man-bullshit if he thinks he was doing this for your own good. He just doesn't know how to be happy again. After Olivia. And everything else. That wrecked him. And it doesn't make it okay, but don't you believe for a second that he didn't have feelings for you.

Me: I know you're trying to help. But … it doesn't matter if I believe it. Or you. Or everyone in your family. As long as Erik believes it … I've got to accept it.

Adaline: But he's SO DUMB. The dumbest. And I hate it. Because you guys were perfect for each other.

"Did I lose ya, kiddo?" Dad asked.

I blinked. "Sorry. I was … thinking about a text from earlier."

He studied my face. "I know you don't want to talk about what happened."

"Not really."

"We can if you ever change your mind, though," he continued gently. "I know I'm not always the most rational when one of my girls gets hurt." I snorted. "But I can listen. And attempt level-headed advice even if it means setting aside my fatherly instinct to fight your battles for you."

I sighed, curling up against his side when he held his arm out. "You and Mom did too good of a job raising us for that. We can fight our own battles because we know you've got our back when it comes down to it." Laying my head on his shoulder, I closed my eyes. "But it's still nice to hear that you're willing, even if it means I may not move out of your house until I'm thirty."

"Hey," he said gently. "You've taken on a lot this year, Lydia. And you've faced all of it with grace and humility and the kind of determination that most elite athletes would kill for."

"I don't feel very determined right now," I murmured.

Immediately, Dad slipped into his *I'm a quarterback, let me make a motivational speech* voice. "A bad couple of weeks does not undo what's meant for you, Lydia. You know that."

What was meant for me.

I still saw my future at Washington, the one I'd dreamed of for years, ahead of me in technicolor. But it was everything else that seemed a bit foggy. What I wanted to see was a bearded smile aimed in my direction. Someone complaining about my music and holding my hand while I faced my fears. I wanted to wake up sprawled over his big, warm body and laugh when he made fun of how my hair looked when I woke up. I wanted to dance with the man who never danced and know that those sweet pockets hidden inside him were meant just for me.

If I closed my eyes, I could picture a little girl with big brown eyes and blond hair or a little boy with dark hair curled up at the edges. He'd be such a good dad. And if he let himself, an amazing husband.

After two weeks, I couldn't let go of wanting that. And I didn't think two months would make much of a difference either. I'd miss him for so much longer than I ever knew him, and even if that made no sense to anyone else, it was perfectly logical in my own heart.

"It feels like more than a bad couple of weeks, Dad."

"A broken heart then," he added gently.

I hadn't cried in five days and sixteen hours. Give or take. But the tally card was wiped clean when my eyes watered. "And how do you live with one of those?"

Dad turned to the side until I was forced to face him. "Is that what we're dealing with? Not just disappointed hopes?"

Slowly, I nodded. "I know I've got time … to find someone else. But I don't want anyone else. He's … grumpy. And bossy. He's so hard on himself when he thinks he's failed. And I think, I think he never learned how to live with a broken heart. So he just pretends he doesn't have one, but he does."

My dad blew out a slow breath, tilting his gaze up to the ceiling before he answered. "Lydia, you don't do anything by half, do you? When you find someone to love, you find the one that is going to make your father go gray in less than a year."

I laughed through my tears. "I guess. I didn't mean to, you know. It wasn't in the plan to fall in love with him. But now I don't know how to …" I paused, shrugging my shoulders in a weak gesture. "Not."

Dad cupped the side of my face. "Your mom would probably be ten times better at this kind of pep talk. But you know I speak from experience when I say that, in general, men are complete and utter horseshit at talking about what they feel or how to deal with big, scary love feelings in a healthy way. I know I was back when I met your mom."

"Really?"

He nodded. "She terrified me. I'd never met anyone like her. She was so … unapologetic in who she was. And I fought my feelings for a long time. I cheapened them. Convinced myself they were anything but love."

Hope bubbled dangerously in my chest, and I had to squash it down when I imagined Erik having the same realization.

"I don't know what happened between you and Wilder," he continued gently. "But if he can't see what it would do to his world to have you in it, then he's a fool."

"Not that you're biased or anything."

"Nope." He kissed the top of my head. "That's a universal truth. Life is better when you have a Lydia Pierson in it."

I leaned forward, squeezing him tight around the neck. "Not too bad at the pep talk thing, Dad."

"Thanks." We settled back onto the couch, and he gestured to the TV. "We still taking bets on whether the Cleveland offensive coordinator is gonna get fired before the end of the season?"

I scoffed. "They're crazy if they do. He's in a building year. They don't deserve him if they let him go before he has a chance to strengthen the O-line."

"That's my girl," he murmured. He ruffled my hair again.

I took a deep breath and settled into the feeling of a good talk with the man who raised me, even if it came at the expense of a broken heart. But I felt—just a little—like I understood Erik better than I had in the past two weeks.

I just wasn't sure what I wanted to do about it.

Chapter
TWENTY-EIGHT

Erik

"W HY CAN'T I CLEAR THAT GROVE OF TREES, THOUGH? You said you wanted some fruit trees, and if we knock some of those firs back, you'd have the perfect space."

Across the table, Mom and Tim shared a look.

I hated their looks. I'd gotten a lot of them in the past couple of weeks, and I was about ready to punch a hole through a wall if they gave me any more.

They were a perfect mix of pity and frustration and love.

"*Someday*, I'd like fruit trees, Erik. My casual mention at supper last night does not mean you need to clear me a half an acre of land this morning." She spoke so patiently, like I was a little kid. That had me sending her a look of my own. "Don't you give me that face, son."

"I need something to do today." I stood, taking their dirty plates with me before moving to the sink. "You said you wanted fruit trees, and that is something I can do. It's either that or I'll start re-tiling Poppy's bathroom."

Tim snorted. "Despite what your sister says, she does not need a newly tiled bathroom. Hers is perfectly fine."

My hands flexed uselessly. Didn't they understand? This is why I was at home. To do the things that normally got pushed aside.

"Besides, Cameron said he'd help with that." She nudged me away from the sink. "He is the builder, you know."

"Cameron is too busy overseeing the construction of three different houses at the moment. He can hardly make time to sleep, let alone come do a bathroom for you." I nudged her back, snatching the sponge and dirty dish from her hands. "I can do this."

They were quiet as I washed the dishes, cleaned the skillet that had made our eggs, and placed them to dry in the drying rack next to the sink.

"Erik," Tim said quietly, and I pinched my eyes shut at the way he said my name. "You gotta stop sometime, you know. You can't distract yourself out of this."

"Wanna bet?" I muttered under my breath.

"We are so appreciative of your help," he continued. "Come on, sit down so I can see your stubborn-ass face while I'm talking to you."

With a heavy sigh, I slung the towel over my shoulder and sat back down at the dining table. It was the same one we'd eaten at growing up, the surface scarred and stained, rings of water damage from all the times we ignored my mom's requests to use coasters. If I looked hard enough, I'd see impressions from pressing too hard with our pens while we did homework growing up.

I was no different than Lydia when Luke first hired me. I'd had to face that truth after my first week back home. It was easier to surround myself with people and noise and busyness, than face the things I didn't want to face. Oh, I'd been running from things I didn't want to face for years, but now I was using home as the tool to distract myself from her.

That always caught up with me at night.

The bed was the worst. Sprawling myself across the middle made it all the more apparent that she wasn't there with me, and each night when I closed my eyes and replayed the nights she shared it with me, I convinced myself it was the last time I'd ever do it.

I'd allow myself one more night to replay all the details, catalog all the things I missed about her, and when the sun came up, I'd never do it again.

I'd move on because that was the best thing I could do. And every day, I proved myself a liar.

"You look like shit, Erik," Tim said.

"Thanks."

At my dry tone, my stepdad smiled. His energy had returned after his last round of chemo finished, and now we just had to wait to see if it was enough to put him back in remission. It was good to see him smile and have breakfast with him, even if he had no filter when it came to telling us the truth.

It was why he and my mom worked so well, parenting such a mix of kids after they got married. There was no time for BS. No time for ignoring the truth of our situations. Mom had come into their marriage, abandoned by her husband, and Tim had come into it losing his wife to cancer. All six of us kids had different scars from those two things, and it served no one to pretend they weren't there.

"What he means is we can tell you're not sleeping," Mom amended.

I rubbed my forehead. "Just … still getting used to that bed."

Tim shook his head. My mom was less subtle, and she rolled her eyes.

"We've given you two weeks," Tim said. "Enough is enough. You miss her. Go talk to her."

My eyes flashed to his. "And say what? That I don't know how to be what she wants me to be? Lydia's life is a fairy tale, where everyone lives happily ever after, and her white knight will carry her off into the sunset someday. And that knight will probably be as loaded as she is with better hair."

"It's amazing," my mom said evenly, "your reasons for why you can't reach out to her have shifted quite a bit."

I slicked my tongue over my teeth.

"At first, it was a lie. There was no truth to what we witnessed, and the reason you didn't worry yourself over it was because she was a kid who would get distracted—"

"I remember what I said," I interrupted. "But thank you for the reminder."

Tim slid my mom a grin.

"Are you two enjoying this?" I snapped. "Because I don't find it funny."

He raised his eyebrows. "My, my, you're giving me flashbacks to high school, Erik."

"Of course we don't find it funny that you're suffering," Mom said. "But you are so wildly obtuse about your own heart that the only thing we can do is laugh. Otherwise, we'll cry. Because the alternative is that you will live here for the rest of your life, and you'll drive me insane with your tree clearing and house projects and landscaping ideas and crop rotations. If I think too hard about you pestering me for what to do with your time until the day I die, I'll end up rocking in the corner."

Begrudgingly, I smiled. "And here I thought you wanted me back home."

Mom patted my hands with only the kind of condescending pat that a mother can manage. "For visits. Yes. We have slowly emptied this house of everyone but Poppy for the last ten years, and holy crap, I do not need more children coming back home to roost."

The sound of the door opening had me look away from the table, and Cameron walked in, blowing warm air through his hands. "Does this mean I shouldn't come in for food?"

Poppy was behind him, wrapped in a bright red scarf. The temperatures had dropped in the past week, and somehow, the cold had felt much more in line with the state of my emotions. She pecked Tim on the cheek and smacked the back of my head.

"*Ouch.*"

"I can't help it," she said with a breezy smile. "Anytime I see your mopey face, I want to hit you because you're *such* an idiot."

Cameron nudged her sideways, reaching across the kitchen island to grab a muffin from the large plate next to the sink. "Go easy on him, Pop."

"Thank you," I muttered.

Cameron's nod was serious. "Of course. It's gotta be hard to navigate when you have a smart, funny, beautiful woman love you for the giant horse's ass that you are, and you're still sitting *here*. Not with her."

I looked around at my family helplessly. "Did you guys decide en masse to have an intervention?"

Mom gave a stern look to my siblings, who knocked their muffins together in a sign of solidarity. "We were making progress before you two barreled in."

"You should be nicer to me, Poppy," I said. "I just offered to tile your bathroom."

My littlest sister, hardly cresting into adulthood, sat at the table and leveled me with those big eyes of hers. "Is that what you think will help?"

As much as I wanted to escape their interference, I knew I couldn't. Not anymore. I'd spent years of my life avoiding the truth of why I'd stayed away from these people who loved me.

It was easier for me. Because I didn't have to face my failure, face the wrong decisions I'd made when I wasn't trying to protect my heart.

And I was doing it again.

But knowing that you're doing something is wildly different than knowing how to fix it. How to change a deeply grooved pattern, something honed from an entire life of decision-making.

"No, Poppy," I said, voice hoarse and rough. "I don't think it'll help. But I don't know what else to do when I'm walking around feeling like she carved my heart out and took it with her."

She blinked at the naked honesty in my answer. Cameron clenched his jaw and stared down at the kitchen counter.

"You didn't hear what I said to her," I admitted. I laughed humorlessly. "Lydia accused me of setting my own life on fire, and as usual … she was right. I don't know how she managed it with how little I was willing to share. I was so scared of what she made me feel, but she just … barreled right through all of that fear and made me fall in love with her anyway."

My mom blinked back tears, and Tim watched me with pride shining in his eyes.

Poppy swiped at her face. "You should be telling *her* this, Erik."

"Poppy, the last time I made a decision with my heart, I walked away from a career I loved, for a future that was never mine to dream about, and I was left with *nothing*." My voice cracked. "I don't know how to tell her this without the constant fear that I'll lose everything again. I've made so many wrong decisions that I thought were right, convinced myself that a little bit of her was better than nothing, and I was so fucking wrong. Because now I know what I'm missing."

My mom didn't even attempt to stop the tears streaming down her face, and neither did Poppy.

"We all lost something," my mom said quietly, "after Olivia left. I won't pretend we didn't. When she called and said the baby wasn't yours …" She let out a small sob. "The look on your face will break my heart for the *rest* of my life, Erik."

I tilted my chin up to the ceiling and stared at the blank whiteness until my eyes burned.

"But what will keep breaking my heart," she continued, "is if you let that be a reason not to try to find happiness."

When I dropped my gaze back down, my family was blurry, and I blinked away the tears.

A voice joined from behind me. "Imagine if they'd done that."

Ian strolled into the kitchen, eyes avoiding mine as he plucked a muffin from the plate. Cameron said something to his brother that I couldn't hear, but Ian simply rolled his eyes. "Calm down, I'm not going to attack him."

"If who'd done what?" I asked him.

Ian leveled his dark eyes on me and didn't look away for a few long seconds. "Them," he said, lifting his chin at Mom and Tim. "They had every fucking reason not to try again."

I pushed my tongue into the side of my mouth while the truth of it sank in. Mom sniffled again, waving a hand in front of her face. "Goodness, you boys certainly know how to hit me in the feels."

Tim curled an arm around her, laying a kiss on the top of her head when she laid it on his shoulder. "He's right," my stepdad said quietly. "When I lost my wife, loving anyone else seemed impossible. But I hadn't met you yet."

"We wouldn't have this family," Ian continued. "We wouldn't have had each other growing up. We wouldn't have Poppy. If either one of them had let fear hold them back, let an … unknown future become bigger than a possibility, we wouldn't have had any of this."

He walked out of the kitchen and snagged a chair, flipping it around so he could sit backward. He faced me in a way where I had no choice but to stare at him head-on.

"You're no coward, Erik. And I'll never admit this out loud again, but if you are stupid enough to fuck this up with her, then you're not the man I've always looked up to."

I could hardly speak, the lump in my throat was as big as a house, and my eyes blurred dangerously. "Did that hurt coming out?"

"Like a bitch," he said dryly.

I exhaled a laugh, and thankfully, my eyes cleared as I blinked the emotion down.

Cameron handed Poppy a tissue, and she blew her nose, a loud, graceless burst of sound that had all of us smiling. Even Ian's usually stern mouth softened.

I rubbed at my chest, the weight of the conversation causing a strange, heavy warmth that was foreign.

It took me a moment to recognize it as hope.

"Now what?" Cameron asked.

My family watched me with expectant eyes.

"Now I try to give her the only thing she's wanted from me."

"Your bleeding heart served on a silver platter," Ian drawled.

I laughed.

Mom leaned forward and laid her hands over mine. "That girl just wants you, Erik. The good, the bad, and the ugly."

"I know," I told her. "And that's what she'll get. If she'll still have me."

Chapter
TWENTY-NINE

Erik

I JOGGED BACK TO MY HOUSE AND TOOK OUT MY PHONE TO TEXT her.

Call her.

Anything.

But I didn't want to hear her voice through a tinny, mechanical connection.

I wanted to look her in the eye and be in the same room as her. I sank into the chair on my front porch, trying to picture how it would play out.

What I'd say. How she'd react.

And just that … conjuring an image of her face was enough to steady me now.

Knowing Lydia—and I did—the only kind of gesture that would matter to her was exactly as Ian phrased it: serving up my heart—every ugly, hopeless piece of it.

She wanted something real, even if it hurt.

So many parts of my past hurt that it was hard to think about which one to hand her first. I sank my head into my hands and fought against the wave of terror that swamped me.

To seek her out in this way, show up at her door and hand her the piece of me that I'd protected at all costs was the scariest thing I ever could have done.

Lifting my head, I stared out into the trees, listened to the birds, the wind, and let the fresh air hit my face.

Terrifying or not, I knew that I couldn't stay in this place any longer. Not without trying. For her.

And for me.

Ten minutes later, I had my bags packed, a dusty box wedged under my arm, and sent a text to my mom that I'd be back. Eventually.

On Tuesdays, Lydia studied at home. In all the time I'd spent with her, that never changed. Luke spent the day at the practice facilities, Allie was always busy with foundation work, and Lydia focused better in the quiet.

The security guards waved me through the gate, and even though my stomach threatened to spill out onto the concrete, I only took one moment to gather my thoughts before I strode to the front door.

The box under my arm felt like its own living, breathing thing, just like it had sitting in the passenger seat for hours as I drove back into Seattle. Carefully, I moved it into a more comfortable position before I reached out and pressed the doorbell.

Inside the house, the bell chimed gracefully.

For a moment, there was no movement, and I fought the wave of disappointment that I'd assumed wrong. That her life had gone on as usual in the weeks that we'd been separated.

A shadow appeared from the direction of the kitchen, and I straightened.

Too tall for Lydia. Too tall and too big.

As Luke approached the door, I blew out a slow breath.

The door swung open, and he did nothing except stare, arms crossed over his wide chest.

I might have been taller, and I might have weighed more, but this was not just a former elite athlete who'd kept himself in incredible shape. This was a pissed-off dad who loved his daughter, and he was looking at me like he was imagining all sorts of creative ways to remove my balls.

"Luke," I said, keeping my tone neutral. "Good to see you."

Nothing. Just a tic in his jaw.

"Is Lydia here?"

His eyes narrowed.

Right. Avoidance of the issue would not work with him. "I know you're probably not happy to see me, but you know I wouldn't be here unless …" I swallowed. "Unless she was important to me."

"Important is such an ambiguous word, isn't it? My phone is important to me. So is the fridge. The keys to my car. I can't seem to function without them, yet none of these actually matter in the big picture of my life." His voice lowered, and the dangerous edge had me taking another deep breath. "I won't think of them on my deathbed, and I certainly wouldn't do bodily harm to anyone if they hurt them."

"I deserve that," I told him.

"No shit, Wilder." He took a step closer. "You deserve that and more because I hired you to protect my daughter, yet you are the reason she came home in tears and hardly left her room for a week."

My heart curled in on itself. This was the mental image of Lydia I never wanted. And worse, it was the one I caused.

I chose my words carefully. "I cannot tell you how sorry I am that I hurt her. But I hope to make amends today."

He studied me, jaw clenching again. "I don't know whether I

should trust you, Wilder. You haven't exactly proved to stick around when it counts."

The aim of his words was true and lodged right at the intended target, but I held my tongue and offered no defense. "That changes today."

Luke grunted. "So you say."

"No offense, Luke, but whether I stick around after this isn't really up to you." I held his gaze, prayed that he could see the respect I had for him because I wasn't completely sure I could take him in a fight when he had righteous paternal indignation on his side. "It's up to her. And I believe you and Allie raised your daughters to think for themselves."

He offered a begrudging nod, and I could see in his eyes what it cost him.

"She's downstairs studying," he said, moving to the side so I could walk in. "I'd tell you to keep the door open, Wilder," he added dryly, "but I find myself feeling generous enough to tell you that I'm on my way out the door."

I sighed, fighting the flush that crawled up my neck. "Got it."

Following the curve of the house, I found myself walking faster, simply because I knew I was closer to her. The energy in my veins was a palpable shift from what I'd felt over the past two and a half weeks.

Maybe that would fade with time if she forgave me. Maybe I'd take it for granted … the ability to walk into any home where she was waiting without feeling like my heart was about to burst out of my chest, but at that moment … it was the best thing I'd ever felt.

Sure, it was scary. But beneath it, what had my heart beating faster, was hope that I'd found from being around her.

Soft piano music came from the end of the hallway, her preferred choice when she studied. I quieted my steps and let out a deep breath, shifting the box into my hands.

At the open doorway, I stopped, leaning my shoulder against

the frame. I needed that extra support at the sight of her. Amazing how I could remember every detail vividly—the freckle on the slope of her shoulder, the slight dip above her hip bones, the fuller curve of her lower lip compared to the top.

She sat cross-legged on her bed, typing away at the laptop balanced on a fluffy white pillow in her lap. Her hair was pulled back into a messy braid, something that fell apart about halfway over her shoulder. And as she typed, her mouth moved along with whatever she read on the screen.

"What?" she asked.

My head snapped back. "I, uhh—"

Lydia squeaked at the sound of my voice, eyes wide as she slammed the laptop shut against her chest. "Holy *shit*, I thought you were my dad."

I exhaled a laugh. "Let's not tell him you mixed us up. I don't think I'm his favorite person right now."

She let out a slow breath, setting the computer down on the bed. Her eyes traced my face, and whatever she saw made her sad.

Right.

As Tim said, I looked like shit. And in my haste to find her, I hadn't stopped to check a mirror. My hair was a disaster, my beard longer than she'd ever seen it, and without a doubt, I still had dark circles under my eyes.

Lydia unfolded her legs and slid toward the edge of the bed, doing a horrible job of hiding the cautiously optimistic look on her face.

She was so beautiful. It took everything in me not to crowd her back against the bed and take those lips in a deep kiss, feel her body pressed against mine in the way that I missed so much. And even more than that, I just wanted to see her smile. I wanted to hear her laugh. Have her tease me.

I wanted every piece of her. Everything she'd give me.

Which was why I approached slowly, tugging her desk chair away from the wall so that I could sit facing her.

"You look—"

My eyebrow quirked at her pause, and she breathed a laugh.

"Terrible," she admitted.

"So I've heard." Settled in the chair, I traced the edge of the box before I held it out to her. Her brows furrowed, but she took it carefully. "This is why I left football."

Her mouth fell open. Her gaze darted between the box and my face. At first, she didn't open it, and I smiled.

"Go ahead," I told her gently.

Even though I knew what was in it, I held my breath while she pried open the front of the simple cardboard box. My heart clattered unevenly when I saw her gaze sharpen on what was underneath. Her mouth fell open into a shocked O when the lid was off.

Tucked into a ball on the side of the box was the yellow crib sheet, a simple pattern of happy little ducks covering the whole thing. Her forehead creased as she ran her hand over it.

"I'd never bought anything for a baby," I told her. "And the very first thing that came into my head was that they'd need somewhere soft to sleep."

Her eyes darted from me, back to the sheet in her hand. With a soft, loaded exhale, she set it aside and reached back into the box.

Next, she pulled out the mobile, three small footballs and some black stars dancing on a circle of soft gray.

"Poppy bought that," I told her quietly. "She was fifteen, working at the ice cream shop downtown, and she saved her tip money."

Lydia touched the edge of her finger to the stitching on one of the stars, and I could tell her eyes watered.

"Even though Greer fought her on a football theme for a gender-neutral nursery, she told us that little girls could love football too, so it didn't matter." I laughed quietly. "And when they saw the duck crib sheet, they wouldn't let me make any more design decisions without them."

Her hand covered her mouth, and her chest rose and fell. She set down the mobile and reached back in the box, a tear spilling down her cheek when she pulled out the impossibly small Wolves onesie.

"It's so small," she whispered.

"It's a newborn size, which I learned later was not a wise choice." The edge of my mouth hooked up in a wry grin, and Lydia simply stared at me with her heart pouring from her eyes. "I guess most babies never fit into that. But … what did I know? My wife had left by that point, and I was staring down the road at a future as a single dad." I let out an unsteady breath and refused to drop my gaze. "The week before I found out it wasn't my baby, I terminated my contract with Washington because I wanted to be there for everything." I shrugged. "I knew I'd have shared custody—it's not like they would've been with me full time—but all I wanted from the time I could remember was to be the best dad in the entire world. I'd change diapers and do feedings and teach them how to throw a football and change a tire and be at every single school event because I remembered what it was like not to have that."

"Erik," she whispered, the onesie still clutched in her hand.

"When Olivia had her ultrasound, and the timelines didn't match up with the last time I'd been home …" My voice trailed off. "She took a test to be sure. I had to tell my family that they weren't getting their first grandchild, first niece or nephew, and I had to walk back to that house that I'd thought would be mine to raise my child in."

She cried freely now, setting down the onesie so she could scooch closer and wind her fingers through mine while I spoke. At the touch of her hand, my entire body relaxed, a soothing hum in my veins at the feel of her skin on mine.

"I never thought I could break someone's heart like I had to break theirs." Then I slid my hand up the side of her face, sighing at the way her eyes fell shut. "Until the day I broke yours. Everything I did to run from my own past still ended up hurting someone who meant the world to me." I leaned forward, resting my forehead against hers. "I was so afraid to make the wrong decision, to let someone in to the point where their absence would wreck me all over again. And you, Lydia, you've already wrecked me in the best possible way. I'm willing to risk any hurt, if it means I can have you in my life."

Lydia pulled back and gave me a soft smile. "I'm glad you told me."

"I'm so sorry I did that to you," I whispered.

"I forgive you," she said, voice hitching quietly on her tears. She cupped the side of my face as we sat there and simply breathed each other in. "I wish that hadn't happened to you."

I pulled back to drink in every detail of her face. For the first time in years, maybe in my whole life, my heart felt whole and strong and sure. "You know why it's okay?"

Forehead furrowed in a slight frown, she shook her head.

My thumb touched to the bottom curve of her lips, I leaned in again. "Because I found you. And you are the *only* one who could've snuck through those walls."

Lydia exhaled a laugh. "Yeah?"

I nodded. "Because you're stubborn." I kissed her waiting lips. "And smart." Another kiss, longer this time. "You're so much wiser than I am."

"That's true," she murmured against my lips.

My tongue slipped into her mouth, and she hummed. "You're intuitive. You saw through me like I was made of cellophane, which made you the most dangerous person in the world, Lydia Pierson."

Her hips canted forward, her hand sliding around the back of my neck. "You're so good at dealing with danger, though." She kissed me, tilting her head as I moved closer, winding an arm around her waist.

"I'm good at dealing with you," I said. "And if you let me, I'll love you for the rest of my life."

Her face broke open into a wide, happy smile. "Let you? Erik, you couldn't get rid of me now even if you wanted to."

I prowled off the chair, pressing her back onto the bed, settling my full weight over her warm, soft body. Her lips were soft and giving, her tongue soft while it slid against mine.

The taste of her hit like a jolt under my skin, a warm, sweet sense of welcome that tugged a groan from my chest. Lydia arched underneath me, pressing her chest against mine. There was no space between a single inch of our bodies, we wound together, trying to erase the days and weeks of distance in one deep, unending kiss.

Slanting my mouth over hers, I traced the wet roll of tongue with my own, the sucking motion of our lips moving in a perfect rhythm. Her hands clutched my back, and where my hands cupped her face, I felt the damp trail of tears left behind.

We rolled to the side, her thigh clamped between my legs, and for long, endless minutes, we were content to stay like that. My hands running up and down the warm skin underneath her shirt, along the length of her thigh so I could pull her even tighter against my body. Her fingers traced along my face while we kissed and kissed and kissed, then slid down my neck, my shoulders, until she let them settle over the steady pounding of my heart.

I curled my body around hers, holding her as tightly as I could with our bodies interlocked as they were. Our kisses slowed to something sweet and innocent, her nose rubbing against mine while she sipped on my top, then bottom lip.

Nothing had ever felt as good as this moment. As right as she did in my arms.

If I dug deep into who I'd been before I knew what it was like to love her, I might be able to find traces of who I was. But all of that hardness, the armor, it was powerless against the way she loved me.

After a moment, her nails dug into my hair, and she tugged my head back.

At my dazed expression, she laughed. "Just to set the record straight of who said the words first," she murmured. "I love you, Erik Wilder."

I sat up on my knees and tugged my shirt off. Her eyes warmed immediately. "Is this going to turn into a competition now?" I asked.

She shucked her shorts down her legs, arched her back when I slid my hands up her thighs. "Maybe."

"Good." I tugged the straps of her shirt over her shoulders. "Worst taste in music? You win that one too."

Lydia laughed, sitting up to yank her own shirt off. "I'll get you to love it. You just wait."

I slanted my mouth over hers in a deep, tongue-swirling kiss, and when she sighed, I pulled back. "I can't wait to prove you wrong."

When I slid my palm over her chest, she sucked in a hissing breath. "All a part of my plan, Erik. It's all a part of my plan."

"Do you know the first time you said those words, I thought they were the scariest thing I'd ever heard?"

And to the sound of her delighted laughter, I set about loving her and letting her love me in return.

I couldn't be sure what came next for me, for us. But for the first time in a long time, I knew that I was exactly where I was supposed to be.

From where I was sitting, with her in my arms, the future couldn't have been brighter.

Epilogue

One year later
Lydia

"I PROBABLY FAILED."

"No, you didn't." He dug his thumbs into the knot of tension in my shoulders, and I groaned, dropping my chin to my chest.

"You can't know that."

Erik hummed, eliciting a gasp when he pressed the muscle just right. "I'm always right though."

Even though he was rendering me boneless through those magical, strong hands of his, I managed a snort. This was a familiar cycle. I finished a paper, or a project, and when I hit submit, Erik would work out all the knots that I'd been holding through weeks of hard work.

While he did, I'd lament the fact that I probably failed (I never had. Proud four point oh still going strong with one semester left in my program). He'd slide his hands over my skin and as the relaxation took hold, I would listen to his deep, wonderful voice tell me that I would be just fine.

My big grumpy man turned out to be the very best kind of cheerleader in the entire world. There'd never been anyone so steady, so solid, and like everything else he did, he was born to support me in exactly the way that I needed him.

Erik never diminished the things that caused me stress, he never talked me out of my fears, simply sat back while I proved those fears fruitless time and time again. And when the grade would come in, he'd hold me in those great big arms, kissing me sweetly through the relief and excitement.

This particular research project had been brutal, and Professor Pena warned me that it caused even the best students in the program to doubt themselves. Erik knew, without me saying a word, that I'd need a quiet place to focus, renting us a cottage on Wautauga Beach for a month, with pristine views of Elliott Bay and the Puget Sound stretched all around us. Far enough away from home that it felt like an escape (home being my apartment where he'd moved in a few months after we started dating). But still close enough to Seattle that he could go into work when they needed him.

Not long after we reunited, Erik had slipped seamlessly back into the Washington Wolves organization—with a role in the Player Engagement department. Rookie Readiness, to be more specific. In the end, it was a perfect fit with not just his personality, but his past. He knew, better than most, how important it was to be smart with your money, to not allow the worst parts of the league to ruin a player's chance of long term success before they had a chance to start. To balance the sport and real life, keep your mind and your body strong. To stay grounded and not let the big stage consume them.

And he loved it. Those protective tendencies of his now extended beyond his family, beyond me, and to the rookies he was assigned to mentor. More than one of our family dinners at my parents' included their eager faces. They'd need a bigger table soon.

But the last month, he'd been able to work remotely, for the most part. Other than going into Seattle for one home game, we'd hardly surfaced from our little haven.

The white walls and ceilings, soft leather furniture and panoramic views were amazing. I loved the size of it—there was enough space that I could take over the kitchen table with all my stacks of books and papers, and still be close enough to catch a glimpse of Erik where he worked at the butcher block island.

But the setting—something plucked straight from a magazine—came a distant second to the simple pleasure of being with him, and being loved by him. Waking in his arms. Knowing what he looked like when he laughed. Trusting that my heart was safe with this one person, for the rest of my life.

At night, we'd talk quietly until my eyelids felt heavy. About our future, which had been unfolding like a fairy tale since the moment I looked up to see him framed in the doorway of my old bedroom. We talked about our careers. The babies we couldn't wait to make. We wanted to get married. Eventually.

I'd have married Erik the week after we started dating, but he insisted that I finish my schooling first. That there was no rush, because I was already going to be his forever. When I told him waiting was for chumps, he set his jaw and got that hot stubborn look on his face that made me want to rip his shirt off.

Then again, everything he did made me want to rip his shirt off. And I did, frequently.

Just like I wanted to now, when he slid his thumbs down either side of my spine and I groaned. I stretched my neck to the side to give him better access, and pressed my thighs together.

He chuckled under his breath, because of course he saw that. "None of that, I have a phone meeting in fifteen minutes."

"Fifteen minutes is plenty of time," I grumbled.

Erik leaned in, nipping the side of my neck with the sharp edges of his teeth. "Speak for yourself."

I turned in the chair, eyebrows raised imperiously. "And you think biting me helps?"

He grinned, wolfish and handsome, and I got a flash of that dimple he kept hidden. "No."

I laughed, leaning in to capture his lips in a decadent kiss. He tasted like coffee, and I sighed happily when he touched his tongue to mine, tilting his head to exactly the angle that I loved.

When I pulled away, I cupped the side of his face. "You're sure I can't talk you into one more stress relieving activity?"

He hummed, holding my gaze steadily. "I think you can store up all those ideas for when I'm done with my call." He tapped my forehead gently. "You're the brains of this relationship, so I trust you to come up with some really good ones."

I kissed him again. "How long will this phone call be?"

Erik dropped a kiss to the tip of my nose. "Thirty minutes, max."

Honestly, I tried not to pout. But I failed, because Erik laughed.

"Now you know how I felt the other day," he said, standing from the stool and stretching his arms over his head. I eyed the flat muscle of his stomach when his shirt hem lifted. "You had those glasses on. And that pencil stuck in your hair."

I grinned. "Got a librarian fetish, do you?"

He braced his arms on either side of me and leaned down to snag my mouth again in a voracious kiss. I clutched his shirt and whimpered when he tugged on my bottom lip with his teeth. "I've got a Lydia fetish," he growled. "And in," he paused, looking at the clock on the kitchen wall, "forty-three minutes, give or take, I'll show you."

Standing from the chair, and curling my arms around his waist, I let my forehead rest against the broad wall of his chest. "Fine," I sighed.

He rubbed his hand up and down my back soothingly, dropping a kiss onto the top of my head. "Maybe less."

I looked up at him. "Who's the meeting with?"

Erik brushed his thumb along my cheek. "Miguel. His agent sent him an endorsement deal he's not sure about. It's good money, but I think he still wants to make sure he's being smart about what he puts his name on."

"I hope he knows he's getting excellent advice to think about that ahead of time."

His eyes warmed. "All my rookies get you as part of the package when they're assigned to me. Of course they know they're getting good advice."

I smiled. "Tell him I said hi."

But instead of moving away, Erik stared down at me, a world of love and affection shining from his gaze. No one had ever looked at me that way, and every time he did, I fell in love with him all over again.

"What?" I whispered.

"I love you." He told me every day. More than once.

"I love you, too." I pushed up on the balls of my feet and gave him a soft kiss. Erik wrapped his arms around my waist, lifting me up as I curled my arms around him.

His face was buried against my neck, and he inhaled deeply. Tears pricked my eyes, as they often did, because sometimes it seemed like the most impossible stroke of luck that he was mine. That I was his.

"And I'm going to marry you," he continued. His voice was a deep rumble in his chest, and I closed my eyes, tightening my arms.

"Yes you are." I kissed his cheek, hiking my legs around his waist, crossing my ankles behind his back. "Any idea when?"

He sighed, which made me grin. I asked him weekly. He never answered.

When he pulled his head back, his eyes were serious. "Soon," he said in a low, quiet voice.

"Thank goodness," I sighed. I pecked his lips, hopping out of his arms when his phone started vibrating. "I'm going to go take a bath while you talk to Miguel."

Erik's eyes darkened.

"I'll keep the water warm for you," I said over my shoulder, tugging my shirt up over my head and tossing it onto the ground.

"You're a horrible tease."

With an arm over my naked chest, I blew him a kiss from the doorway of the bathroom.

Just before I closed the door, Erik pushed into the room after me, sweeping me up in his arms and depositing me on the bathroom counter as I shrieked in surprise.

He took my mouth in a ferocious kiss and I laughed breathlessly when he adjusted his height down to place sucking kisses along my chest. "Erik, what about your meeting?"

"I told him I'd call him in ten minutes." He licked a tight circle over my flesh, and I gasped, bracing my hand on the counter. When he lifted his head, his eyes were dark with delicious intent. "I just needed something to tide me over. Is that okay?"

I cupped the side of his face, heart racing with delirious love. When I pulled him close for an achingly sweet kiss, I realized that everything about my future had unfurled in exactly the way I'd hoped.

"Yeah," I whispered. "That's more than okay."

I didn't have to try to imagine anything anymore, of what it could be. What I hoped for. Because the reality of what I'd found with Erik was so, so much sweeter than anything else I could've planned.

The End

Curious about Lydia's sister, Faith Pierson and her protective bad boy boyfriend, Dominic? Here's a sneak peek at their book, *The Lie*, available now on Amazon, Audible and with your Kindle Unlimited subscription.

Allie's door was cracked open, and when I approached, I heard the rumble of a low voice. He came into view before Allie did, and if someone had written a caption for the image of him that I saw, it would've been *pissed-off bad boy bucks authority*. His arms, big and tattooed, were crossed over his chest, and he stared at Allie like she'd done him personal harm.

His jaw was a sharp line coated in dark stubble, and there wasn't a hint of emotion on that chiseled face. For a moment, I stared at him. Something about his demeanor made me feel very much like I was approaching a wild animal, and that danger made the air vibrate at a different frequency.

"There you are, Faith," Allie said as she appeared into view. With a warm smile, she opened the door for me. "Come on in."

"Thank you for waiting," I told her, tucking some of my brown hair behind my ear. "I know I'm a little late."

She rubbed my arm. "Dominic and I were just getting to know each other before you got here."

He snorted, and my brows bent in on my forehead at the derisive sound. Allie's eyes met mine, and I saw a gleam of humor in them, which made me relax a little. Then she gestured toward me. "Dominic, this is my daughter Faith. She runs the foundation I was telling you about."

I gave him a friendly smile and held out my hand. But instead of standing to take it, he gave me a head-to-toe study without rush, then nodded curtly.

Ahh, okay, so he was one of *those* football players. That was Camp Three. The ego-the-size-of-Everest,

I'm-too-talented-for-basic-manners football players who made me want to shove bamboo splints up my fingernails rather than spend time with them.

Those players made it very, very easy not to break my no dating the players rule. Kinda like when you went camping and they told you not to feed the bears because they might eat you alive.

Allie cleared her throat sharply, and Dominic sighed, reaching forward to shake my hand. His skin was rough and warm to the touch, and I fought a shiver when his palm scraped against mine.

"Do you need to finish up with him?" I asked Allie. "I can come back at a better time."

She shook her head. "No, this is perfect. Dominic is actually going to be spending some time at Team Sutton, and I'd love it if you could find one or two of our grant recipients that would benefit from his presence."

My eyebrows shot up. Benefit from Oscar the Grouch's presence? When Dominic's glower intensified, I realized just how transparent my reaction had been and tried to smooth my face. Another thing I needed to work on now that I was in charge of the foundation. "Umm, sure thing. We can find ... something."

Allie's beautiful face split into an amused grin because she knew me all too well and just how horrible I was at hiding my feelings. "Perfect. I was thinking maybe a couple of hours a week for the next month?" She turned her gaze to Dominic, and oh my, I saw the way she was not even remotely asking for permission from him. "Sound good?"

"Like I have a choice," he muttered.

I blew out a slow breath, eyes wide.

"We all have choices in life, Dominic," Allie said, unfazed by the attitude. "Spending time with the kids who benefit from Team Sutton might not be something you get to choose, but I promise you, I expect glowing reviews from Faith once your time is done."

If I thought my eyes were wide before, they must've been taking up half my friggin' face when she finished that little speech. Now I was his babysitter?

Keep reading with your Kindle Unlimited subscription!

OTHER BOOKS BY
KARLA SORENSEN
(available to read with your KU subscription)

The Ward Sisters
Focused
Faked
Floored
Forbidden

The Washington Wolves
The Bombshell Effect
The Ex Effect
The Marriage Effect

The Bachelors of the Ridge
Dylan
Garrett
Cole
Michael
Tristan

Three Little Words
By Your Side
Light Me Up
Tell Them Lies

Love at First Sight
(Published by Smartypants Romance)
Baking Me Crazy
Batter of Wits
Steal my Magnolia

Acknowledgements

I am so thankful to so many people for helping me cross the finish line with this book. Writing never seems to get easier, and because of that, it becomes increasingly important to surround yourself with a core group of people who will listen to your meltdowns and hold your hand when you feel like the story is going to get the best of you. And I'm so grateful for those people in my life.

As with every book, thank you to Kathryn Andrews and Fiona Cole for encouragement, plotting help, beta feedback and ass-kicking on a regular basis. I genuinely don't think I could do this without you two helping me every step of the way.

Amy Daws and Michelle Clay for reading the final product and making sure everything was smoothed out where it needed to be.

Najla Qamber/Qamber Designs Media for another amazing cover and beautiful graphics.

Jenny Sims and Julia Griffis for making me look like I know what I'm doing.

Dani Sanchez at Wildfire for the promo help, and Michelle and Tina for keeping me sane.

My husband for being an endless well of support and encouragement, and always helping me carve out time when I need to finish.

"For I know the plans I have for you," declares the Lord, "plans to prosper you and not to harm you, plans to give you hope and a future."—Jeremiah 29:11

About the
AUTHOR

Karla Sorensen is an Amazon top 20 bestselling author who refuses to read or write anything without a happily ever after. When she's not devouring historical romance or avoiding the laundry, you can find her watching football (British AND American), HGTV or listening to Enneagram podcasts so she can psychoanalyze everyone in her life, in no particular order of importance. With a degree in Advertising and Public Relations from Grand Valley State University, she made her living in senior healthcare prior to writing full-time. Karla lives in Michigan with her husband, two boys and a big, shaggy rescue dog named Bear.